About th

Catherine McNamara grew up in Sydney, ran away to Paris, and ended up in West Africa running a bar. Her collection *Pelt and Other Stories* was longlisted for the Frank O'Connor Award and was semi-finalist in the Hudson Prize, and her short stories have been Pushcart-nominated, shortlisted and published in the UK, Europe, USA and Australia. Catherine lives in Italy.

Praise for *The Cartography of Others*

"McNamara's work has a fierce, vital beat, her stories robust yet finely-worked, her voice striking in its confidence and originality. She writes with sensuous precision and a craft that is equally precise. This is fiction that can stand up in any company."
– Hilary Mantel

"Catherine McNamara's haunting stories map landmarks of psychological encounter. Hers is an international canvas, marking the points where contemporary lives cross with sensuality and finesse. Beautiful work."
– Cathy Galvin

"McNamara does things with words (most) other writers cannot. Her stories are sensual and assured. Not a writer to be ignored."
– Tom Vowler

"Catherine McNamara's writing is superb, this latest collection presents a unique way to talk about displacement and sensuality."
– Eric Akoto

"A master of mood and atmosphere, Catherine McNamara has a keen eye for the startling image that so often holds the heart of a story – a blue tent the morning after a party, a naked woman spreading herself across a window high above Hong Kong. Her theme is desire – its ambiguities, betrayals, bruises, and joys – and this is fearless, sensuous writing. Her prose is meticulous, the stories rich with insight and empathy. Highly recommended."
– Annemarie Neary

By the Same Author

Pelt and Other Stories

THE CARTOGRAPHY OF OTHERS

THE CARTOGRAPHY OF OTHERS

CATHERINE MCNAMARA

This edition first published in 2018

Unbound

6th Floor Mutual House, 70 Conduit Street, London W1S 2GF

www.unbound.com

ISBN (eBook): 9781911586579

ISBN (Paperback): 9781911586562

Design by Mecob

Cover images:

© Shutterstock.com
© iStockphoto.com

Printed and bound in Great Britain by Clays Ltd, Elcograf S.p.A.

For D

Dear Reader,

The book you are holding came about in a rather different way to most others. It was funded directly by readers through a new website: Unbound.

Unbound is the creation of three writers. We started the company because we believed there had to be a better deal for both writers and readers. On the Unbound website, authors share the ideas for the books they want to write directly with readers. If enough of you support the book by pledging for it in advance, we produce a beautifully bound special subscribers' edition and distribute a regular edition and e-book wherever books are sold, in shops and online.

This new way of publishing is actually a very old idea (Samuel Johnson funded his dictionary this way). We're just using the internet to build each writer a network of patrons. Here, at the back of this book, you'll find the names of all the people who made it happen.

Publishing in this way means readers are no longer just passive consumers of the books they buy, and authors are free to write the books they really want. They get a much fairer return too – half the profits their books generate, rather than a tiny percentage of the cover price.

If you're not yet a subscriber, we hope that you'll want to join our publishing revolution and have your name listed in one of our books in the future. To get you started, here is a £5 discount on your first pledge. Just visit unbound.com, make your pledge and type CARTOGRAPHY18 in the promo code box when you check out.

Thank you for your support,

Dan, Justin and John
Founders, Unbound

Super Patrons

Mary Abercrombie
Eric Akoto
Jenny Antoine
Mark Appleton
Von Mac Attack
Judy Birkbeck
Michael Chuah & Merlyn Bowman
Victoria Brigggs
O C
Teri Carter
Jimmy Cathy
Paola Cecchetto
Gina Challen
Karen Champniss
Ingrid Christensen
Lisa Colley
Ruby Cowling
Maurizio d'Amore
Rupert Dastur
Frank Deconz
Emily Devane
Lucy Durneen
Roma Ellis
Tracy Fells
Liz Fenwick
Nancy Freund
Claire Fuller
Linda Gahan
Frances Gapper
Pia Ghosh-Roy
Ambra Gobena
Miranda Gold

Kim Golden-Malmgren
Michele Goldsmith
Rhoda Greaves
Rachel Hore
Penny Howard
Denny John
Rae Joyce
Dan Kieran
Andy Kissane
Georgina Lippiett
Alison Lock
Rowena Macdonald
Alison MacLeod
Linda Mannheim
Linda Martinez
Agnes Marton
Alan McCormick
Jarred McGinnis
Danielle McLaughlin
Maria McManus
Paul McNamara
Paul McNamara
Kay McNamara
Julia McNamara
Alexandra McNamara
John McNamara
Rachel Chuah McNamara
Evi McNamara
Tony McNamara
Christine McNamara
Diana McNamara
Kevin McNamara
Paul McVeigh
Julio Mendoza
Erinna Mettler
John Mitchinson

Damhnait Monaghan
Fran Mulhern
Annemarie Neary
Lyra Nelson
Luke O'Connor
Eileen Or
Jeremy Osborne
Susi Owusu
Imogen Pelham
Sylvia Petter
Jonathan Pinnock
Stef Pixner
TCE Wyee Point
Lou Pollard
Justin Pollard
Julia Pucci
Jimmy Pucci
Leo Pucci
Fred Pucci
Flaviano Raschietti
Barbara Renel
Pauline Jansen van Rensburg
Jane Roberts
David Rose
Stuart Rosewarne
Yvonne Roy
Marta Sagui
Lisa Smithies
Anna Solding
Anna Southern
Sherry Stanfa-Stanley
Alice Stuart
K&D Sunshine
Susan Swindells
Jane Telford
Mike Scott Thomson

Janine Trapp
Meret Valtwies
Jose Varghese
Alessandra Verona
Barney Walsh
Laura Windley
Alison Woodhouse
Olga Zilberbourg

With grateful thanks to Stuart Rosewarne, who helped to make this book happen.

Thy body is a natural paradise,
In whose self, unmanured, all pleasure lies,
Nor needs perfection

John Donne, *Letters to Several Personages: Sappho to Philaenis*

Contents

Adieu, Mon Doux Rivage

There are four of us on the boat. Jean-Luc and myself, and Belgian music manager Raoul Vidal and his Japanese soprano wife Mieko Inoue. Raoul, big as a cupboard, stands on the deck with arms folded, squinting back at the coast. After a few days he's discarded his shirt. When Mieko comes on deck he bends over her like a poised wave and whatever they say is soundless. Jean-Luc has read that she sang at Covent Garden twice, but he is pretty sure her career has flatlined. Jean-Luc has a nose for these things. He was the drummer from my old band in Marseilles.

They've booked for a week-long cruise around Corsica, emailed me strict diet instructions (no gluten, no sugar or cheese, preferably grilled fish). Looking at Raoul, I'd say he was brought up on *moules frites* and tankards of beer. I once toured in Belgium with an all-female group and this is the truth: they fry pig's blood sausages in butter. This is something that requires an explanation.

Raoul has sought me out a couple of times when I am having a quick puff at the stern. He has a range of slight criticisms and needs. Do you have sanitary napkins? Could you chop the cabbage in the salad a little finer for Mieko's digestion? All over his body, his skin has surrendered to the sharp summer sun and it explodes in blisters wishing to be pricked. His nose is peeling and he doesn't care, which in turn means that Mieko doesn't either.

He asks, 'Do you have any copies of *The New Yorker*?'

I shake my head. I imagine he is used to long lunches.

Their suite at the bow of the boat must be agreeable to Mieko. She stays there a lot. On my way to the laundry cupboard I think I hear a sound – a voice ascending – but this ceases on its path. The boat moves ahead with a steady rolling. When I back into her with clean linen in the galley, I hear a word that is released almost inaudibly, at great cost: 'Sorry.' She looks at me at with my pile of clean towels and fresh sheets. It seems as though she wants to take this word back. I should ask if she wants anything, or remind her that I have seasickness tablets if she feels unwell. She is carrying a big hat and a Japanese novel, wearing loose ivory trousers and a cotton shirt. Most probably because my ragged blue-painted nails are on show, and Jean-Luc says

I have feet like a platypus, I have made it my mission to see the opera singer's toes. Mieko wears a pair of closed black espadrilles and her feet are pressed into their jute spirals.

Jean-Luc has given Raoul a Michel Houellebecq novel in French, the one where they massacre the tourists. Raoul sits on a bench and reads it through like a man on a train, his back in burning shreds. Mieko drapes herself on a deckchair, fully clothed. For a long while she does not read. They sit far from each other, uninvolved. Before it's time to prepare lunch I sit with Jean-Luc at the stern. We've just come through a rough patch. Jean-Luc misses the band life. He's come to sailing late and has doubts on the water. He doesn't like me questioning him and stresses out when we anchor or come into port. Jean-Luc puts his hand on my thigh. As his fingers dig in, I watch the fuzzy-edged scorpion inked into his skin. His nails are broken and black. The wind is high, higher than he'd like, and he has trimmed both sails as we cut as close as possible to the coast. We can see the point of Nonza now, the village stranded high above the pebbled grey beach as though washed up in a storm. Once we are anchored in the bay I will set up lunch on deck, the *sole meunière* Mieko just tolerates, with an avocado salad that perhaps she will not. Though initially she said she would eat prawns, her face dropped yesterday when I grilled a dozen scampi. Raoul removed the platter.

'There has been a misunderstanding,' he said, after tilting the plate in the boat's wash. 'Mieko does not eat prawns.'

If the couple nap after lunch, and perhaps swim at the beach through the afternoon, I will have time to borrow Marianne's scooter in the village and do a quick shop at the bigger town of Saint-Florent. Our supplies are dwindling. Jean-Luc removes his hand, eases off the sheets, prepares to tack the vessel and veer in towards the coast. I watch his tattoos, some of them are busty women who seem to be feasting upon his physique. We don't speak much when we are at work, not even when we are anchored for the night in a star-swept bay. If his heavy arm reaches around me it feels almost inanimate, like a stranger's cool skin.

Though Jean-Luc hasn't entered me in a month we have laid bets on who will hear Mieko and Raoul at it first. People get frisky on boats, in confined spaces. I see it happen always. We have had a man and woman groaning and growling on deck for hours. In the morning they were sedate, reading books and newspapers. The woman had a dental issue and had to be taken ashore.

Mieko stretches up an arm and unfurling hand against the glare of the sail. Raoul looks over to her, watching the boom move across as the vessel turns. Jean-Luc's orchestration is gentle. The sails rattle like stage curtains above the small soprano, then the wind throws them into shape. Mieko's hat falls back as she stares up into the grandeur of the mast. We are no longer shouldering against the open sea but are propelled to the land in the bellies of long emerald waves without crests. These make a lulling washing sound. Mieko's hand falls away and she raises her book in the glossy light. Raoul resumes rifling through his novel.

Jean-Luc tramps across the deck to see to the jib and I hold the tiller while watching his body. He was with another woman in his prime. I have seen the photographs of his thick hair and bright teeth and leather jackets. Jean-Luc came down to the south from Lille on a motorbike.

After lunch Jean-Luc untethers the dinghy and rows me ashore. Mieko and Raoul retire below deck – the meal has gone smoothly. There are two other boats at anchor but the vast beach is empty. It is the hottest hour of the day and the island looks wrought and faded, pressed against the distance even as it begins to loom. Bushfires will roar down these hills again. Beneath us, the sea floor of black-green pebbles inks the water with cold tones and the waves are dark and sharp. It is an awkward, remote place that Jean-Luc likes. Guests enjoy viewing the hellishness of the land's ascension, but few make the climb to Nonza to have a *gelato* or see the sea stretching in a gauzy endless slate. Most want to move on to l'Île-Rousse or Calvi where there is a marina and nightclubs. Our guests like to get dressed up at night.

Jean-Luc pitches the dinghy onto the stones and when we kiss goodbye my tongue flicks into his mouth. The water withdraws, fizzing over wet black knuckles. I step out barefoot and push the boat off, holding up my sandals and shopping bag. There are a few sunbathers in the strip of shadow under the gouged cliff thrusting the village into the air. The pebbles shimmer all the way to the scrub where the path begins. Some are oily gems, others are lozenges the size of children's feet. I drop my things. With Jean-Luc staring at me, rowing solidly, I strip down and wade into the water, diving under the bucking waves.

Two hours later I am back on the beach with my full shopping bag, grateful that Marianne's brother Pietro took me all the way to Saint-Florent in his van. We've had two beers at the summit – Corsican red beer brewed with chestnuts – that spill through my head. I've hiked down the path at breakneck speed to save the groceries, and torn across the hot stones to the shore. I see Jean-Luc on deck and wave for him to row out. There is a man's head in the water which I recognise as Raoul's. The seabed carves away quickly and Raoul thrashes through the waves, letting them belt over his head which pushes out of the foam, his fair hair whipped around his cranium. His red face splutters and he spews water from his mouth, paddling as more waves crash upon him. For a minute, I worry he is in trouble and I will have to set down my bag and rescue him. But then his body scrambles out of the surf. He is naked. He throws himself face down in the shallows as water streams over his glowing back. His white bottom has a surprisingly round shape.

I look back out to the boat to see if Jean-Luc has registered me waving. I have fish and vegetables in my bag. He is speaking to Mieko, which hardly seems possible. Mieko, dressed in baggy black trousers and a long-sleeved cream top, stands watching her husband in the water. Soon enough, Jean-Luc is metres away from me in the dinghy and I hand over the shopping. There is wine in there to chill for this evening. I am certain Raoul will succumb to chilled Sancerre. I toss my sundress and sandals into the bag and push Jean-Luc off. He looks at my body as though it is an outline on the landscape.

Mieko appears for dinner in a floral dress that is not becoming. It is as though she is indulging Raoul, who may have Belgian floral leanings. Watching him in the surf may have invited her hands to hover over this dress. I prefer her in dramatic blacks and whites that denude her features. Mieko totters across the deck in a pair of low gold heels, an expensive mesh covering the fretwork and toes of both feet. There are contrasting copper and white threads woven through the sheer substance. I see the glint of nail varnish, but there is no sense of shape or proportion. Before the week is up, I will see Mieko's toes.

Mieko refuses a glass of wine and walks the length of the deck. I wonder when she will get cabin fever. After a few days they all do, they have to set foot on the ground. Today, she had no wish to go ashore. I suspect she'll come back on board with shopping bags when we sail on to Calvi. The soprano likes to shop.

Jean-Luc has anchored a little further from the shore for the night and has gone below to take a shower. The lights of Nonza sway high above us. I wish I were up there with Pietro and Marianne in the piazza drinking beer. Strains of folk music cascade towards us, from the bar a guy from Ajaccio has built on the cliffs. He has a jazz band on weekends but tonight the bay is almost soundless. Waves barely stir. The forecast is for more of this. Jean-Luc joins me after his shower and I know he is not relaxed. He, too, would like to go ashore, but he would sleep alone in the dunes. He kisses my cheek, takes Mieko's glass over to her. She accepts it from him and they clink glasses. I watch them, the man I love and the tiny floral soprano. I haven't asked Jean-Luc what roles she played at Covent Garden, whether she was allowed to stray from the confines of her race. I imagine Mieko in a kimono with a powdered visage. I see her collapsed in fabrics on the stage with a trickle of fake blood.

Raoul climbs the steps. He wears a loud shirt and is redder and more blistered than yesterday, his washed hair feathery. He is exhausted. His face droops and he snatches up a glass of wine. Raoul asks me what is for dinner but doesn't listen to my reply. He tells me he has just finished his book. He says, 'Did I already ask you if you had copies of *The New Yorker*?'

I tell him he has, and I'm sorry I don't. I ask him if he liked Houellebecq's novel.

'Not much,' he says.

He puts out his glass for a refill, looks across the deck and notices Mieko's dress. For a moment, his eyes dampen.

I ask him what he usually reads.

'I don't have time to read,' he says.

At the table this evening I see Mieko's face close up once again. We have passed the three-day marker, where people's barriers soften and they remember our names. Raoul is satisfied my cooking is delicate enough for Mieko's tricky digestion and Mieko no longer looks aghast at her plate. I watch food entering Mieko's mouth. The crepe has just started around her eyes though she has a young woman's taut plump skin, well–hydrated and radiant. Her face is a broad palette which I can see would transform in light, with song. Her eyes are exquisite marbles that reveal kindness in their spheres. When Mieko smiles at Raoul, he looks a better man. A third bottle of wine is opened, this one a local rosé from the burnished hills. Raoul raises a glass and makes a toast to his wife. Jean-Luc's hand smooths my thigh. I try to remember my bet with Jean-Luc and who wagered whether Day Three would be the night. I see Raoul's eyes slide over Mieko, over her lifted breasts, into the folds of flowers. Dishevelled, they spill with veneration.

I go below deck for our desserts, a crème caramel made with almond milk. I arrange my tray, putting a bottle of Muscat under my arm. I stand there, smelling wood varnish and the bleach in the cupboards, the whiff of diesel at this end of the boat. I listen to their voices above. I wonder if what Mieko and Raoul will rediscover tonight is any different from the clumsy relishing we have seen many times over, each couple so mortal under the night skies, so afflicted by the feigned simplicity of sleeping on a powerful boat. When I reach the deck they are dancing. The folk music drifts on the air and Mieko is pressed into Raoul's oversized embrace. Jean-Luc holds his glass. I distribute the desserts and slip beneath his shoulder. The geography of his body is weary. I worry that this life will make him ill one day. I nuzzle his rough cheek, his neck.

Raoul sways back to the table with his wife tucked beside him. Mieko's face is bright, new dimples have appeared in her cheeks. She takes a few spoonfuls of her dessert, then dabs her lips. Clearly, her doubts about my cooking have come home. Raoul empties his dish, goes to the stern where he pees into the motionless water and Mieko can't contain her laughs. Raoul brings up a bottle of Calvados from their suite and fills everybody's tumblers. His wife lies down along the seat, nestles into his lap with her eyes open. I see it is a very long time since they have made love.

Our band had quite a following. There was a year that my voice was good and we'd taken a string of Cassandra Wilson songs and transposed them into higher keys. Jean-Luc and I were the only ones who had any music theory, so we worked on the songs together. He could play classical piano as well as drum like a god. He could also dance. After the gig we'd go to nightclubs in Marseilles, the darkest, meanest ones with Algerian bouncers who would push a guy in the chest, knock him down in the street. There were absinthe cocktails in dirty glasses and Jean-Luc unrolled our magic pills from his trouser hem. There we would dance until we were raw and dawn spat on the harbour.

The boat cruises, they were my idea. I thought we were getting washed out. I thought that one day Jean-Luc would wake up and walk out the door, remembering he left a wife and kids in the north. I thought the band was fading and we were seeping into the crowd. There was a fuzz in between songs and you knew they were waiting for something bigger. I started to get scared. In the end Sonia and Beaté brought in a half-Tunisian girl and it fed them.

I know Jean-Luc will want to sell up at the end of the season. And I'll say yes, just to stop his soul from getting any harder, anything to the change the flavour of his eyes.

I wake on the cusp of dawn. Jean-Luc has pulled over the bed sheet and I am stiff from lying for hours in the damp. I lift the sheet and trace a finger across his shoulder, down along the fold of his back, the crevice of his arse, his hairy thighs. He doesn't feel a thing. I tuck him in and rise. I won't make noise now, but I still have the dishes to do from last night. I didn't hear Raoul and Mieko come downstairs after their murmuring on the sofa after dinner, so I'm pretty sure Jean-Luc has won our bet.

I go up on deck. This is the time when the water is a silken mass you could glide into, never needing oxygen again. I have always known I would end my life in water. Of course they are here, under a blanket that doesn't come from the boat. I can't see how their bodies are entwined, whether Raoul simply cradles her from behind, or if their faces are mirrored together, sharing breath. In a band, you see the way people sleep. I light a cigarette and I guess the smoke travels over to them. There is not an odour, not a sound written on the morning. Mieko pulls away the cover and her eyes flutter, she pulls it up again. I sit down and inhale. Sleeping out here can't be good for a soprano's voice.

I head to the galley to start the dishes. Above, I hear moving limbs, speech. There's not much you can't hear on a boat. She speaks so quietly to him that I still don't know what language they use to communicate in intimacy. I hear them step down to their cabin and the door clicks shut. I hope we can make it to l'Île-Rousse today. There are friends I'd like to see in town. Jérome, who runs a bar now; Mélanie, who sells second-hand books in the square. I doubt that Mieko and Raoul are browsing types but there is a sophisticated food market under an open-air structure just off the piazza. It has thick chalky columns and the grace of a temple.

I think of going back to stir Jean-Luc but instead I spray down the surfaces. A boat is always grimy, so even this doesn't help much. All metal develops green encrustations, all wood swells beneath its thick varnish. I bring a pot of coffee upstairs, the flan I bought at Saint-Florent and a basket of yesterday's croissants. There is a splash from one of the other anchored boats. A man has dived in. I drink a coffee, remove my shirt and ease off the ladder, paddling softly. The dry mountains are purple, while Nonza sits on her outcrop. I hear cars in the village taking the tight turn before the rust-coloured church to Sainte Julie, so beautiful that one of my deepest wishes has always been to have that name, but I do not. Perhaps my life would not be so different if I did. Inside the church there is a painted, beckoning statue of the young woman whose short life ended in torture on these shores. Sainte Julie is the patron saint of the island. I backstroke to the beach and lie stretched out on tiny pebbles, a carpet of beads. I see

Mieko on deck wearing a beige shift, then Jean-Luc, who sits down to speak with her.

By the time I join them on board Raoul has surfaced. He is wearing a crushed business shirt. He looks cranky. His hand shakes before it lifts a glass. He dunks a croissant into his *café au lait* and eats more slowly than he did yesterday. Mieko sips the tea she brought herself. Neither of them wears sunglasses. Her kneecaps are just visible and they are finer than I had thought, encouraging me to imagine that her feet are sinuous sculptures. I see short strands on her almost hair-free legs. On her feet are the same espadrilles as before.

As he stares at a piece of flan on his plate, Raoul announces that he and Mieko would like to go ashore. In fact, he says, this area pleases them a lot. Jean-Luc and I look at each other. The sun, bound to her course, already makes a blazing sweep of the bay. The sea here is windless and there is no shade on deck. Raoul says they'd like to spend less time at the other ports along the way and relax here, along the unending grey beach he now points to while Mieko nods. They'd like to investigate the bottom of the cliffs. They're keen to hike up to the village. Raoul says he has heard about this place. Perhaps he read something in a newspaper supplement.

I am already thinking of the long trips to Saint-Florent for supplies rather than the easy walk to the supermarkets at l'Île-Rousse and Calvi. But Jean-Luc seems mesmerised by the idea. I see him unlocking. He is pleased to anchor here because the pressure is off for him.

Mieko reappears in trousers and a navy long-sleeved top, wearing a hat and carrying a large bag woven of the finest straw. Jean-Luc helps her into the dinghy. Raoul, wearing his open business shirt and a pair of baggy shorts, has trouble transferring his weight to the smaller vessel and Mieko grasps the gunwales as the boat rocks. They set off. I light a cigarette watching them, watching as seagulls swoop for crumbs I have thrown into the sea. Raoul carries her ashore, sets her down and rights her. Gingerly, she takes a few steps like a cat out of a cage, then advances to the cliffs, Raoul following. I turn away to take the breakfast things below deck. When I come up I see Jean-Luc has overturned the dinghy on the beach and walked a few hundred metres in the other direction. I see Mieko and Raoul as figures beneath the earthen mass of the cliff face, treading over rocks to the placid beach that lies further on. They look like a pair of runaways.

When Jean-Luc returns I am dozing under the canopy I have set up under the boom. His hand runs along my thigh but then stops as I awake. He climbs over me, naked, turning me face-up so our bodies fit together. He is aroused. He slides across my bikini pants and pumps hard, gripping my body. He kneels back, his genitals in a dark, wet cleft. He leans over and kisses one of my platypus feet.

Mieko told Jean-Luc she lost her voice while performing in Paris a year ago. She was onstage singing when her vocal chords became two arrow shafts in her throat. She was taken away in an ambulance. She thinks the video is on YouTube. She asked Jean-Luc not to watch. We have no signal here, but I know that Jean-Luc never would. Mieko said that she and Raoul had been married for eight years. Normally, they went to Osaka in the summer, but her parents had recently died. Raoul had no family left in Leuven, except a sister he didn't get along with. They were childless. They lived in Paris in the 14th *arrondissement*. Mieko was a singing teacher for Japanese students at the international school and the children of diplomats. She hoped to get her voice back, but the process had been lengthy and disappointing so far. Doctors had been unable to diagnose a specific problem apart from the strain of major performances. Mieko herself said she suffered from nerves, and a Japanese doctor in Paris had been treating her. They were here because he had advised a week on a boat in the Mediterranean.

Jean-Luc tells me that they won't be coming back until late. He showed them the steep path to Nonza and told them to order pizza at the bar, to get a cool table by the fountain. He said Raoul should tell them they were from one of the sailing boats anchored off-shore. They'd get treated better that way.

But the morning passes and we do not see them cross the stones. The shade has been stripped from the inlet and I see their heads bobbing on the water for a long time. Mieko comes out and she is wearing a white one-piece costume. She sits down, opening a small umbrella, covering her legs with a towel. Raoul thrashes in the calm sea. He backstrokes out a fair way, then frog-kicks to the shore where he floats with his ruddy stomach in the air. He lurches out of the water, throws himself on the pebbles.

There must be a cusp of shade growing in the rocks and they transfer there, no longer visible. I open a bottle of white wine and prepare a salad. Jean-Luc takes a mask and dives into the water to remove seaweed from the propeller. When he returns, we finish the bottle and he lazes on deck. I start re–reading the Houellebecq Raoul has left on the table.

It is quiet at first, a vocalise more than a song. Mieko has returned to the shore in her white swimsuit, a sarong around her waist. Raoul sits half in the water, letting the waves slap his side. Mieko bends over and stays down for a long time. She rises, begins the vocalise again, a heartbreaking crescendo. Jean-Luc looks up, growing aware of the sound.

The breasts of the young Sainte Julie were cut off by Romans stationed at Nonza when she refused to worship their pagan gods. Corsicans believe her severed breasts were dashed against a rock wall below the village, and this produced a spring called *la fontaine aux mamelles*. Expectant mothers now come to this place as barefoot pilgrims to secure their supply of milk, it is on the trail leading up from the beach. Sainte Julie's body was draped on a fig tree and all versions of the story say a dove flew from her mouth at the moment of her death.

The Wild Beasts of the Earth Will Adore Him

My new colleagues were backstabbing and merciless and came through inching, dust-choked traffic from the hinterlands to work. In turn, they wasted no time in blasting each other over milky Liptons in mugs or warm Guinness bottles passed across the desk. Very quickly the office mystery was established as Meredith. Meredith was creamy white, with coiled blonde hair dropping down her back and the way she moved was staunch. I was informed that Meredith slept with her dogs.

The dimensions of the Accra agency were tighter than the huge Jo'burg office where I'd been stationed before, but there was just as much piss-taking with the accounts. Everyone else was tar-black except the caramel secretary. I was looked at warily (mixed-race, shaven head, *Eraserhead* T-shirt) for good reason among their yellowing business shirts, and they didn't ease up until Kwame Djoleto made a lewd crack and they could see I wasn't a jerk.

More than once, Meredith glided from the staff room with a flowery mug and wearing a pleated apricot skirt, a shade of Sunday bazaar. Someone blurted that the husband had left her for a Nigerian hooker three years ago and she was frozen here, the sickly salary better than any amputated return to her confectioned home town. Kwame said the hooker had been squealing on top and Meredith had burst in with a gun from the kitchen, the dogs howling and the husband in grovelling tears.

This brought forth light, worn-through sniggers.

The company had rented me a house off a road of better streets and I was told that Meredith was a neighbour. She'd had to scale down when the husband's salary moved away. I didn't envisage us having stilted drinks on the porch but Meredith, one afternoon while handing in a budget estimate, said it was a tranquil part of town. Ingrained along her forehead and the grooves either side of her mouth were deepening lines of hardiness. I asked what breed her dogs were.

'Labradors. Black Labradors. They suffer in this heat.'

Never once in my life had I owned a dog, wished for a dog, even studied a dog. I find them breathy.

In the mornings a group of local soldiers jogged along the street in front of my place. This area of town backed onto the sprawling military camp with its crooked fences and colonial bungalows. The soldiers carried guns across their bodies and shouted marines' chants as they jogged to the end of the street. Every morning I watched their caps and olive shirts through the blinds. Some time afterwards, just before the driver swung around the corner to take me to work, Meredith would engineer two sleek black shapes down the empty street. Their spines snaked along, their thick tails levered and whacked around, their mouths were large, pink, wet.

I soon realised the nucleus of my clan of colleagues was not Kwame Djoleto, who made a lot of noise and was wide and pungent, but a thin man named Solomon who did little more than retrieve the post. Solomon sat straight-backed on his seat. He walked with a polio limp. A son of Solomon's had died recently and the funeral notice was still on the staff board, showing a bright boy with buck teeth. Though I was the boss I realised that it was Solomon who commanded the team's fluctuations and temperament. He looked congenial, long-suffering.

All hands came on deck any time there was a photo shoot as these were few and far between, dogged by many interpretations of the theme at hand. Take cooking oil. Weeks were spent on divergent storyboards, meetings were left in disgust. Brainstorming in the overheated conference room took on the dimensions of outright warfare as each colleague within the creative department (and several others without) unfolded his or her heartfelt story of Frylove. Kwame wanted a romantic scene: husband comes home, embraces wife from behind while she is cooking. There was a valid debate about the trappings of the kitchen, about whether the wife should wear Western dress; whether the husband should be fat or slim. How dark their skins should be. I noticed Meredith paying attention in a freefall way. Was she thinking about her dogs? When a handful of ideas had been cobbled together, Solomon was consulted and the fine-boned man mentioned his preferences while twisting a leaky pen. Kwame's scene, for example, didn't involve any offspring. The grasp of the husband could be perceived as sexual (guffaws). Western dress was better, though the food should be rigorously local. As Kwame attempted baldly to defend his idea I stopped scribbling and saw that Meredith's eyes like a watershed were upon me. But I was just in the way of her blinding thoughts. It was probably not the dogs she was thinking about.

Discussion reignited in a bullying way when Kwame insisted upon the wife's fair tones and narrow waist. I glimpsed Meredith roll her eyes.

The two black Labradors were also walked in the evening. That was when I sat on the porch with a neat gin. Like Meredith's, my spouse had taken off. But with good reason. I hadn't had an email since. I watched Meredith's arid walk behind the two animals with their slack leather leads. The dogs progressed slowly, heat-stricken in the musky air, heads bobbing, tongues gluey. Meredith filled out a tracksuit and wore a peaked cap.

I was still sitting there in the dark eating peanuts when Kwame and two of the others made the visit they had been promising, wearing tight open shirts. Kwame was carrying a further bottle of gin. Their faces were beaded with sweat and the youngest man wiped his temples with a handkerchief. Kwame looked up at the rusted fan blades suspended from the teak-cladded awning and said that Solomon knew a good electrician in Tudu. The fluorescent light made my skin look green, while they were a trio of black faces with violet flints. I brought out extra glasses.

Kwame drove us up through the suburbs to a nightclub called the Red Onion. I held onto a bottle of beer as women became wavy before me. Cocks were crowing when with ringing ears we came outside into the damp. I wondered whether Meredith, in the arms of her Labradors, was awake.

Solomon was absent and the office was in disarray. It was not known whether it was something connected to the son's recent funeral, or whether fresh problems had arisen in his household. No one knew where Solomon lived. No one knew which *trotro* he caught to work. We went ahead with the Frylove photo shoot. The kitchen of the house next door served as a set. Lights on stands were placed apart and Meredith positioned fans. But there was an uncertainty, a negligence, in the air. Everyone looked lethargic. Kwame snapped at the Frylove models under the hot lights. The woman who was the 'wife' snapped back at him and folded her arms, while the 'husband' slumped in a kitchen chair and sent text after text. Any sort of orchestration dispersed. Meredith came across with her folder, standing between Kwame and the woman. I couldn't understand Twi and didn't know if Meredith in all her years of living here had grasped their tongue. It didn't seem to be the case. As she led the woman up the hall to the bathroom I heard her say, 'Now just come this way, Nana Yaa. You don't want to spoil your makeup now.'

The model 'children' rolled up bits of paper and flicked them about the room.

As boss, I knew I had to call Kwame into line and re-establish the dynamic of the day. Kwame scowled at me in anticipation, his head swinging on his considerable neck as he looked around for Solomon among the helpers one last time. The maps under his armpits clung to his skin. He went over to the cooking pot and stirred the cold stew. He checked the yellow Frylove bottle was in sharp light. He told the unruly girl and boy to behave themselves before he took them outside to beat them. After Jo'burg's tetchy egos and gauzy models, it was hard not to laugh.

Meredith brought the 'wife' back from the bathroom. They had agreed upon a tawny girl, far too young to have produced the preteens at the table. Meredith positioned her over the pot, showing the lumpy 'husband' how to clasp her. Kwame nodded. Someone had handed him a mug of tea. I waved away mine and watched the white woman giving a 'honey-I'm-home' embrace to the ticklish Frylove 'wife'.

The end of the day produced two feasible shots we uploaded onto the computer: 'The Hug' and 'At the Table', the latter an alternative that showed the mother arranging a platter of jollof rice and chicken on a printed tablecloth, flanked by husband and children. Given 'The Hug' was devoid of any sort of sexual or marketing charge, I preferred the rigid table shot with its acidic yellows and greens, its gasping comedian faces. There was an irresistible lyricism at the base of its poor logic and composition.

Kwame wasn't happy with either and roamed the set like a lost dog. Two weeks later the table shot, plus titles, was on billboards about the town.

Solomon refused to surface over the next few days and voices trailed along the corridors. Where did he come from? Was it Teshie? Did he catch a bus from Nungua? A chair was kept for him at the next round of meetings, where Kwame clashed severely with a colleague called Patrice. It was about a hair–straightening product, one of the agency's ongoing campaigns. Patrice's first ideas were overturned and sliced in the belly, then given a final pounding on the head. I noticed Meredith looked distracted, someone or something had pulled the plug on her concentration. The conference room was cramped and full of bad breath.

I watched Meredith walk the dogs in the evening and almost felt like calling out to her from my porch. One of the dogs seemed to lag a little, and directly outside my scrappy hedge she crouched to the road and massaged the dog's ears while the animal licked her face. I recoiled. The other dog turned around limply.

A staff member who travelled a long way into town along the coast had found a funeral notice on the *trotro*. It was Solomon's. The funeral was to take place the following week. Employees gathered in the office foyer and the poorly printed sheet was passed around. Kwame pushed into my office. Shaking in his hands was the streaky photograph showing Solomon's face tilted upward, his mouth open and front teeth tugged slightly out of line. It was clear that he was the father of the bright boy with buck teeth. Kwame cast down the sheet of paper, taking out a handkerchief to wipe his face. His trousers had an oil stain on the thigh and I saw he had tiny, clenched ears that wanted to hear very little.

Meredith entered the office and examined the page with a depleted expression. Outside a man burst into tears while a woman named Comfort led a procession into the conference room, where sobbing and moaning began. Kwame followed his colleagues and I soon heard his voice lifting above the others in a reverent, stilted backwash. Meredith and I stood staring at each other. I felt as though I were bagged inside her head and looking at myself. I saw my jaw harden and lines rippling my forehead.

Meredith flushed and we followed the others into the room.

What I in no way expected was to see a hired *trotro* parked outside the office a few days later and a coffin being unloaded under Kwame's sweaty direction, then slipped through the narrow front doors. The driver squatted by a roadside tree in ragged shorts as staff members filed into the building after the swaying cargo.

Inside the conference room the tables were jammed together and I heard shoes scuffing and the creaking of wood. I stood transfixed in the doorway to my office, fingers hooked in the belt of my jeans. Meredith walked grimly to the staff room, came back holding a mug of tea. I heard the box jemmied open and there was a chasm of silence, a collective exhalation mixing with the aura of Solomon's embalmed body. A chemical smell arose. My stomach heaved. I turned away to my desk and switched on the monstrous air conditioner plugged into the wall. Then Kwame was at my back looking like a man plummeting, his fists empty and his face stripped. The whites of his eyes had red hairline cracks.

Solomon's face was puffy, like he was in the process of chewing a mouthful of food. His skin looked sheer, the lines on his forehead fleeting. The stretch of skin between upper lip and nostrils was more rounded than it had been when he sat here twisting the leaky pen. He wore reading glasses, a beige suit, a bow tie, a late-1970s ruffled shirt. A part of my brain was laughing, scavenging this experience, while another examined the cracked leather shoes that were boats on his feet, the tennis socks, and wanted to buckle over. The body already looked flattened and false, a rasping snakeskin with all moisture erased, though there was oil or shea butter combed through his hair. I stood in line around the tables as each staff member waited for a moment with the odourless corpse. When my turn came I spoke softly, a few words. But as I walked away I felt a powerful excavation building up in my body. I wanted to shit, or vomit, writhe on the ground, pluck my own eyes from my head. I wanted rapture before it would come to me. At the door I turned back to the coffin with a pit in my chest, currents shunting in the spongy ellipse of my brain, each organ inside of me vaporous. I sat on the loo for a good ten minutes, then poured gin for everybody.

Solomon's funeral notice joined that of his bright young son on the staff noticeboard and they became a pair of comrade saints. Staff members glanced at Solomon's easy–going manner in the photograph as they passed and Kwame, hands on hips in conversation, looked up to his quiet colleague as though for confirmation or advice. Kwame's aggression moved someplace else and Patrice's ideas for the hair–straightening campaign were revived.

There was excellent dope to be had in this country. After a string of demolishing hangovers I had organised a good supply of undoctored weed and smoked every evening. Kwame disapproved. He refused even the slightest puff, folding his arms like an old woman and curiously watching me filling a skin. The week after Solomon's funeral Kwame sat on my back porch and stared at me lighting up, his forearms on his thighs and his large hands thrown together. He eased back into the cushions to avoid the cloud I exhaled. He had no companions this evening. His shirt burst apart in scallops and dark ovals of his belly showed through. His chest was hairless and his neck had rings of flesh. His eyes caught on the rusty fan I had failed to have fixed, its blades tilted on their axis and the knot of wires escaping the dislodged plastic cup. I knew he was kicking himself for not finding out in which Tudu slum Solomon's electrician lived, before Solomon had died.

I inhaled again, beginning to feel the easy fissuring, the wandering explosions. I dropped my head back on the thick bamboo of the chair. Kwame shifted and I told him there were more beers in the fridge. He went into the kitchen and came back outside, uncapping the bottle tops in some mysterious local way, his movement wobbling the light given off by three candles on a saucer. As usual, there was no power. The neighbourhood lay black and dense beyond us. I inhaled a third time and the memory of love in my bowels, my brain rank with it, sprang forth inexplicably. My heart rate surged and I felt my body veering. I looked down at my belly and thighs, my arms on the varnished armrests.

Kwame stared into the darkness. In Solomon's absence the office staff clustered around him and I knew he came to sit here in silence. Perhaps he had begun to understand his own deference to the slim man, and the fixation of listeners whenever Solomon had whispered his words. Kwame saw me studying him and he jerked around to point out a bright beacon of electricity up the road through the trees. A generator rattled loudly. It was where Meredith lived, he said.

Sniggering, I asked him who the hell had started the rumour about her sleeping with the dogs, whether it was some sort of fixation or score-settling, or a sick way of wanting the broad blonde woman.

'I did,' said Kwame.

His teeth shone and we both laughed loudly, crazily, until our laughs tailed off. I did not ask him why. I felt the full throttle of the overloaded spliff and wanted to roll downward, brakeless, curl in a ball, think of Solomon meeting the buck-toothed boy in the other world, on a corner somewhere in a place as merciless and rundown as this.

Meredith came to me with a problem. She said that Patrice's ideas for the hair-straightening campaign had been plagiarised. She pulled out an African-American magazine she had found in the staff room, and I could see why Patrice's lavish storyboard had initially been slaughtered by Kwame. It was damned good. A light twinkled on above Patrice's head.

I convened a meeting in the conference room. I decided to exclude Meredith and not reveal my source. I sat there, Kwame and Patrice before me nursing tea, both bristling. I saw that their newfound collaboration had thin and knotted roots.

I swung around the magazine. Kwame glowered. Patrice's eyes popped out. Kwame instantly began a tirade in the local language which I allowed him to conclude. He apologised to me. But not to Patrice who sat glumly in the chair, his first gainful moments now stamped in the dust. He confessed he had found the magazine at his sister's house; she was just back from Atlanta.

Kwame shook his pointed finger in Patrice's face and both men shouted. I wondered whether I should have told Meredith to pipe down and forget about the magazine. But the company was a conglomerate, our work traversed borders; lawyers might have been flown out. I tapped my pen on the desk and neither of the men heeded me. I had a flash of the most galvanising moments in my extinguished married life. The sense of being a faceless, fleshless absentee in the room.

'Kwame,' I said.

Kwame pushed back his chair and stood. He suggested I sack Patrice on the spot.

'Otherwise I will be leaving here this noon,' Kwame said.

This is when I longed for Solomon's counsel. I knew enough of Kwame's volatility to avoid agitating him further. I noticed the undersized ears were like creased flowers, the central folds bearing no stamen. I saw that nothing would stop him from travelling this tangent to its absurd end.

'You will choose. One of us will go.' Kwame walked over to the frosted windows with his hands on his hips. Patrice stared at the desk. I saw he'd put a lot of effort into his haircut. He was an earnest young man, an asset. I looked at his embarrassed face and remembered when a priest had placed his fingers on my forehead at school. My prime thought had been to knee him in the groin. Until a current had passed through the intersection of our skins. Heat. Transmission.

I heard Meredith pass outside in her squeaky wedges.

'Patrice, you will leave us,' I said. 'You realise this is a very serious error in judgement. It's unacceptable, as Kwame has pointed out.'

Kwame nodded at the window without appearing satisfied or easing his stance.

I left the room. Meredith tagged after me in the hall and I turned around and looked at her face. It was downy, it had been licked by dogs. I thanked her for her astuteness and her lips pursed.

I closed my office door and made a strong cup of instant coffee from a tin of Nestlé and the kettle atop a filing cabinet. I sat there swallowing the hot, dirty drink. I turned on my computer and began an email to my estranged wife.

The following day a shabbily dressed woman stood in the hall and was ignored by everybody. Finally Kwame swung around and demanded to know what she wanted. I had just visited the bathroom for the third time and saw him descend upon her. Her voice was a weak whisper as Kwame bent over. She wore busted flip-flops that had been wired together and her feet were covered in dust.

Kwame turned to me with his face draped in guilt. He took the woman's fine arm, leading her to the conference room. I saw her hair had been straightened many times and she had lost patches of it. As they walked Kwame's hand opened on her back.

Before Kwame strode into my office to inform me, I knew what he would say. The woman was Solomon's sister. She needed money. I felt another cramp shifting through my gut.

'I cannot believe,' said Kwame. He sat opposite me at the desk, head rocking in his hands. 'That we have forgotten his family. This cannot be.'

I asked what the common practice here was.

'Gifts of rice,' he said. 'Gifts of rice.'

I opened the top drawer of the filing cabinet and took out a wad of greasy cash in an elastic band.

'How much?'

These words seemed to devastate Kwame a great deal.

'How much is a man's life worth? And an innocent, stolen son?'

I stood there waiting. I felt very light-headed.

'Might it be better to send someone out to buy some bags of rice?' I said.

Kwame released a mighty *humph!* 'Who now shall go out to buy rice? When we are even without Patrice?'

I handed him the wad of cash. The money came from my own pocket. Kwame's shirt was tight across his back as he left the room.

Three days later a second woman was standing in the hall. Where the first woman was eroded and unobtrusive, this woman was large and gay, staring up and down at everyone who passed. She wore a bright print and her feet and cheeks were plump and scented. A glittery scarf was tied over her hair. Kwame stopped by her and the woman announced that she was Solomon's wife. I saw him march her into the conference room and command cups of tea.

I walked into my office with the armful of back files Meredith had just retrieved. I half-closed the door and sat down. The dust made me sneeze and the massive splutter travelled down the ratchets of my spine. My watery intestines had made a wreck of my body and I'd been living on flat Coke and rice crackers for days. I pushed the files aside and stared at my hands on the table. They were shaking. I wondered if you starved a human body of love or food or kinship – which loss would be the most ruinous? I continued to look at my hands, recalling the lifeless fists beside Solomon's body. I touched my fingertips to my neck and they were cold. I heard Meredith's heels squeak into the conference room. Kwame introduced Solomon's spouse. Other office staff joined the trio and I heard laughter. It sounded as though the woman was telling stories. Kwame led an eerie applause that rose through the building.

I juggled with the idea of making an appearance but felt that Kwame would have called me if my presence was required. I was not informed of the arrangement he came to with the woman, and when I next went to the bathroom Solomon's spouse was gone. The office was silent for the next few hours. Kwame and two colleagues had gone to scout for a location. Before lunch I abandoned the files and had the driver take me home, where I dropped to my bed, head pounding.

I woke in the afternoon. I showered and the water was icy on my skin. I ate some cold rice and opened a tin of local tuna. On the porch the heavy air felt chilly. I wore an old sweater of my wife's that was laced with her smell. I sat there in the midst of the neighbourhood. Children were crying out; there was an argument at the fruit stall down the road; a shoe-shine boy trudging along drummed his wooden box with his brush. I made a cup of hot black tea and sat with its fusty heat beneath my face, making me perspire. I opened my laptop to the email I had begun to my wife on the day I had sacked Patrice. I wrote two more sentences before all sense, all emotion, failed me. She had used the word *irretrievable*, many times.

Meredith appeared at the far end of the street, heading out from her gate with a single dog this time, on its leather lead. I watched her pace down the road. She wore a peaked cap that shadowed her face, but today she held her head higher. Glancing left and right, she looked strangely mobile and engaged. The dog's head was low, close to the road surface, a slinking along more than a walk. The lead slackened between them. When Meredith was level with my house she looked directly into my porch and saw my eyes trained upon her. She stopped. I had the feeling she had been hoping I was there. I waved, motioning to her to open the gate. I lifted myself out of the chair and moved to the railing as she crossed the gravel. The dog followed her, nose roving over the new terrain.

'Hello, Meredith. Anything I can do?'

Meredith's erect walk became a stagger and I saw how hard she had been pushing herself before. Why the fuck had she stayed on here?

'It's Bobby McGee,' she said, hauling herself closer. 'My other dog. I think he's dead.'

After she spoke, a suffering shudder collapsed her shoulders. She removed the peaked cap and brought her hands to her eyes, her forehead shiny and flushed. The dog folded its black shape on the ground.

Meredith peered up. 'Would you mind coming to see?'

I closed my computer and went down the steps. She pulled her cap back over her coiled blonde hair. I felt her eyes comb my chest and realised I was wearing a woman's sweater. I did not wish to explain. I noticed the day-glo orange laces in her running shoes.

'This is Janis,' she said, indicating the Labrador now swinging a thick tail.

I opened the gate for Meredith and the dog, and followed them the short distance down the street. In this direction the houses increased in size before the road terminated at the crooked fences of the military camp. Meredith's place was freshly painted and ringed by leafy coleus plants, with twin traveller's palms fanning upward either side of the steps. She unlocked the metal grills over her carved double doors.

I followed her down the hall. The house smelled as I would have imagined. Soap and hair products: it was clear how much Meredith prized those long blonde coils. There were no photographs, just clean surfaces, empty chairs, a shocking emptiness. I wondered if her cheating husband and the Nigerian hooker had lasted longer than three months. It was probable that they had. I thought of young, bright

Patrice who had been quashed by Kwame Djoleto, and how Kwame would soon have the final word on every project in the office. I thought of the last time I had made love with my beautiful wife, how we had lain there erased, the bed sheets blank, the room vacant, our fluids leaking from us into crevices where they would drain away and there would be no embodiment.

Meredith showed me the dead animal lying on her bed. The front paws were crossed, the hind legs a little astray. There was urine on the sheets and the belly seemed swollen. She had left the air conditioning on high so there was no smell. The dog's eyes were open. Meredith sat on the end of the bed. I stood there looking at the dense black carcass thinking of the weed sitting in a drawer of the wall unit at home, thinking that if I phoned Kwame he would know who the hell to call and what to do with this.

The Ukrainian Girl

When Louise came downstairs the next morning the Ukrainian girl was tying up rubbish bags with swift double knots. To anyone else Louise would have said there was no need, but she let the young woman shuffle outside with the two smeared bags. Louise even pointed to the bins by the gates of the small villa so that she might feel obliged, and checked out the girl's pert bum screened by a pair of rose Capri pants. She couldn't recall exactly what the girl had been wearing the night before but it had been busty and sheeny, and she knew the males had groaned after her, holding their loaded crotches. Louise also had a gut feeling that the Ukrainian girl had ended up in her brother-in-law's tent. How else to explain this act of contrition?

Louise glanced at the kitchen counter, now freed of her husband Daniele's stoned cooking efforts. A coffee percolator sat on a blue ring of flames. Louise put on the kettle for some green tea. The Ukrainian girl's name was Yulia. She was new to Verona and a friend of someone's girlfriend, invited to help redress the gender imbalance. For Louise always provided far too many men at her annual summer party, single men who thunked to AC/DC when the couples had melded into the dark corners of the garden.

Yulia came through the back door holding Louise's son Pietro on her hip. Louise opened the tea tin, feeling hangover-lousy.

'Did you wash your hands after touching that rubbish?' she said, not really wanting Pietro's outstretched arms.

'Of course. We play now. Where are Pietro's toys?'

'They're out the back on the terrace. In a big trunk. Those are his outside toys.'

Yulia smiled a gooey smile at Pietro and swept outside. Graceful, Louise thought, after all that gyration last night. Louise heard the toy box open, and Pietro pitching trucks onto the tiles. She exhaled. She knew that the right thing to do now would be to call Francesca, her brother-in-law Diego's wife, and see how she'd passed the night. Francesca had a stitch in her cervix and the baby was due next month.

But Louise walked back to the cooler front rooms of the house with her cup of tea. On her divan was a sleeping man wrapped up in one of her kente cloths. It was Ross, Daniele's best mate, who'd flown out from London for the bash. He'd also been vying for the Ukrainian girl through the first phase of the night, until it was clear her brother-in-law had somehow scooped the evening's prize. Louise was almost certain she'd seen Ross throwing himself about to an AC/DC track on his own after the DJ did a runner, which was when she noticed Yulia and Diego hand in hand crossing the wet grass. Around dawn she'd finally tucked under Daniele's shoulder as Ross rolled yet another joint, a dozen empty Prosecco bottles across the tables between them.

She unlocked the door to her study and sat awhile. She heard the gates creak open and a car drive out up the hill. As the day drew on guests would either drag themselves back to town or dig in for the day-after party. Someone would revive the fire, some younger person would put the music on full blast, some jazz or mild hip-hop. The dogs would lie sated under the trees, bellies full from the barbecue last night. There was still a plastic bag of meat in the spare fridge.

She could just see one end of the bright blue tent her son had helped her erect yesterday afternoon. She'd set it up for Diego who'd had a stressful year and didn't much like to be bothered, who had driven in alone from Milan, sweaty and strong-smelling, and headed straight for the downstairs shower. This was before she had rushed inside to finish the flans. Now the tent zipper was open, wafting, a woman's summer skirt. No sign of Diego. Strong sunlight was starting to douse the grass and two men she didn't recognise were shifting a cane chair under the trees, both with bare tattooed chests.

The door pushed open and Ross popped around the corner.

'Louise? All on your lonesome?'

'I thought you were dead to the world,' Louise said.

'I think I was for a while there. I can't sleep any longer on that godawful sofa.'

He turned to the window as Pietro crossed the garden kicking a ball, a robust Yulia behind him. She was all muscle and flying raven hair.

'Hey,' he said. 'She even comes up good in the daylight.'

'They all do, don't they? That kind.'

'That's a bit harsh. You said you needed some fillies to join up the dots. She's a great-looking filly.'

They watched her tumble to the ground and let the child's ball pass towards the fence. Yulia rolled over and Pietro straddled her belly, bouncing while the young woman laughed. 'You were tailing her for a good while last night,' Louise said. 'Looks like Diego beat you to it.'

'It wasn't really like that,' he replied.

'What were you talking about all that time?' Louise had seen them on one of the outside divans, Ross wearing an unusually disarmed face.

'We were talking about education, really.'

'Oh, come on.'

'It's true. She said she's brought her son to Italy because the schools are rotten where she is, and now there's the war. She said her husband used to beat her. He cracked her cheekbone twice.'

'Right, pull the other one,' said Louise. 'Next you'll tell me her family perished in Chernobyl and she walked all the way here in those nasty stilettos she had on last night.'

'She did lose her grandparents there. And both her parents died young. She grew up in an orphanage outside Kiev. She told me her daughter died of leukaemia last year. She was four.'

Louise gasped, her eyes knitting together, propelled towards her son. They both watched as there was a flicker or beckoning from Diego's tent and Yulia fell to her hands and knees and crawled inside.

Louise settled Pietro in front of a cartoon in the only childproof zone of the house, and went upstairs to the bedroom. Her husband Daniele was still outstretched on top of the sheets. He opened his eyes as she walked in.

'*Vieni qui, bellezza.*'

'Not now, Daniele.'

She sat down on the rumpled bed, thinking of the pale-faced daughter in the hospital ward and Yulia's bone cracked by a man's fist, her cheek swollen and the bruising seeped around an eye. It couldn't be true. She told herself that Ross had been swayed by the dope and the loud music, the girl's cupped breasts. Daniele nuzzled her back, cradling himself to her. She pulled away from his hot body and went to the bathroom, where she sat on the laundry basket. From the window she saw the bright blue tent in the middle of the garden. A couple lay entwined in the hammock and the two bare-chested men drank beers in the shade; a woman from her office sat cross-legged on the grass wearing a burgundy straw hat.

Daniele came in, sat on the rim of the bath.

'He fucked her, didn't he?' she said.

Daniele was the older brother and now his face remained steady. He kneeled down on the bath mat, a little cautious on his dodgy left knee, opening her with his chin, stroking her thighs with bristly cheeks, pulling across her panties and reaching her cunt with his cool tongue. She clasped his head, felt the oil in his scalp. Louise had been to Moscow for a conference once and hated it. The men with grey swabs under their eyes, the statuesque silken women who would one day decompress into their pillowy mothers with pincushion faces and arms. She had marvelled at the flower stalls on a freezing Saturday morning until a colleague told her they were 'forgiveness flowers'. Forgive what?

Forgive me for beating the shit out of you.

Louise stepped out of the shower and her son handed her the downstairs telephone. The music was on loud outside and she shut the bathroom window. Louise sat on the laundry basket again. It was Francesca, Diego's wife. Francesca had spent the last five months confined to her bed. Most nights, apart from when he had his tennis matches, Diego had been stationed in the next room reading the newspaper.

'Do you have any idea when Diego's heading out? I've had a pretty bad night.'

Francesca sounded teary, ever so bleak.

'Sometimes I can't feel the baby moving any more, you know? And then I lie there waiting. I even tap my tummy to get him to move. Is that stupid?'

Louise remembered pushing tent pegs into the soft ground, wanting Diego to be comfortable, feeling guilty that her cousin and her kids out from Bristol had taken up half the house. She had thought he might feel out of the fray there, able to bed down if he got tired of the dancing under the portico around the back. She had never imagined the warm enclave might provide a shroud for two fused bodies.

'It's fine,' Louise told her. 'It used to happen to me all the time.'

'Is Diego anywhere nearby? I suppose they must all be sleeping still.'

'Well, yes. I've hardly seen anyone yet. They're beginning to surface downstairs and someone's just put the music on. I haven't seen him so far.'

'Another long one, hey? Gosh, I bet you worked so hard. I'm so sorry I'm stuck here and can't give you a hand.'

'Don't worry, Fran. You just sit tight. Next year we can get legless.'

'Next year I'll be bloody breastfeeding.'

Francesca was on the verge of crying but all Louise could see were Yulia's flimsy Capri pants being thrown aside, and Diego ascending her flesh. They were sensual stocky brothers, both with round, jutting bottoms and heavy lips. Before her love for Daniele had triggered, it was Diego that she had wanted. She and Diego had once kissed.

'Are you okay there?' Louise said.

'Yes, I am,' Francesca replied. 'I'll be okay. I just don't like being on my own too much. I'll be fine. Tell him I called.'

Louise stared down at the blue tent in the middle of the garden. The couple in the hammock were snogging, arms wrapped around each other. The trio in the shade were leaning over eating sections of watermelon.

Daniele pushed open the bathroom door and turned on the shower.

'That was Francesca,' she said.

He opened the linen cupboard and took a towel from the top. Water splattered against the glass door until he reached in to lower the pressure.

'What must it be like,' she said. 'Throwing yourself at anything that moves?'

Her husband took two tired steps towards her. She loved him infinitely for what he was about to say, but knew she would do her utmost to batter it down.

'Louise,' he said. 'You are not responsible.'

Now Louise recalled the look on Diego's face as he danced with

Yulia. Astonished and bold, a face activated by rebellion. And Yulia so vulgarly agile in his arms in that shiny dress falling from her shoulder, bending her body around his.

'I am responsible for my lies.'

Louise took a short sundress from the wardrobe and rubbed sun cream into her face. She stayed barefoot and went downstairs. Fresh coffee sat brewing on the stove and she greeted her cousin's teenage daughters, all part of the tireless dancing clan last night, who were teasing her enraptured son. Biscuits were stacked on a plate and croissants were being tipped from an oven tray into a basket. It was a good thing the Ukrainian girl had bagged so much rubbish before as the bins were quickly filling again, and these young girls had no intention of tidying.

Ross, shirtless, was sitting outside in the sun wearing a pair of women's sunglasses. He was drinking from a jug of Pinot Grigio someone had refreshed with ice. She poured herself a full plastic cup and edged into the shade. The tent was a dozen metres off in the middle of the bleached lawn, whose fringes were now dotted with chatting people lounging in the shadows. A smoke plume rose from the barbecue. The tent flap had been zippered, its blue flanks were still.

'Do you think she tells the story about the dead child and the smashed cheekbone to every sucker she meets?' Louise said. 'It must be rather stifling in there by now.'

'Louise,' Ross replied. 'They left an hour ago. She had to pick up her kid and Diego gave her a ride into town.'

Louise looked at the painting above Francesca's head. It was by Daniele's grandfather, a provincial painter who'd managed to sell a lot of work. His was a strain of localised surrealism, unfriendly to the eye and – Louise had always thought – to women. In this work, long knuckled fingers clutched at elusive shapes. The dynamic seemed uncomfortably sexual, bearing a wet pulse, and revealed a cloying internal diorama. She suspected maternity to be the muffled subject: the parting of childbirth, the jostling of organs; the renewed filling of that gulf by penetration. It was as close to an heirloom as the family possessed and she had never wanted it in her house.

Today, the painter's great-grandson lay in Francesca's lap, her massive dark brown nipple pressed to his face. Francesca was sweating, her neck and breast glistened as she touched his damp curls. The strain of these months, the final bursting through of the child, had left her a ruin. Louise filled her glass with another nip of frothy Guinness. She heard the men in the kitchen. Daniele was tipping pasta into the colander and a hot chute of water coursed into the marble sink. Diego was setting out plates and cutlery. They were laughing together as brothers and speaking in dialect.

That day, that blistering morning after the party, Louise had shaken down the address from someone. She'd made a stubborn, torn Daniele drive her into town, had sent him upstairs into the ugly apartment block near Porta Nuova station. Twenty minutes it had taken. Then Daniele had brought his younger brother out onto the footpath like a criminal. Diego had stood there collecting himself, his blunt hands dropped before his jeans. As they pulled into the street Louise saw the Ukrainian girl come outside and stand on the narrow balcony. She leaned over to see who was in the car, watched them drive away.

Three Days in Hong Kong

You fly in. He says he won't be there, there'll be a sign with your code name. *Philomena M.* He likes secrets. You know he likes living between several worlds suspended in the air. He likes flight. He risks collisions. He travels way too much.

There is the card with your secret name. *Philomena M.* The driver has pointed sideburns like Nick Cave and caramel skin pulled tight over his cheekbones.

You drive onto the motorway into the night, past cheap housing blocks with scabbed facades, balconies crammed as though the life is oozing out of them.

The city pulls you in, sucks you under, chucks you up, then streams around you. Chasms, rafts of lights, a Prada shop; the black numb sky and nowhere water.

You pull into a ritzy place. The driver carries your half-empty suitcase, lopsided by books. You see a shabby Caucasian couple, hear them speak Australian.

Your room number is 537. A slim porter manoeuvres your bag.

The room makes you start. It is layers of ruffled smoothness and finally the deep ink panel of the harbour. Buildings corded in light.

You have barely sat down on the loo when the phone rings and you waddle out, knickers around your thighs.

'You've made it then,' he says.

'Well, I was booked,' you reply.

'I can't wait to see you.'

'I'm wet as—'

'I'm full as—'

He is fiddling with something. His phone. His trousers?

'Touch yourself,' he says.

'I am, darling.' You are not.

'I can't make it tonight. Just sit tight. Rest yourself. I'll drop by early tomorrow. I'll wake you up with a little morning attention. Make sure you're naked between those sheets.'

You go to the window. The city is a wide sweep of glitter. In the story of your life you are love-struck and yearning, lucky and crazy. But you are not. You feel like laughing when he looms over you. You don't like the *ahh* sound that escapes through his nose after sex. You don't like his bum. You run a bath, trying to imagine his apartment, his groomed wife, the people he employs to keep his life clean. You think he has three young sons.

In the morning you wake up to his phone call. Jet lag.

'I knocked, baby. You didn't answer. I knew you'd be tired after the trip. I nearly came in my trousers outside your door. You make me drown in you. I'm at work now. It's a beautiful day. I'd like to take you out on the harbour.'

You crawl over. You are in Hong Kong. Outside, everything is fumy with light.

'My office is not so far from your hotel. I should be able to pop in later. Don't shower. I want to savour you. I can't believe we're not in grimy London and I have you all to myself.'

You murmur. You hate air travel. You fell asleep with your book on your chest and didn't move all night. You wander over to the bathroom to pee, telephone to your ear. Your mouth is rancid. This room feels bigger than your apartment.

'Why don't you order some fresh fruit? Have them send up something. How I wish I could lather you with mango and papaya, my beauty.'

'I will, darling,' you say.

'That's a weak little kitten talking there.'

'I'll perk up.'

'You've perked me up already. I'll call you later, sweet one.'

You look at yourself in the bathroom mirror. Thirty-seven, no children, you know you are muddling along. And now you've slipped into this crevasse and you are dangling.

The last time you fucked him you told yourself it was glorious. But it was June for Christ's sake, two months back. His friend's place in Highgate. You look at your face beginning to twitch with lines, your still-beautiful eyebrows in high Arabic arches. You think of the man you walked away from who loved you, and went on to marry another woman who bore a disabled daughter. How you felt so guilty over that, as if you were the one who made it happen. You had to be.

After breakfast you are stuffed. A package arrives at the door. You hope they haven't made a mistake and close the door swiftly. It is a Chanel shopping bag with a ribbon. There is the most delightful handbag inside and you inhale the scent.

The distrustful side of you thinks: a copy? As you hunt for the guarantee, some sort of certificate.

It's there all right.

You lounge in front of the television. You switch it off and read your book. You close that and look out at the harbour which has a hard flat light, not blue like other seas. You wonder if it is a big harbour, or an inlet. You didn't buy a guidebook; he said he would whisper it to you, write it all on your skin.

'You won't believe what's happened. There's been a lot of movement at the office. I've got to put in the hours today. My honey, it's just not going to happen this afternoon, our harbour cruise. Can you hold out? You didn't wash your lovely skin, I hope.'

'I'll let you do that, my darling.'

The long empty hours make you feel a form of love unfurling towards him. Is it the waiting, the stretchy irrelevance of time in this ludicrously luxurious box? You're in love with him for a minute.

'I can't talk any longer. Get yourself a bottle of champagne. I'll help you finish it off. The handbag – it's not too classic, is it? I wouldn't want to label you, my love.'

'It's adorable. You are too good to me.'

You head to the shower.

In the afternoon you doze, and then it is dark again. The day has been upended, it has swept you by. Normally you are such a productive person. This is insane. You feel drugged. Your thick hair is still damp from the shower. Frizzy. Awful. You hang up the three dresses you have brought for the three days, now minus one. You've packed slinky things, things that will slip off your skin, fabrics that will show up its warm sheen. You hope they are not too vulgar. You haven't a clue what people wear here, or where he will take you. You slide on a cobalt blue dress that throws your breasts into relief. You wish your tubby tummy didn't have to show too. You should probably take a visit to the gym downstairs.

An hour before he is meant to pick you up, your phone rings:

'This is totally unexpected. Our anniversary, I'm afraid. It's next week but my wife's sister will be here and my wife has insisted we celebrate tonight. My darling, I can't risk putting her off. But I've managed to book a table in a restaurant in one of the buildings opposite your hotel. Can you believe it? I'm so close by. I can see you, my lovely.'

You look out. Masses of lights. Layers and layers of cubicles. Some empty, some with people still working. Boats plot the harbour. Planes thread the sky.

'Where? Where are you? I can't see you.'

'My wife has her back to the window. We're in the corner. She's just gone to the ladies.'

You are standing staring into infinite rooms, infinite faces, infinite lights.

'I don't believe you are out there.'

'You don't believe me?'

'What colour is my dress? What colour are the knickers I am flashing now?'

'Your dress is blue and you are not wearing knickers.'

You are shocked!

'I cannot speak any more, my darling. Remove that dress.'

You stand naked over Hong Kong, your hands in tepees on the glass, your legs apart. Your hair falls down your back, over your breasts. It is hard to believe anyone is watching you. For him, you touch yourself. You are not very wet. The man you left used to arouse you in a moderate way that you felt was not enough. You would lie awake, your lips to his shoulder. You were so mad he never probed your body hard enough, that you made sure his efforts were in vain.

You want to hug his disabled daughter. You decide that when you go back you will call him and do this.

The next morning you rush to the door naked when you hear a

knock. As you unlock the door you feel sweat between your hairless buttocks. Everything has been carefully waxed. Your sex is a peeled fruit. Your fingertips like to wander over the moist skin.

It is a woman in a mauve uniform holding flowers. You snatch them from her.

You throw them down and go to the bathroom where you look at your parts which are much more beautiful than the flowers. Then this disgusts you, the way the folds are so prominent. You love to pull a man's cock into you.

You go back to read his note.

I'm being a bore, I realise. Flowers! The most divine ones I could find, for the woman I long to embrace with love and lust.

No signature.

They are too perfect to allow them to gasp to death. You put their severed stems into a cut–glass vase on a bevelled glass table. They are orchids, the saddest of all flowers, but in the vase they spread as though in an embrace. They open to you and they are flawless.

'My darling! You were so gorgeous last night. I saw the way you touched yourself. So slowly. Your fingers pushing inside. Quite a spectacle you were. I kept asking myself, "What is she thinking up there?" My princess. My lover. My pristine baby. The way you opened yourself. Tell me.'

You breathe in, peering over Hong Kong. Today a grey tapestry, the lights are wounds.

'I was craving you, my love. I wanted to straddle you, feel you pounding inside me, feel your hot release.'

You know there is not much point in saying anything else.

'Have you looked outside, my darling? Have you seen the driving rain? I can't see us on the harbour. Or at the gardens. I'll be over to make love to you as soon as I've finished here. Champagne, my love. I want to drink it from every cleft on your body.'

'Oh, you will,' you assure him, shredding orchid petals. Shredding, shredding.

You commence reading your second book.

'Something's happened.'

He sounds upset. This had better be good, you think.

'It's worse than I thought. I never imagined. Please forgive me.'

'What's happened? How can I help?'

'It's my son, J—. My youngest. Appendicitis. Well, peritonitis, they've just announced. I'm at the hospital right now. He was taken from school in an ambulance. They operated an hour ago.'

'Oh my God!'

'I guess that rules out our afternoon tryst. I can't believe the bad luck we've been having.'

'The important thing is that he's okay. Are you worried?'

'Not at all, these doctors are the best. He's in the best hands possible. My wife's pretty shaken up.'

'Of course. What a shock.'

'But kids spring back quickly.'

'They do. Well, mostly.'

'Sorry?'

'I mean they do.'

You are thinking about your ex's disabled daughter, his rotten wage; the way she won't be springing back any time, ever.

'I love you,' you say. It moves through you, a ghastly compulsion to be tied to him at the bottom of the sea, your lungs a matted filigree.

'I love you too,' he says. You would pay to know what he truly thinks.

'I want you inside of me.'

You hear his breath catch, you feel pathetic. You are testing, pushing. He is whispering to you from a walled-in space where his groaning longings are compressed. You hear the noise of machines and a voice on a loudspeaker. You feel power.

'Come to me afterwards. I need to feel you. We can still make this happen.'

'I will. I'll just get my wife settled. Unfortunately, it might take a while. But I'm with you, *ahh*, I'm with you.'

You wake up, still drowsy, head throbbing. There is an empty bottle of champagne near your pillow and a bright-faced woman looking out from the television screen, talking on mute. A perfect face. Hong Kong harbour is chafed by light.

'My darling.'

'It's my last day. I haven't seen you yet. And I'm leaving this evening.'

You are crying, there is too much riderless emotion within you. Perhaps it's the trip, the displacement. Too much inertia, the jet lag. Too much time studying your face in the mirror, bending and hoisting and scrutinising the descent of your body. You've never had the time for such corrosive nudity.

'I've come all this way to see you.'

You are falling, you have fallen into this room, this lavish fabrication. And now you haul yourself before the astounding panorama which is thinly luminous. Your tears are wet with theatre.

'You've been so patient, so unbelievably patient. J—, my son, had a turn last night. We were down there again. His blood pressure dropped. It all went off-kilter for a moment. It was an emergency but he's okay. The doctors here are the best around, the very best. You understand, don't you?'

You know what is implied there. That, childless, you live in an obscene gulf. You can never know these things.

'I guess you'd understand if you had kids,' he says.

You end the call.

That night you tell the receptionist she can go fuck herself and you are not catching any flight to London. You order champagne, you stand by the dramatic window with its view of light-pocked buildings behind buildings and the harbour heaving in its black bucket.

Naked, quite drunk, you plaster yourself on the window. Rolling your body over and over on the glass.

In the morning the hangover passes quickly and you feel normal, more like yourself than you've felt in a very long time. The jet lag has gone and you've eased into this time zone. You dress elegantly and step outside into the city's warm cauldron. You wear a huge horny smile on your face.

You are *Philomena M* and this is your fourth day in Hong Kong.

The Book of Bruises

Renzo brought his sister Monique to the station. He had half-wanted her to miss the train and hovered there as her quilted jacket and trainers climbed the steps. Monique paused in the corridor, tucking her hair behind an ear as someone pushed past her. It was a gypsy girl with a dragging brown skirt. She blurred across Monique's body as the train pulled upon its agonising physics and began to move.

Renzo stood for a moment beside the empty tracks.

Outside the evening sky was still cerise in one corner. He stepped into a bar and drank the glass of red wine Monique had refused an hour ago, she'd preferred another coffee before the voyage. He sat there, fingering his glass. The wine was not good. Last night they had finished a bottle of Merlot and he had brought their father's mountain grappa onto the table, filling a pair of glasses. He had watched his sister's eyelids grow heavy, the way she licked her teeth and asked for water; he followed her lilting walk to the bathroom. Monique had fallen asleep on his sofa. Renzo paid the barman and went outside to smoke, sat on a cane chair as people pushed past. Some went back up to the Gare du Nord with their trolley bags, others to the Metro around the corner. He noticed a second gypsy girl as she wove along. Pregnant, he saw the expelled belly button at the centre of her freighted body.

He felt like eating noodles but he went past his usual *traiteur* and wandered into another bar. He ordered a Calvados. He was familiar with the woman sitting alone in the corner, but he ignored her. Several times he was aware of her eyes cast towards him, then they would return to her glass. Renzo wouldn't see Monique again until after Christmas perhaps, when they all rallied around the minute porcelain woman their mother had become. Monique's husband Serge would make his annual appearance, with his ponytail and wide shoulders and a hand often resting on the back of Monique's neck, under her hair, an engraved silver ring on one of his fingers. Monique would wear short skirts and black tights, boots with a stacked heel and metal chains around the ankles. They would take their mother to her favourite restaurant in the 4th *arrondissement*, where Monique would shepherd talk and locate harbours of recollection, until the old woman asked them all to leave her in peace or she'd call the manageress.

Once Maman's descent was in place, Renzo and Monique's father had left Paris and gone back to his hilly town in north-eastern Italy. Age had skated over him. The last time Renzo had seen him, his father had been wearing a fine blue sweater the same colour as his eyes. Gesturing to a listener in the dusky courtyard of his brother's farmhouse, the vivid azure of his irises had been emboldened by the dye of the wool, caught in the last light. In an older man it had seemed especially flaunting. Renzo had turned away and walked down to the cold lake. Where his father had been a boy there was a brutal, scarred riverbed Renzo and Monique had roved during their school holidays, hunting for gun cartridges or buttons from the young men blown apart by mortars at the end of the Great War. Their father had told them of this last crop of underage boys, brought to the front when all the other soldiers were maimed or gassed or wandering shell-shocked through the villages in rags. They were the *Ragazzi del '99*, born in 1899, clutched by their mothers and sweethearts, given misfiring weapons and cardboard boots and the blood-splashed uniforms of the dead. They were shot down in the dirt, just footsteps from the trenches. While Renzo had loved these stories Monique would look idly about, her damp black fringe pressed to her forehead.

The reason Monique had come this time was that she and Serge had had a fight. She did not show Renzo, but he knew there were wounds on her somewhere. She wouldn't tell him anything further, said it was not so bad this time. Serge had the kids holed up at his mother's place in Lille. Even so, Renzo knew from the start that after three days Monique would want to go back to him. There would be no calls, no contact, just a magnetic pull that would reach into her and start hauling her northward. Monique would become robotic, she would book her return ticket. At the outset Renzo had warmed to Serge, thinking the big ponytailed man had tamed his sister, who'd had abortions and slept with a raft of men. Until Monique turned up with a newborn in a shawl and a purple welt on her face. Renzo had watched the bruise turn violet, then green, then yellow. She wouldn't get it checked. He saw her pat it sometimes, hold her palm against it.

The woman he had ignored now came to the counter and leaned in next to him.

'Hello, Renzo.'

He nodded.

'I'll order us both another round. You don't have to talk to me. I can see you don't want company.'

But she sat at the bar with him when their drinks arrived. Hers a cognac, his another Calvados. Outside it had started to rain and the shower swept down the street. The woman held an unlit cigarette. They went out together under the awning to smoke, feeling the bluster between them.

'I saw you had your sister down again.'

'Yes.'

'She looked well.'

Monique's train would be crossing the flat dark north now. She would not be reading. She would already be communing with him. And Serge would be waiting for her in the unlit house, the children long gone to bed. Renzo's mind couldn't produce any other thoughts. Would Serge pull away his sister's clothing? Trace her bruises or push his fingers into them? Renzo had seen Monique's body when they were children bathing naked in the river near Vittorio Veneto, their father watching in rolled-up trousers from the bank, alpine water coursing in green furrows between the shoals. Monique had splashed icy water over him, made him shriek, her nipples pressed into her chest and her tiny pleat opening as she leaped away. Elfin, with her helmet of black hair. As a young man Renzo had waited to shed those long boyhood years. When Monique started to go out drinking and clubbing he had studied in his narrow room, hearing her bang furniture or moaning when she came home with a boyfriend. But Renzo had been desperate for a celestial love to invade him. At twenty he had moved to Rome, spent ten years there savouring the scrolled facades and the swallow-sketched nightfall. He'd been melded to the carnal, obliging city. And he had loved profoundly too. Every tributary of his mind had gushed with love.

He looked to the woman at his side and saw her grey, serene eyes were upon him.

'I had trouble with my ex-husband,' she said. 'I've seen the bruises on your sister's face the other times. You always go back to them. You always do.'

Renzo stared at her.

'It's an awful thing to see happening,' she said.

He wanted to kick away from her and charge down the street in the rain. Not looking back, swearing at her. But he finished his cigarette and ground it into the pavement. They had a final drink at the bar and when they returned outside a night wind had cleansed the sky and they saw stars. He hoped it was a good omen for Monique's homecoming. But any thoughts he had of his brother-in-law made him feel sick.

The woman said she would walk a stretch with him. Her name was Caroline and she had been a dancer. She walked with light abbreviated steps, her spine stretching upward. It made him walk more erectly.

'I loved my husband as I love water, wine, the night,' she said to him. 'But he was the man who finished me off. I was nothing after that man.'

Renzo listened to her. He had grown used to her talk.

'I hope your sister can get away from him,' she said. 'Do they have children? I remember I saw a boy once.'

'A boy and a girl.'

'I see. That's difficult.'

They were both smoking again. She was wearing cascading, muted clothes. She dressed like this always. He saw her skin was pearly and fine.

'What did he do to you? Your husband?' he asked.

'My husband? You mean the violence? Oh, I cannot tell you that. Each of us is different. We do not have the same wounds. But I can smell it on a woman. I can see it in a man. I can see it on your sister. She is expecting it. Perhaps you had it in your house.'

'Not at all,' he replied.

As they rounded a corner into a dim side street three young men overtook them. They jostled Caroline from behind and she gripped Renzo's arm. They joined as a phalanx in front of them and demanded cigarettes. Caroline gave them three from her packet. They insisted Renzo add some money to that. He shook his head and waved them off, said he'd have none of that in his own *quartier*. The one closest to him pulled back his fist and drove it hard into Renzo's cheekbone. Renzo's body jerked against the wall. As his coccyx hit the ground he thought of his father's *Ragazzi del '99*, those young boys climbing over the trench walls into the sunlight, chests stung by metal, the caress of hot blood before they even knew their bodies had begun to die. Renzo had seen his aggressor's fingers clench and his hand forming its soft club, but why hadn't he tried to block the swinging arm? Was this how it happened with Monique? Did she stand there as Serge balled his fist and it crossed the air?

Renzo smelled blood trickling down his cheek. Caroline dropped to his side as the thugs ran off.

'Put that away,' he said as she pulled out her phone.

'Don't be foolish. You've likely broken your cheekbone. It's not looking good.'

'No doctors,' he said, feeling nauseous. 'Just let me sit here a minute.'

He banked to the other side and vomited on the pavement. The vomit smelled of Calvados and the prawns he and Monique had eaten at lunch. Caroline handed him a tissue and crouched by him, her garments skirting the ground. He moved his palm over the surface, smelled the fustiness at the bottom of the building and saw the city above as a reeling firmament.

A couple walked past, arm in arm. They stepped wide around them, the man turning back to stare.

'Come on,' said Caroline, helping him to his feet. 'You're not a pretty sight on the ground. Let's get you at least to my place. It's just across the road.'

Renzo stumbled and he felt the heft of her arms as she pulled him upright. His feet plonked one after the other.

'The bastards,' Caroline said. 'The bastards. This is when being a woman is so useless. And there were three of them.'

They crossed the road and she punched numbers into a keypad by the door, pushed it open as her arm reached out for the light.

Renzo looked up into the stairwell. It was the same in his building. Flared creaking steps and a sinuous banister, bony doors and a stack of muffled lives.

As soon as they entered her apartment she led him down the long hallway to the bathroom and handed him clean men's clothing. He had never seen her with a man and he wondered where these had come from. His eyes strayed over her jars of cream, an open box of tampons, her eyeliner placed near the mirror. He bent down to wash his face but the nausea rose again, so he leaned against the tiles and tugged off his shirt.

Renzo wandered back to the main room which had an elongated shape and heavy velvet curtains. It was stuffy. There were three papier-mâché sculptures at one end. They were dancing humans or swooping birds, and each figure had half-melted skin like plaster casts he had seen in Pompeii. They circled in immense agony. He smelled cats.

'This is not my place,' she said from the kitchen. 'Just house-sitting for a friend who's gone abroad. It's a tad depressing, isn't it?'

'I was just thinking that,' said Renzo.

She brought out two mugs of tisane on a tray. 'Here, you'll like this. Let me take a look at your face. Oh Lord.'

She came over to where he was sitting, peering all around his left eye. As she dabbed, little puffs of her breath collected on his face and the pain thundered to the surface.

'Perhaps it's not broken after all. Just an almighty bruising.'

When she had cleaned away the blood and rubbed oily arnica into the bone she sat down hunched over her tea, ignoring the cat poised there waiting to tread onto her thighs. Renzo had a feeling she disliked cats. She had pulled her sleeves back and her arms glowed in the lamplight; they were performer's arms. He now knew that they would speak until dawn in this light. Renzo thought back to his father shrugging and gesturing in the dusky courtyard, his azure irises and the fine cerulean sweater, how these reverberating hues had been radiant. He remembered the snap of leather down the hall, and the first weals he had seen across Monique's thighs. He remembered bruises darkening in a grip around his mother's neck. Renzo also remembered the woman he had dearly loved in Rome so many years ago. How that time it had coursed through him too, and he had struck down this woman's beauty and she had stared up at him from the marble floor.

He looked at Caroline, whose hands were closed around her cup. He had never thought that his voice would be heard.

Magaly Park

There is a murder in the new apartment block on the Point, in the garage downstairs, it's all cordoned off. It isn't anyone who lives there as they're not up for sale yet. A woman saw a side-door ajar and ran over when she heard a scream. She saw a guy pull a knife out of another man's gut. The guy knocked her down and ran off. She was a jogger on her way to the bay. I watched her interviewed by a police officer, a paramedic tending to the scrape on her arm. 'It was the last thing I was expecting! The very last thing!' Her voice is pointy and she sounds excited, like she's met someone famous in the loo. She has a badge on her tank top from Tai's school, Sydney Girls High. The action is all over now and I'm sitting on a bench in the park. A RiverCat goes past towards the city, rousing the water and mucking about with the boats. The cops and men in puffy white suits have gone away and the ambulance crawls back to the main road with the siren on a slack dead man's spin, the red light clocking around.

I call Tai to tell her something's happened on the Point. Her mother's been on the balcony all along, shifting up and down the length, going back in to top up her coffee. Coming out again in her jute slippers and baggy pants. Tai is doing statistics problems today and won't answer. I guess Nora's seen me, she doesn't miss much. Down by the water there is a bloke with a fishing rod. He doesn't like the dog that's come up behind him to sniff his bait.

'Cassie! Cassie! Don't do that!' A woman in a peaked cap drops onto the sand from the stone wall, runs to the nosing Labrador. The fisherman is barefoot in rolled-up trousers.

'I'm sorry! I'm sorry! Hope she didn't eat any of your bait,' she calls as she clips on the leash. The man looks at her. The woman is wearing a yellow pair of plastic Croc sandals and an open white shirt. Beneath this her wobbly breasts are contained in a too-small top. She pulls her shirt together. She and the Labrador walk along the sand towards the ridge.

Further along I see the woman who was interviewed about the murder. She has finished her run and is exercising now. She lunges, one leg bent at the front and the other stretching out behind, her butt pushing towards the grass as though a palm is putting pressure there.

Her arms are pointed above her. It's a yoga position I've seen Tai do, but she is not as good as this. Tai is tiny, but not nearly as bendy as this woman. I can see the woman's heart is not at rest and her face is taut. How alone she looks in the still park.

She pulls out of the pose and walks to a bench, sits down and covers her face. She stays hunched there, crying. Why haven't the police taken her home? She is probably a tough woman who said she was fine, just a little shaky. That the jog would help.

I walk over. When she feels someone approaching she braces herself and looks up.

'I saw you interviewed up there,' I say. 'Thought you looked pretty shaken.'

'Oh, I am, I guess. It was pretty crazy.'

'It must have been. Was he a young guy?'

'I didn't really get a look. I mean, I did, but I couldn't tell. I was supposed to go to the station with them. They're coming to my place tonight. I'm not looking forward to that.'

She is older than Tai and me, too old for high school. There are wrinkles around her eyes and across her forehead. Somebody's big sister. Her hair is pulled back with a faded pink headband.

'He was rolling around on the concrete, you know. There was blood everywhere. You know I did first aid once. I did a course. But I couldn't go near him. I just turned away and started calling. I pretended he was a dead dog or something. You know, one you've smashed on the road. Now I think his soul must be floating around above us and he never said goodbye to anybody. I'm thinking, I didn't help him leave this life. I must sound pretty fucked up.'

'I think anybody would be,' I say. Another RiverCat pushes by, sending out its long, deep-bellied concaves. The fisherman backs away on the sand, watches the waves splash. A man has released twins from a double buggy onto the fine grass. A football travels between two boys.

'I told the police I didn't see anything. But they're still coming to the flat tonight. I ought to tidy the joint!' She stands up and her legs are restless. Her tears have left dried salt along the sides of her cheeks.

'My name is Giselle.' She puts out her hand and shakes mine.

'I'm Grant.'

'Wouldn't it be nice to live down here near the park?' She looks at the arc of new, overpriced apartments that have risen on the bedrock.

There seem to be more of them each month, crowding around every inlet cluttered with boats. The brief, sandy beaches are no good for swimming but cleaner now than ever. The guy near the water has caught a fish. Giselle looks up to the Point where the apartment building stands, shining with new chrome and glass balconies. There is plastic sheeting on many of the windows.

Giselle lives in a block of flats under a huge Moreton Bay fig tree. They protect them now. You'd need a permit to cut one down. The pods fall to the ground, crooked husks that look as though they could still be of some use. There is a row of carved grooves inside if you open one up. Giselle's front path has been swept clear and there is a bank of coloured disposal bins.

'I shouldn't really be inviting you to my place. I've had a murderer knock me down today!'

I am wondering whether Nora saw me approach Giselle in the park, or watched me walk away with her along the footpath, by the swimming pool that only residents can use. Tai was adopted from China when she was two months old and Nora has always chained her to her desk. Nora wants manic Higher School Certificate results. Tai wants to change her name and find her real parents.

I check my phone and Giselle glances at me. 'Cuppa or a beer? I guess you're old enough for a beer.'

She places a can before me. She opens a smoky-blue cupboard door that has been painted over many times. She pulls down a beer glass. Giselle's upper arms are bulging with muscles and her waist is narrow. I am certain that guys have tried to circle it with their hands and she has laughed them off, then become annoyed.

'They asked me if I got a good look at him. But I had to say I didn't. He just pushed me out of his way. I was looking at the other fellow, trying to understand what was going on. It wasn't clear at first.'

Giselle sits opposite me. She pulls off her headband and her hair is greasy and thin.

'I think I'll have a beer too.'

As she moves I watch the stubble in her armpits. There is a slit above her nostril from a piercing and her earlobes have rows of silver studs.

'I wonder what he's doing now, the killer I mean. He could be sitting somewhere having a beer, just like us. I bet he's headed interstate. Up north. Well, you would, wouldn't you?'

I see two guys pitted against each other in the garage on the Point, the walls still smelling of wet paint. A knife pulled out. Pants shitted.

'Do you think they knew each other?'

'I'm pretty sure they did. Maybe I'm imagining it, but the vibe was there. It was something that finished badly. Maybe he didn't even want to do it, you know? But they knew each other all right. I'll probably tell that to the police. I mean, they'll want to know why and I'll say it's just a feeling.'

'Maybe you should be more careful from now on.'

'I'm always pretty careful.'

'Well, I think I might head off.'

'Yeah, I've gotta shower and see these guys.'

'I guess you won't be jogging in the park for a while.'

'I could do.'

She takes me to the front door and I see a room in shadow I hadn't noticed before. There is a yoga mat rolled out beneath the window, which opens onto the arms of the massive tree outside. I see a warm bronze Buddha sitting on a shelf and a pale orchid in a pot. One day I would like to watch Giselle do yoga again. The way every inch of her body was tuned, a triumph of equilibrium. Tai isn't there yet. She shakes and perspires and it is a pain to watch her. My other feelings take hold and I have to rake these back. Tai wants to remain a virgin until it's the right moment.

On a table by the door is a picture of Giselle and a much younger girl. Giselle's arm is around her shoulders. The photo is from a few years ago but its meaning is clear. The girl has died. Placed near her box of keys, it looks like a reminder.

Giselle looks smaller behind the half-closed door with its Yale locks, she is glad to be relieved of me. She can't be that careful if she ran into an empty building and saw a man stabbing another man.

I decide to walk back towards Tai's place, though I imagine Nora will have penned her at the dinner table by now. Her phone will be off. The news might be watched afterwards. Or Tai's hands might flutter over the piano keys while Nora knits. If the sliding doors are open, I will hear her. She has to stop by nine o'clock otherwise the old man downstairs will call the police. Nora drops chunks of soil or cherry tomatoes onto his balcony, which juts out far beyond their tiny strip. The old man reports Nora for hanging out her washing, which is not allowed.

If the old man listened to Tai's music he would be healed. He has a tumour.

I first saw Tai at my last swimming competition before I quit high school. She was in her school's relay team, she did breaststroke. I was captain of my squad, a couple of years above her. I swam butterfly and had the best time in the state. Tai wasn't a bad swimmer but their team lost. She wasn't selected for the district team and I knew she wouldn't swim any more with her exams ahead. I went on to the nationals from there. I came in fifth on a bad day, the very worst.

I don't train any more.

But I remembered Tai's small face in and out of the water, its fierceness compared to the other girls. She had the propulsion and slinkiness of a rodent and when she climbed out her skin shone. I watched her shiver with the other girls, all hiding their brazen new chests. I saw how resolute she stood among them, how the losing cut into her.

After I quit I followed Tai home from school one day. I sat on one of the benches in the park, directly below her place. She knew who I was. She came out onto the balcony to look at me, then went back inside. I watched the bay. I remember a man came down and unlocked the metal gate to the marina, with its rolls of barbed wire like a punk bracelet. He walked along the jetty to his boat, turned on the engine, opened up the panels enclosing its frisky noise. A woman stood on the grass as though on a stage, reading from a book to a bunch of sailing boats.

Then Tai came outside, walked past me but didn't stop. On her way back she sat on the bench beside me. She took my hand and placed it on her thigh. That was a year ago now.

From Giselle's flat I walk out along the peninsula in the dusk, taking the road the ambulance went up this afternoon. The first stretch of apartments has been sold. They are two-storey duplexes, curved in a terrace overlooking the bay. Some of the gardens have climbing plants in bark-strewn beds or terracotta vases either side of the front door. A man beeps his car alarm and pushes open his gate. These places cost the most. Tai's block and the ones with the better view on the Point are smaller two– and three–bedroom apartments, probably some studio flats as well. The man has paused at his front door, staring at me as I pass his car. He's probably heard from his wife or girlfriend or boyfriend inside that a guy was knifed a few hundred metres away and he should watch out.

I reach the site of the murder. There is a portable fence around the whole garage area, tape over the doors. I stand where Giselle was standing when the policeman interviewed her. The concrete driveway has a black seam down the middle and I'm pretty sure this is where she was standing. There are two garage doors behind me, with two side-doors flanking these. The one to the left was the one Giselle entered when she heard the screams.

I turn back down the footpath to the bay. As it grows dark I begin to hear the halyards clanking against masts, waves slapping hulls. I slept here once, on a beach towel inside the cave on the rock shelf. Lights have come on in the terraces backing onto the park and in the block where Tai lives. The heaving water seems to rise into the sky, merging with its glittery molasses. I lie down in the grass and my brain feels like an entire galaxy. Tai has told me she can feel the same thing.

I wonder if the old man with the tumour will sleep tonight. The motion of the water, it would help him just to hear this.

I look up to Tai's apartment and there is a grey fuzz. Nora's watching SBS no doubt, some movie from Serbia or Ireland. I could walk around the back of the building where Tai's bedroom lies, just to be beneath her slowly undressing body. I know how much time she spends in front of the mirror. I know she's shaved herself down there. She says it's itchy but she won't let me touch her. She says all the girls do it. My ex-girlfriend from the swimming team had a tufted pod that showed under her costume. I imagine Tai's folds and my mouth fills with saliva. But wanting Tai has made me cleaner. The abstinence roars through me and there are days when it turns into a boundless force. I could climb rock faces, or swim to the other side of the river. It allows me to lie here ridden with stars, my tongue curling in my mouth. I am not even hard for her.

Tai said she had an older man proposition her when she was 15, on holiday with her cousins at the beach. She is the only Chinese member of the family. She wore big hats and didn't tan. He was a businessman from Hong Kong. He came up to her when she was reading Henry James in a café. He asked her if she'd like to come to his room. Tai filmed the guy on her smartphone and her mother called the cops. Now, Tai says, she would never have done that. She would have asked him for money and never told Nora. She would have just fucked him and had it over with, she says. More than once – she says this with regret – she wonders if perhaps he had come for her, maybe he was family. She'd just been too young and dumb, too conditioned by Nora to see every man as a different shade of danger, just because Nora had had two of them and they had taken off. Tai says that perhaps she might have flown away with the businessman to Hong Kong, where he would have found her a job with a merchant bank. She is gifted with numbers. I have listened to this story expand. Sometimes she imagines she is sitting behind him on the aeroplane, watching him eat through the gap between the seats. Sometimes she meets his immaculate wife in their apartment. When she talks, I wonder if it is because of where she comes from that she needs to travel so far and so accurately. I know that in her life Tai has hardly left this suburb. Some days she says Nora should have left her in China where they'd have slit her throat.

Tai isn't pretty. She has a mole on one side of her nose like the final island of a long archipelago. The skin is denser there, flecked with dark hairs. It seems as though it was given to her at the last moment.

She can't get it removed yet, the dermatologist has said. Tai is worried that with Nora's views arching over her, the mole will have to stay.

I sit up, the waves are short and agitated. The tide is about to turn. When I trained I used to know water. I could feel its cohesion, the way it is a cousin of the air. Water has a grip, it just pretends to be porous. Some days even the water in the pool felt like a clinging syrup and you wouldn't be allowed to stream along. Other days it was a buoyant liquid that thrust you down your lane.

I try to voyage like Tai does. I try to modulate the past and make it swing to my command. But for me this is impossible. I see Tai in the shack where she was born, the mother who hated the squall of her voice, who left her for days in her own shit. This is the only story I see on her smooth skin.

The following afternoon I walk along the footpath in front of Giselle's apartment block. I see where the branches of the Moreton Bay fig tree brush her windows with dark leaves. You could almost climb inside and tumble onto her yoga mat. It is brighter today than yesterday. The sky is sharp and the bricks of her block are burnt yellow. Giselle comes outside in a zippered hoodie and jeans, her hair fluffy. She holds a carton of paper rubbish.

'Hello there,' I say.

'Oh. Hello.'

She opens up the bin and tips out a carton of toilet rolls and pasta boxes, then a stream of newspapers and leaflets.

'How'd it go last night?' I say.

She frowns. Today she has put a silver ring through the nose piercing which changes the composition of her face. Everything now radiates from this puncture.

'You mean the police? It was pretty pointless. They showed me photos. One of them did a sketch on the computer. They wouldn't tell me anything about the dead guy.'

She throws the empty carton into the bin and turns away. There is no continuity from last night.

'Have you been down there today?' I ask.

‘Where? To the park? Not yet. I’m headed down there now. I got in late.’

‘Might catch you there.’

I imagine the pair of big constables filling up the stairwell with their shoulders and boots. Polite rapping on the door and two Anglo names announced.

She walks away and enters the building. I back off and cross the street, worried she might stand there watching me from the yoga room, thinking I’m a nutcase. Along the main road the eucalyptus trees lift and whir with the wind carving up the water. They are ragged trees with the bark torn away, or with cinnamon curls stuck to marbled trunks. They are inmates who know this land’s burning colonial past: the smoke drifting after battles, a bullet tearing through black skin. It is written in them. Blue-green leaves lie on the footpath and I wonder if the murders are written into us too. If the map of blood Giselle saw in the garage will have its edges scrubbed hard and some caustic acid thrown onto the cement by a foreign cleaner who knows we are a murderous people. That we have killed here, over and over, dark-skinned bodies thrown into the salt water.

I don’t like the piercing on Giselle’s face. I guess she inserted it before the police came, pushing the silver through the hole and stepping back to see herself in the mirror. Probably it makes her feel stronger. They might have told her to take it off at work.

I pass liver-bricked Federation houses with trellises and brass bells on brackets clinking in the wind. These homesteads have names like Stepney, Mile End, Rudley’s Chase. Sometimes an Italian woman in an apron comes outside to cut roses. Sometimes a worn Lebanese man is rolling a fag on a step. I cut through to the new estate carpeting the Point with its signs saying SOLD! SELLING FAST! Tai says we are a bunch of cowboys here, that we will never amount to much. On days that it suits her she goes on about Chinese history and culture, other days she stares cross-eyed at Vietnamese ladies on the bus. Giselle jogs past me. Her pace is swift and the muscles of her thighs are at work. She ignores me and descends to the park.

I follow her down there. My bench is occupied so I walk along the stone wall above the sand strip, then cross over to a vacant one in the shadows. I am close to the terraced houses backing onto the park. The place behind me has its own swimming pool wrapped in a glass fence. A small girl wearing floaties jumps into the water. She climbs out, runs around, jumps in again. Giselle begins her yoga with some loose stretches, then drops down, flattening her hands on the grass, printing them there. She rises slowly, lifts her heel into her crotch, one leg bent up, arms raised over her head, palms pressed together. She holds each pose long enough for someone to sketch her on a page. From here, she looks supple and poised, but yesterday when I was closer I could see the effort the poses required of her, each one a departure point into a gulf that was bodiless. Yesterday, until she broke down and cried, Giselle travelled to that place. I wish Tai could do this. I would love to see Tai's body extended as a bird's, swooping down to the earth. But I know that Tai is not ready to consign herself to anything or anybody.

When she is finished, Giselle comes over to me. Her features are razor-sharp, the nose ring moves with her breaths.

'Look. You're freaking me out. What the fuck do you want from me?'

'Nothing. I'm just watching.'

'Well stop it, would you? I know people like you. People who check up on you and hang around and try to be nice. I was dumb enough to bring you up yesterday but I was in shock, you know? And now you're freaking me. If I see you again I'm calling the cops. I'll say you're harassing me.'

'I'm not harassing you. I always come to this park. My girlfriend lives here.'

'I don't care where your girlfriend lives. I said you're freaking me out.'

Her arms drop to her sides and I notice a pulse on her stomach skin which is exposed below her tank top.

'I'm sorry,' I say.

'Yeah, the fuck you are. I can't believe you even know where I live! You try anything and I swear I know who you are. They'll find you.'

She twists off, the graceful bird gone from her. I stare out to the water, pushing away my shock. Mostly, these boats are never unmoored. Their wood is sodden, bird crap splatters their decks; they spend their lives yanking on chains.

Giselle half-jogs a few metres then turns back. She stands in front of me, her face fallen.

'Look. I'm sorry. I know you're not a freak. I have seen you here before too. With that Chinese chick. I know you're all right. I'm sorry I lost it on you.'

'That's okay. You've been through a lot.'

'I don't think I should have come here today.'

'Maybe not.'

'Are we fine then?' she says. 'Are you sure we are?'

'We're fine, Giselle.'

She jogs away through the trees.

On Saturday mornings Tai is allowed to see me. It's the gap where she used to play netball, so Nora can't really protest. Tai can't study endlessly. Besides, her exams are not for seven months. At first Nora stands watching on the balcony. She is an ex-smoker and her hands flick in the sun. Below her the old man moves about on his terrace with an aluminium watering can. He stoops at each flowerpot and earthenware vase. From here it seems that there is a neighbourly rapport between them. Tai and I normally do not touch, but today she leans on my shoulder. I think of the businessman from Hong Kong, working up the courage to approach her reading a Henry James novel in Coffs Harbour. I see his silver-framed glasses, a horizontal slit etched in each oval, the café reflected in the glass. One day I know Tai will kiss me and our mouths will explode.

Tai says she wants me to be the first one. She says she used to think it should be a stranger, in case it hurt or she hated it. But she's touched herself down there, put things inside. She tells me she thinks she can feel what's going to happen. Tai says Nora has a vibrator hidden in her drawer, and at times there are snatches of her cries in the night. Listening to Nora has made Tai despise bald, noisy emotion. That is why I wouldn't be surprised if, when the next businessman asks her, she lets him take her away.

It's a crazy thing, entering a girl's body, just to contemplate that you are inside the confines of her skin. I think that I would be overwhelmed if I entered Tai's body. I'm worried I might go blind, like a man who has stared at the sun, or that I could freeze inside of her and we would be stuck together forever – I've read online that it happened. I know it would not compare to the other girls I've been with, their squealing and clenching. I would be engulfed. Just now I have begun to think that if it were possible I would prefer Tai to enter *me* and feel her pushing *my* organs. I would sooner have her within me rather than invade her. I could not handle hearing her disguised grief.

Nora goes inside. She watches the Italian news at ten o'clock, the last night bulletin from the other side of the world. She can't see us from the couch. I have waited all week to smell Tai next to me and now her hair is beneath my lips. I part it with my nose and sense the thick strands flaring from her scalp. Tai draws away. She looks at my face, her gaze moving over every feature. She takes my hands which are furnaces within hers. She releases them and they return to my lap. She slips her fingers under her thighs, tilting, so her hair falls in a black quiver. Her body inches away from mine so that we are no longer touching. My head is reeling, but this is how it is. There are days when she laughs a lot and tells me about her English professor whose freckled hand lingers on her forearm. There are others when we sit like two old people who have no mirrors in the house because each is the reflection of the other. These are very moving days.

Down on the strip of sand, a father walks into the water in a pair of baggy shorts. A small boy bounces around, clapping and skipping. They have a radio-controlled boat. The father sets the boat in the water. It is a racing boat, not really meant for the jerky shallows. The waves push the boat to the shore and the father splashes back to retrieve it. They walk out further. The father holds up the boat and the propeller starts to buzz. He places it on the surface and it does one furious circle.

I know Tai hasn't got much time left before Nora calls her up and tells her they have to go food shopping. I look at her knees, shaven too, and the opaque length of her thighs. Tai's phone lights up and she doesn't answer.

There is a cry. The speedboat has gone straight into one of the anchored sailing boats and lies still, already far away. The father wades in a little, then pulls back. He is a non-swimmer. The backwash tugs the boat around the other side of the hull and soon the tiny craft is being drawn out through the moored vessels, its red plastic less and less distinct. The pair stand on the shoreline as the boat reaches the body of the river.

Tai turns to me. 'Why don't you swim out there and get it for them? You can do it.'

I look at her, to see where this request might be coming from.

'It was a stupid place to put it in.'

'If you swim out there, I will do it with you. Today. Now. We can go to the cave in the rocks.'

My heart jolts. It is a seedy cave, horrible with fires and brutal sex.

'Don't say that.'

'You don't want to?'

'No, I don't. Not there I don't.'

She moves as though she is getting ready to go. She swings her dusty feet. 'You won't do it?'

'No.'

The boy is crying. The father's shoulders have rounded. I think of the green water gripping my legs. The water is cold here and the riverbed is clean enough, but years ago it was full of trash and jelly blubbers and putrid slicks. Not even the sharks came upstream. It's probably about 200 metres out there, four lengths of the pool, something I used to thrive on. I've done ocean races where the waves slap you about, currents snaring your limbs and sea creatures smearing your thighs.

'Kiss me now,' I say to her.

Tai's jaw moves. Her toes splay in the dirt and she looks out. There is a RiverCat crossing the bay now, the racing boat is drifting towards its path. The boy squats in the sand with his arms wrapping his head. The father tries to see through the masts.

'It's too far now anyway,' Tai replies. 'Look at that fool.'

When she leaves she says sorry, it just came into her head. I watch her walking back to her place. Nora is on the balcony.

I don't go to the park for a few days. I have my own stuff to do. There are times when I forget Tai. Not for long, but she is far from my thoughts. She calls me once, but I see the call afterwards. I do not call her back. I will wait until next Saturday to see her in a better mood. When I am in a big shopping centre I see Giselle sitting in a café, wearing a blouse and a plum-coloured skirt. Her hair is pinned back and sits in a curl above her neck.

'What are you doing around here?' she says.

'Just picking up some trainers. My old ones have had it.'

'I'm on break for another ten minutes. Like a coffee or a juice?'

'Sure.' I edge through the tables and sit down opposite her. She looks well rested; the nose piercing has been removed.

'I work in the building society over there. Been a slow one. Haven't seen you around lately. Look, you don't need to stay away.'

'I'm not staying away.'

'So you'll be back then?'

'Yeah, I will.' I order an orange juice and a bright cupful is poured out from a machine.

'Health freak, are we? Did you read about the guy that was stabbed?'

'No.'

'They were cousins. The dead guy owed him money. The killer came all the way in from the country and then he caught the train all the way back. He was waiting for the cops in his kitchen. Came away without a fuss. They even looked the same in the newspaper. Weird, hey?'

'Yeah.'

'I guess that'll be a hard block to sell. Or maybe not. People can be weird.'

The orange juice is chilled and acidic with metallic-tasting strands. I used to get a navel orange in my lunchbox when I was a kid. I thought they had something to do with the sea, the navy. There is a swirl of pulp and liquid at the bottom of the glass.

'Your girlfriend doing her HSC?'

I nod. 'She doesn't get out much. Her mother is strict.'

'She looks really brainy. Not because she's Chinese, I mean. I bet she studies hard.'

'Yes, she does.' I feel like telling Giselle that Tai is perfect. I imagine putting the words out there, seeing Giselle's face take them in.

'Well, I'd better head on otherwise my boss'll have a fit. See you at the park one of these days, then? Maybe you can pop upstairs and we can have some pizza.'

'That would be great.'

She slips through the tables and pays, walks a way down the main thoroughfare and then through glass doors into the place where she works. In the darkened yoga room, under the boughs of the Moreton Bay fig tree outside, I can see our bodies pushing together. Giselle would be firm and soundless, never looking into my face. She'd be glad when it was over. I watch the woman opposite eat a big piece of fluffy cake with caramel icing. She forks it into her mouth slowly, staring at passers-by.

I end up at the park on my usual bench. The sun is still high and the water is drained out. The fisherman is sturdy in the sand, newspaper cupping his bait like a desert flower. I look at his line sloping into the water. The boats all point east, none of them bucking against the tide, no sound except for the *cark* of birds. The fisherman looks back at me, nods. I turn to Tai's apartment, knowing she will be wandering down from the bus stop now. I'd pick her up from there but her mother won't allow it.

I see Nora on the balcony in a pair of red ballooning trousers. She sees I am on the bench. Tai says she is exasperated by my constant presence. She has told Tai I am a dropout who is surely on drugs. I think of Tai's offer the other day, being played by her. I might have held her in the dirty cave last Saturday. It could have happened. I reel back to what I should have said, but the only way I can regain some sort of control is by imagining my limbs slicing through water. I imagine swimming hard, against a current, a gruelling distance.

I get up and walk along the sandstone wall to the rock face, climb up to the same level as the cave. I round the Point and stand in front of its mouth, now an open tomb layered with pebble-smattered rock.

I crawl in but it is too much. There is a whorl of wrath and the hole smells of shit.

I move outside, standing with the burdened peninsula at my shoulders. If it were possible to dive here I would spring into the shallows and swim as far as my limbs would go, no matter the ferries and vessels, I would just swim and swim until something carved me into shreds.

I see Tai approaching me on the rocks in her school uniform. Her white socks are rolled down. She is coming to apologise for last week. I sit on the ancient stone, turning away from her. We will walk together to our grove, here above the water's milky tissue.

Enfolded

For a time she called him Julio. It wasn't his real name. When that game ended, she had stayed Esmé for a while, but he would slip. She used to enjoy calling him Julio, partly because that game tickled them both so hard. But now it is a half-forgotten trace and they are all but nameless to each other. There had been another game where she was 'O' and he was 'M', but that was a sexual game, grinding and full of spluttered words, burrowing and friction. There are no more games now. She sits on her suitcase outside his local airport waiting for the driver he will send, because he has fallen from a ladder and lost the use of his legs. He couldn't piss, he told her on the phone. Couldn't drive. Couldn't have an erection.

There had been no need to say that. She notes a young man heading her way from the parking area.

At the house he is dressed for her, wearing a printed shirt she bought for him when they were together, three decades ago. He wears this shirt every time they meet. Winter in Amsterdam, spring in Addis Ababa. Harmattan here in Accra. Always this shirt. At first, she stands a few metres away from him. The room is messy. A creative man's disorder. She sees that crankiness has just left his face and his chin juts out, raised, ever-searching. He lifts an arm that has become feminine. His fingers are lean, reptilian, nails bitten to the core.

She takes his hand, feels the cool pads envelop her sticky digits. She folds to her knees and cries in his lap. It smells of an old man's trousers, old man's urine.

The same young man pushes his wheelchair onto the veranda. Before following, she removes her espadrilles and feels her feet embrace the tiled floor, a kiss on the tarmac. She looks at her bent toes, black nail polish. It hits her that he can't feel his toes any more, he has to look at them like distant mementos in a house-girl's soapy hands. She remembers his toenails scratching her in bed, his knees cool behind hers. She smells food, the oily red palm nut soup she hasn't eaten in an age; she hears him summoning her from outside. If anything, his voice booms louder now. Perhaps because he feels imprisoned? But he has always snapped at her, snapped at most people. Her views of him have not yet shifted from able to disabled. She thinks of centaurs. The upper body fused to another creature, the surging of the arms, the tossing of the head and neck. She remembers sweat clinging to the fine hairs of his chest, the taste of it. She thinks his smell has altered.

It is a shock to see how crowded the yard has become. The palms are now lofty above the rooftop. Nothing has impeded them. His fingers plunge into the soup, wear a glove of its viscous colour.

'Sit down.' He points to her. 'You know I hate to eat cold food.'

The young man uncaps her beer. She sits down. The soup steams. The scent reaches into her. The sea, too, sends tendrils through the clacking leaves. It's not far from here. The veranda rails are rusty. Chunks of concrete have fallen off, landing in the dust below where she hears children's cries. Are they his children? Begotten long before he fell to the ground here? A friend – Nana Yaa – had told her there were dozens of them, an unchecked almost tribal reproduction. But Nana Yaa always had a bitter tongue.

'You don't look any different,' he says to her.

She raises her eyebrows and looks out. Once, they were accomplices. Now she wonders about the smell coming from his trousers and whether the young man takes him to pee or whether there is a bag for it. And whether this mercy mission is going to include sitting on the loo all night after downing his cook's food.

'Not used to this chop any more?'

'Not really,' she says. 'But I'll give it a go.'

He pushes his plate away, half-eaten, and drinks his beer from the bottle. She thinks he drinks a lot of beer sitting here. He has a paunch. He watches her wash her right hand in the side bowl and begin eating her soup.

'You know I like to watch you eat.'

He stares at her, as he has often stared at her. Occasionally her eyes cross his. Long ago she begged him not to make a study of her, of each quaver of her nerve endings. He once wrote a poem to her nipple: *Morning nipple, mid-morning nipple, my nipple.* Better poems have been written. The soup is hot and her eyes water. Her mouth feels like a ravaged cleft and she feels the food sending a marker into her chest. A flag planted deep.

He looks away from her when one of the children downstairs screeches. She sees his lips twitch: she's guessing he usually shouts at them. He casts his eyes back at her.

'They your kids?' she asks.

'No, why?'

He has always lied to her face. They weren't meant to last more than a minute. A gasping fusion, hotel rooms; they were secretive. Then one airless night she let him tower over her. They were in a street bar. The street bar closed. They stayed on grubby metal chairs in the breeze block cubicle next to the gutter. Talking first, his arching talk, her spilling answers, until the city was quiet and he climbed over her and a baptism took place, water coursing along the open drain from the bowels of somewhere, cheap beer fraying at the back of their throats. She now thinks this initiation was risky and theatrical. She has had better lovers on clean beds. Men who didn't need an arena or the night's clawing.

She finds a hard meat rind in the soup and removes it from her mouth. *Wele.*

'You know I hate *wele* in the soup.'

He smiles. That used to be another game between them. She was Pig Meat. He was Bush Meat. She loved him because he had found what was common between them, had shone a hard light on her.

'You know,' he says, 'I can't believe I have you sitting here across from me. This is what I have always wanted.'

Sitting before her, flanked by palms scoring the punch-blue sky and the powdery wall beside him, there is no evidence of the wheelchair. He is a free man sitting here, free to wander to the railing and light a cigarette, lean on the rail showing off his shapely rump and long thighs, turning back to peruse her at the table. His scruffy beard has grown. His legendary dreadlocks are gathered together. He looks like a man in one of his own documentaries.

'So where shall I take you this afternoon? What would you like to see?'

She hasn't given any thought to what she would do here. She knows nothing about this country now. There is almost a week before them. Her throat tightens. He called her only recently, eight months after the fall. Initially he had been to the States for an operation. There had been a glimmer of hope, a keen doctor, cousin of a filmmaker friend. It hadn't worked. The soup sits in her stomach, a queasy burning. She flushes her throat with beer.

'I don't know,' she says.

'Are you tired?'

'No, not at all.' Perhaps she expected him to be more miserable, more of a recluse, even ashamed of what has happened to him. Perhaps she is ashamed. She isn't used to it yet.

'I want you to have a good time here,' he says to her.

The young man drives them to Labadi Beach. It is a trial to watch him being parcelled into the car, the young man sweeping him from one seat to the other, one arm under his bottom, the other curved around his shoulders. She watches him belt himself in. She sits in the back seat holding her straw hat. She has changed into her swimming costume and now wears a sundress. Her arms feel flabby, her skin mottled. She is self-conscious. The dress is fairly long. She has brought flip-flops.

In the car as they drive she starts to cry and he turns around and sees her. She places her cheek on his shoulder and he holds her other cheek with his hand, which is cool. There is a snatch of his familiar smell between his fingers, deep where the skin forks apart. Her tears finish and she pulls away. He looks out of the window. He has bundled his hair into a knitted Rasta hat.

Though the car park is full his driver heads directly to the sandy entrance to the beach. She sees the water shimmering, waves crashing, hears loud reggae. Helpers rush to the vehicle, standing in a circle when the driver lifts out the wheelchair, pulls the arms apart, placing a worn cushion on the seat sling. She sits there, watching him scoop up her ex-lover, arrange his trousered legs. She gets out. The crowd of hawkers and ragamuffins jostles around her, hands extended with peeled oranges, cinnamon gum, nail clippers. Ahead, the young man has tilted the chair and pulls him as a donkey would a cart. She looks at him and he is laughing at her grim face, telling her to get a move on.

They settle under a beach umbrella in the sand outside one of the bars, a shack really. It is a busy afternoon but a table has somehow been freed for them. She senses he comes here a lot. With friends from the past, not family members, the people he caroused with. Mostly men. She knows that the women who interested him all became lovers. Many would be weary of him now. She gets the impression he also comes here alone and likes to strike up conversations, offering a beer to the coconut boy or a Danish pilot. She remembers his world views were almost sensual. He chiefly talked about himself.

One of the waitresses gives him a warm kiss on the cheek and his arm reaches along her back, fingers in a star. She wonders if he can still have an erection. The girl is ripe and very dark.

They are served beers. The driver has disappeared. Later she sees him standing under an awning alone, sipping Fanta.

'Would you like a swim?' he asks.

'Not yet, not really.' She doesn't want him to see her body. Before, they used to glide together. Hours were spent naked, examining each other's orifices, plunging until pain or fear or eclipse brought them back. Their intimacy has always haunted her. She wonders what he has done with other women.

'You're afraid I'll check out your bum?'

'Something like that.'

'Like to see mine?' He laughs. 'You know, I'm going to make love to you before you leave this place.'

She shakes her head slowly.

They would always have the blueprints for each other's bodies.

Before she is too drunk she takes her towel down to the water's edge. She needs to pee and figures she'll do it in the sea. She wonders how long he will last after two beers. Maybe that is why the driver is waiting there. She doesn't know how it works yet. She takes off her dress and wades in, dunking herself in the water's cold clasp. Tropical, but the sea is always freezing. Beyond her the waves crash down and few people have gone out this far. She pees, a hot cloud on her leg. She was once caught in a rip here. Another time a turd floated by her shoulder. She breaststrokes a little.

Refreshed, she walks back to where they were sitting but his wheelchair is gone. She looks about, he can't have moved far. Then she sees the young man pulling hard, flicking up sand, the wheelchair tilted behind him. The chair is swung around and parked. She feels like embracing him, knows the alcohol and drowsy sun are conspiring. She wonders if it is still illegal to go on the beach at night. They were encircled by soldiers once, near one of the fancy hotels. The soldiers pulled down his trunks and played with him, laughing at his fine spent cock.

The young man walks off to his shady spot under an awning, stands there squinting at the surf.

'How was the water?' he asks her. 'I'd like to have a swim with you. In the morning if you like.'

When he called to tell her what had happened, he said he wanted to buy her a plane ticket. He said he had to see her. He asked her about dates. She could not speak. Eventually she told him some dates when she would be able to get time off work and foster out her animals. It had been a fretful trip, partly because he had rewired her all over again and she knew she was returning to his orbit. The keenest, most grievous thing she had ever done had been to leave him. But he had spoken so plainly on the phone. She had never heard him speak so plainly.

Two fresh beers are opened on the table before them. She wipes the rim of the green bottle, chinks hers with his.

'Let's sit awhile,' he says.

The light softens after its bright peak. The day ends early here, it is dark by six o'clock. The sun seeps into her legs. She feels her skin tight and dry, wet behind the knees. Sand covers her shins. The chair is uncomfortable and she shifts from one buttock to the other. Her costume has dried already. She sees him looking at her arms. She covers her slight belly with her towel. He has never worn sunglasses, his eyes have always gazed at the world, even in the hottest places. She noticed reading glasses on the table at the house. A hawker comes up to them with a tub on his head piled high with useless things. He studies the man's headdress, then points to a shred of blue netting that the girls use here when they scrub their skins. The seller has calves like yams and removes the contraption from his head; places it on the sand, bringing forth socks, soap, chalk for ants. *Do they not want any of these fine tings?* But again, her ex-lover points to the bright blue netting. He buys it with some greasy notes and gives it to her. It is a coarse blue spider web.

'A gift,' he says.

'Thank you.'

He calls behind him to the ripe waitress who comes out laughing, her tray flat on her hip. The girl loops her arm around his neck and their faces are close. When other women came up to him she used to feel so scalded. But now she identifies this impulse, it feels innocuous. She looks away. The driver has stepped out from under the awning and is speaking on his mobile phone. People are beginning to trail back to the car park. A tiny girl with masses of beaded plaits wears a sagging swimming costume and sucks her thumb. Her mother has tattoos sunk into her amber shoulders, one laced across her chest. Other people have just arrived. Two men in wide trousers and printed shirts, two girls with groomed hair. They set out a little way from the reggae-blaring speakers, then drop to the sand in a group. No hand-holding, no kisses. There are still religious people here with staunch values.

The waitress leaves, her bare broad feet kick up sand as she sashays off. He has bought a Guinness for the hawker.

She glances at his beige trousers and the socks and canvas shoes the young man has fitted on his feet. He looks like a slim girl wearing cast-offs. He always wore jeans before. Jeans everywhere. Through deserts. Shirtless in the house when she was drenched with sweat. She tries to imagine him naked. His slack upper body tapering to the inert twins of his legs. She remembers taking him in her mouth, stroking his thighs. She remembers the weight of him, can feel the different textures of him on her tongue.

'Perhaps we should go to the house now. I have a couple of things I have to do.' He says this as though he has forgotten an appointment. The young man comes over, manoeuvring him through the parade of people headed home. Their vehicle is at the head of the car park and again she watches painfully as his body is transferred. She will have to get used to this. He seems tired. On the way home he does not speak and she feels as though it was a mistake to have come here. He stares at the neighbourhoods. At the house his chair is smacked apart again and his body is lifted and he is wheeled to the stairs. The young man carries him up into the house.

She steps out of the car into the yard. Children and mistresses have gone someplace else and she smells smoke from a charcoal cooker. The walls of the house downstairs are brown with grime and palm trees are pushed deep into the dirt all the way to the back fence. She walks over and touches one. Looks up to the clutch of coconuts at the top, genitals under a skirt. It's been a while since she's had sex, she supposes he can see it on her. She walks over to the next tree and flattens her hands around it, feeling the dry ridges and ruts. She remembers how he used to make her lie on the rooftop and describe clouds, a thing she hadn't done since she was a kid. It never rang true, his delight in unmarred things – she knew his childhood had been stolen in boarding school. She still doesn't know what she should ask him. Why she is even here. She looks up, imagining he is leaning barechested over the railing, smoking, looking rangy, hungry for her. She hears a sound from the shower block at the back. A toilet is flushed and a squat, untidy woman walks out and back into the house, wiping her hands on her shift.

Upstairs the door to his bedroom is closed and she hears water running. She wants to shower but doesn't know if there is enough pressure for two of them to run at the same time. She leaves her things in the spare room, goes out onto the veranda and rubs the sand from her shins with a towel. She is still wearing her swimming costume. She can smell food cooking downstairs in the kitchen area. He has always had mediocre, cranky cooks who would leave after dramatic fights with everybody, usually involving theft. She doesn't care for food right now and doubts she will this evening. On the table there is a carafe of water and two glasses, one with droplets inside. She drinks.

There is still no sound from his bedroom. She knew there would be a lot of dead time here, when he would rest or have other things to do. She has brought work with her but she doesn't feel much like it. She sits outside drinking water. The neighbourhood is quiet. They were all stylish homes once.

The young man comes out of the bedroom and closes the door. It's hard to read his face. It is as though he embodies what has happened, even more than the paralysed man in the room, and when he leaves he takes away a portion of the tragedy. She is glad the young man is remote. She would not have liked some chatty nurse. She hears a voice from the bedroom. It is a clean, clear voice that fills the room, reverberates into the next. She gets up and glances at her face in the mirror before going to him.

'I'm sorry,' he says. 'I had a bit of a spell there. I'm not supposed to drink alcohol.'

She thought as much.

'I needed it, you know. Your fault.'

She looks about the room, sees a photo of herself. There are photos of other people too, some of whom she remembers. She sees him next to a tall woman with a broad forehead, the image of him. And then a pixie child with dreadlocks, grinning on a swing. She looks back to the photograph of herself. Her hair used to reach her buttocks and he would dress her in it.

'I'm happy to have you in here again.'

He has showered and wears a different shirt. He wears drawstring trousers and looks more like himself. His hair is pulled back and his beard looks combed. The young man has placed him in a wider wheelchair by the window. His feet are bare. He sees her looking at them, watches the journey of her eyes.

'Come here.'

She shakes her head.

'You're not afraid of a little guy in a wheelchair?'

Now she wants to know what happened. Why he was up a ladder. Why him when there are idle men on every street corner here, all of them more able than a 60-year-old filmmaker.

It's not the first time he's read her thoughts.

'I was stupid. Very stupid. I was checking the phone cable. It was worn through and the wires were exposed. I wasn't getting an internet signal. Couldn't get a technician to come over here. You know how it is. I fell onto a cement ledge you can see down there. Didn't feel a thing. Just flying. Descent. And a crack inside. A horrible crack. They did their best, you know.'

She worked out it must have happened in February. The heaviest time of the year for her. Winter. Her favourite dog put down. And over here, this.

'I wanted to call you,' he says. 'I wanted to hear your voice. I waited because I thought there was a chance. Now I know there is no chance.'

She wonders who walked him through it, who was there when he woke up. A wife? A daughter? A sturdy friend or half-brother? She doesn't know what the fuck she is doing here. And yet she knows, she knows.

'I'd like to swim with you,' he says. 'Shall we go for a swim together tomorrow?'

She nods.

Neither of them is hungry in the evening. She finds a tin of tea leaves next to the kettle on a small refrigerator in the corner of the living room. She makes two mugs of tea and wheels him onto the veranda.

In the night she hears his door open and close quietly. She hears voices. She can't get back to sleep. The hot food completes its course through her and she sits on the loo listening to mosquitoes whining. She scratches bites on her legs. Back in her room she drinks more water, feeling cramps in her stomach. It is dark in the room though there is a green fluorescent light left on outside somewhere below; there are bars on her window. She lies down again. The sea is silent, only the palm leaves stroke each other. She wonders if he is listening to the same sounds, if each night has become an endless tunnel of lost sensations. Or if there is a woman from downstairs spreading heat through his body, pushing its force against the border where his nerves dissolve.

At daybreak he is dressed and showered, then wheeled onto the veranda to sit waiting for her. He looks composed. He motions for her to come over and she feels creased and puffy. He tugs down her arm and kisses her cheek which is loose against the bone. His lips are warm, she knows their pressure. She feels a spring, a fountain. She pulls away, closes her cardigan around her. The damp morning surrounds them. She never rises this early.

She knows what will happen. Somehow, she will lift him onto the bed. She does not know how their clothes will be removed but they will be removed. He will tug his upper body near to her back, a hand across her breasts, hooked under her shoulder. She will haul his knees behind her knees and her feet will enclose his dormant feet. Later, she will trace the rim around his body, the fault line, the front. She will bring her wet cheek to the neat laceration on his spine.

It begins to rain. They both watch the morning shower, a clean curtain.

Love and Death and Cell Division

It is eight months since Shaun has come out of a North London hospital. He parks the silver car and steps down first. His hair has grown back curly instead of straight, the waves are reaching out, conspiring and rich, blacker than logic. Shaun has fought off the same malady that leached my brother's bones. He used hardiness supplied by his Slavic mother, the one who ran off. Shaun also fell in love with one of the nurses who is now eight months pregnant, whose elbow within a denim jacket he gently lifts out of the car; her hair is arranged in neat braids. She is brown and sleek with a basketball plumped above her jeans.

They walk steadily together and Carlotta barks. Their kiss is a small note of harmony. Shaun points to something at the back of the house.

Carlotta rushes at Shaun with instant recollection and I recall the months Shaun stayed here, helping with odd jobs and the garden. How, listening to the young man moving about the rooms of the house, I would place a hand upon my heart and feel an uneven rocking. Minor things used to disappear from my cabinets and one day I found Shaun collapsed in the garden. Blue-lipped, his skin drained. A spread-eagled Bacchus in shorts. The paramedics rushed wordlessly through the house with a stretcher banging doorways.

Shaun runs his hand along Carlotta's bristly back until she flips over, presenting her teats and recent scar. The girlfriend smiles, tucking her hair behind one ear. Shaun prevents Carlotta from lunging over to sniff the new odours of her person. The dog sits, eyes moored on Shaun's face.

Introduced, the girlfriend extends a hot hand that has been planted in a pocket. Shaun leans across for a pertinent hug.

'You've shrunk, Mary!' He seems taller, fair skin aglow, on the verge of a strategic, masculine beauty.

'And you look so very well,' I say to him. 'Do come inside.'

Shaun throws their jackets onto the coat pegs and follows me down the hall, to the living room where a fire pulses.

'You see what a wonderful place Mary has? It's like this all the way through. Stunning, Mary. Looks as stunning as ever. Who's doing your gardening?'

'I have two older chaps. They come over from the estate.'

Shaun stands still on the carpet for a moment, rubs the back of his hand across his eyes.

'I'm sorry, bit overwhelmed for a minute.' The girl folds her arm around his waist. 'Thanks, love. Thanks, babe.' Shaun's hand steadies on the ball shape above her jeans.

The day the ambulance took my nephew down the lane, I stood on the flattened patch of grass made by the paramedics kneeling around Shaun's strewn body. I tried to understand what had taken place. My own heart had felt a surge of palpitations that slowed into incinerating relief – for I had failed to warm to my brother's son, and I knew I was once more in full possession of my house. I felt a luminous sense of liberation as the ambulance changed gears on the hill.

Shaun assists Efua with a flourish as she lowers herself onto the chair. 'This is the woman who saved my life. It's all in her hands.'

Efua's fingers knot together beneath her cargo.

'This lovely lady used to read me stories after the end of her shift. It was mesmerising. She comes from Ghana. She took me to her country. She's made me see everything, the lot of it. Illness, disaster, joy, simplicity. I owe everything to her.'

I make a round with the teapot. When he was in hospital I visited Shaun rarely. He was in my brother's old ward, lizard-like.

'We'll be getting married traditionally in Ghana after the birth. And then the official thing in London after that. My mother – you remember Dina? – she's making the dress.'

'Dina? She's resurfaced?' Unfortunately, this comment escapes.

Carlotta trots over to Shaun, provides her broad head for a rub. Carlotta's jaws slacken and her tongue lolls on the carpet. The fire–spun air in here is soft. Cinders reach up into the chimney shaft. The girl removes a cardigan.

'You all right there, Effie?' he asks.

She nods.

Shaun looks around the room, at the floral wallpaper and pretty oils, the urns on the sideboard and porcelain platters on the walls. He massages the dog's belly and I am alert.

'It's so good to be back here, Mary,' Shaun says. 'I know it wasn't always easy between us. I know bad words have been spoken. Perhaps – perhaps there's a chance it was the illness talking. We know it had already seeped in.'

In an argument, Shaun once let fly what he thought of me: *You are a frigid, uptight bitch who hasn't been humped in an age*. The words were muttered as he slammed the glass door across and stormed down to the garden shed. I don't think they were meant to be heard. Shaun had come in late and vomited in the downstairs bathroom. Carlotta had finished off the mess on the bath mat and stank to high heaven.

'I've seen the bottom, Mary. It was hell,' Shaun continues. 'I can't even explain. I had to learn to trust in my body. Trust in a bunch of cells. I can see goodness now.'

Efua leans across and touches his knee. She has a fresh point. 'We had the baby screened, didn't we, Shaun? They did a genetic test. They said everything's normal. Nothing to worry about.'

She halts, perhaps remembering something blurry Shaun has told her. My malformed daughter, born when I was 44, her violet face mistakenly shown to me. A nurse should know better.

'How is your mother?' I ignore the girl and question Shaun.

'Dina? She's all right. She went home for a while. Then came back to London to start a business. I have a kid sister, you know.'

I see my poor brother's emaciated body turning in his grave.

Efua asks to use the bathroom. She looks quite frantic. Carlotta waddles over to sniff her boots and she shuts like a flower.

'I'll take her,' Shaun says. 'I doubt I've forgotten the way there.'

He saunters back into the room. Efua follows, pulling the cardigan around her shape.

'Those windows don't look very secure out the back,' Shaun says. 'Have you had any more burglaries in the area?'

'I have Carlotta. And an alarm. I sleep well at night.'

I cast my eyes out over the garden. The roses are thriving, catching dabs of sun. Several of the trees show off their shaggy moss coats while the lawn gleams. I am pleased with my new gardeners.

'Dina asked after you,' Shaun says. 'She wanted to know if you were still hiding out in the woods.'

'I'd hardly call this hiding.'

'Don't miss the big bad world?'

'I've seen enough of it.'

My visions of his mother come forth. Shoulders. Breasts. A way of steering her body into a room. How my brother hungered after her and the upholstery used to soak up her scent. And then this son, brewed from the pair of them in Dina's womb.

'What does she look like now?'

'Dina?' he says. 'She looks older, I guess. She still packs a punch.'

Shaun runs his hand through the black currents of his hair as though even he can't believe it has burst back. Before his cells went wild he was so reedy, a slice of my brother's physique. We are a tall, fine-boned people. It is easy to recall the boyish frieze of his body. But somehow, the illness has heightened different, vital genes. His features have widened and his eyes have a stinging elemental quality, now directed at me.

'Mary, the truth is, Efua and I would like to ask you something. I don't have a job yet. And Efua is about to give birth to, well, we weren't going to tell anybody, but your great-niece. You wouldn't care to rent us out a room for a couple of months? The back wing – I know you never go there. We'd keep to ourselves, of course.'

I look at the woman with my nephew's offspring folded within her abdomen, her body a vessel Shaun has filled over and over with wriggling matter.

Those foul words Shaun once muttered about me were correct.

The afternoon they took away his blue-skinned form in the ambulance, I at first stood in a stupor on the grass, wrestling with this drama. When the garden sharpened into focus I saw that my flower beds were being assailed by a strange flat worm. Seconds later, my hands were holding a cloudy rubber condom! I looked about and there were further congregations everywhere. Hanging from the rose bushes, draped across the azalea and hollyhock, crushed beneath the peonies and zinnias; even hurled over the papyrus stand on the artificial island in the canal.

Near the garden shed, I found a stash of coloured wrappers kicked into the dirt.

I remember standing on the grass, my outrage crisp, recalling cars along the lane and the summer-long moans in the dark. I thought back to fleshy shapes on the lawn and Shaun gulping glass after glass of water by the kitchen sink at first light. That day, while the paramedics revived my nephew's body, I plucked out Shaun's used condoms from my plants using a washing peg. One by one I watched them descend into the bin.

As we sit in silence Carlotta comes across and rolls over at my feet. She's grown a little stout after her operation. She gives me the closest expression to a smirk that could be expected of an animal.

The Kingdom of Fassa

Two years after her death they agreed to do a commemorative hike up the mountain that had taken her life. He flew out from Gatwick to Venice and caught a train up to the Dolomites, where he had lived as a boy. They'd chosen a few days in late September when he and his father could both schedule time off work, a fortnight short of her anniversary. That date stalked them both. Before, there was still hope and the kitchen bustle of bootlaces being tugged and boiled eggs wrapped in worn tea towels, the skin moving in pleats over his mother's forearms. After that date there was horror in every object, and when the search was over the seam of the mountain ridge divided the earth into rank shadow and a porous lilac world, where her plummet would be ceaseless and her bones remain whole.

He heard his father in the kitchen. Bruno could be trusted to turn this into a worthy day, a day that would have brought about Annette's chipped smile. He heard his mother's terrier barking, shook his head thinking there would never be an end to Scottie's vigilance. His father had moved into his uncle's unused house, one of a handful raised on the hillside in the '60s boom, too flimsy to heat with their warped window sashes and faux-baroque tiled floors. For two years the family palazzo had been standing nakedly open in the village piazza. No one would finish the renovations now, and his father could barely glance towards the cobbled square without growing stormy.

He pulled on jeans and walked barefoot into the kitchen, zipping up a fleece. His bowels felt full, crimped with nerves. He had his mother's finicky stomach lining and felt the corrosive pang of coffee every morning, but that had stopped neither of them from drinking a half-dozen espressos a day. He looked at the kitchen clock and saw it was later than they had planned to set out, but they had drunk Malbec deep into the night, knowing that this morning lay ahead of them.

Bruno's staple before these long treks was a bowl of watery plain spaghetti and he sat on a stool eating this, eyes on the table surface. The dog stood still. At Bruno's back the dense ridge loomed: a backwash of rucks from the ancient motion of the range. The three thousand metre summit was visible from the other side of the house, and behind Bruno you could see the village stacked in the valley's shadowy watershed. The kitchen window view included the palazzo on the square, with the slate roof tiles and copper eaves and drainpipes that his parents had argued over for months, which he knew Bruno would have erased if he could. After arriving yesterday he had walked into the village and said hello to his cousins. He'd looked up and the copper piping was still so vital, embracing the deceased building with a fuel of caressing arms and fused joints. At the bottom of the square, an open tap endlessly replenished a trough with spring water and he'd put his hand inside, watched it become fishy yellow and felt the flesh burn.

He began to slice salami. He peeled off the skin and threw a piece to the dog. Bruno poured coffee for them both, producing a single spoon and placing a supermarket packet of sugar onto the table. Today there were no boiled eggs wrapped in worn tea towels, no mint tea in flasks. Bruno wore the leather hiking boots with rusted eyelets he had been wearing that day, a torn flannelette shirt tucked into shorts that showed the muscle grooved above his knees. At 56, he had the body of a young climber and every movement of his was choreographed by purpose, where Annette had grown plump and flaccid, her breasts becoming pillowy cushions she used to chide as she waved hands down her front.

His father's face dropped towards the chewing dog.

'We'll bring Scottie,' Bruno said. 'She'd have expected that.'

They set out to the steps behind the house. These were wooden planks a prior resident had lodged into the side of the hill, now pitched unevenly and several refusing to bear weight. Some families had vegetable patches up there, basking in the light. There were serrated leaves hiding courgettes grown gargantuan beneath, and tomato plants with acid-yellow flowers, and a cherry tree whose late fruit had been removed. The steps gave way to an earthen furrow between grass tufts and this cut across to the north of the village, where all paths to the mountain intertwined. These paths were the language of his boyhood; he had once hobbled down here dragging a broken leg. When they were far above the houses they heard an engine turning over – it sounded like a woodcutter's empty pickup – before it rattled down the gorge. His father walked on with a hunched gait as the white dog tore through the grass in a mechanical frenzy. He followed, already short of breath; his synapses seemed to be carrying his mother's voice.

Where am I, my child? Where am I, my child?

That day he had barely seen her falter, had barely believed the disappearing act that started with a stumble, a waver in equilibrium. But Annette's unsteadiness had become a cartwheeling, a battered rotation that he and his father stood watching, immersed in fragments while all logic became savage. Not a cry as her body shot over the line of rocks above the wide fogged-out gulf, as Scottie trembled and whimpered in a flurry of fur.

Bruno twisted back towards him. He felt salt secreting into his mouth and his senses were jammed.

The path continued its wide swoop towards a border of blue pines. He concentrated upon this and knew that the smoky light and smell of resin within the forest would ease his nerves. He needed these moments before they trod upon the mountain's bare Triassic surface and they would revisit that day, when it would open up unmarked ahead. He prayed the weather forecast would not betray them, that fog would not claw up the peak, choking as a cold gas.

He watched his father trek into the trees, the dog in white flashes at his heels. He knew Bruno felt differently about the forest. For Bruno it was a thing to be passed through. Inside there were fenced-off patches where cows grazed, and these *bestiame* were shepherded by youngsters who came up from the cities on the plains, feral men and women with Rasta plumes or hair shorn over their mangled ears, tattoos down their arms. They camped out in the deserted *tabià*, lit fires and had all-night parties. Bruno always said that he hated them, he thought they had no place here. Yet there were no more shepherds born of the village. All youth had gone from the valley as fast as funds or initiative would allow. Some to Milan and Padua and Venice to study, while others crossed the mountains to Cortina or Arabba or Val di Fassa where there was work. Annette, who had grown up in London, had never wanted him to stay in Italy. She'd enrolled him in university as soon as his results came through, had found the flat in Camden and put paid to his homesick mourning.

Not for the first time he wondered how his mother had survived so long in this forgotten hamlet stuck to the mountain's backside. The village with its sour sunlight sat at the end of a road of hairpin curves, that was prey to landslides and hefts of collapsed snow. In August, its single restaurant might be crammed with out-of-town vehicles whose owners strode laughing through the streets, while woodcutters and deer hunters stared up at lottery results on the television in Amelia's bar, or leered at the pregnant Cuban one of them had snagged on a holiday abroad. These were men who shot russet deer, seduced by their great bodies folding to the ground, heads reeling and eyes bulging with torture. They gutted them, pushed their hands within sweet, slithering organs; they sectioned these beings into drained cuttings for freezers, ate platters of this flesh, extruded into moist salami scented with grass and blood.

He knew his mother had been a prize here. He also knew that she had danced on tables and Bruno had ploughed into her at night. In the summer she had read Dylan Thomas to them both, the three of them sitting on wooden chairs carried outside under the tree. He'd found it embarrassing, the way his father's eyes foraged over her, hands quivering as though the language had borne him away.

Let me shipwreck in your thighs –

Bruno couldn't speak English to save himself.

Ahead, his father held open the last wooden gate and the forest passed behind them. The mountain stood ridden with raw early light. Scottie ran off. As the older man latched the gate he began to feel pressure in his throat. They halted at the edge of the grassy maze before the colossus. He could not remember standing here with Annette, their conversation, or whether they had even lingered. He could only sense the sheets of colour and the timeless fracturing of geology, and that at this point his mother had entered the last hours of her life. He realised how little he had touched her since he had left the valley, how their bodies had developed strict perimeters and she would watch over him when he visited, rather than share her eyes. He gulped and the air that entered him was saturated. There was no oxygen more luxurious than this. He looked up at the summit, tapering off and made half-invisible, the incandescent surfaces they would traverse where the light was sheer. He saw the trail cut into stone above the treeline. This was the one that would bear them upward in tramping silence, sweat raining from them.

For a moment he remembered how he had doctored himself months after the accident. After the fall, Annette's body had lain trapped in a cleft all night; they didn't find her for a full twenty-four hours. Back in London he had loitered in a city park at nightfall then settled down to sleep. He had crawled under a low tree, digging into the dirt, clutching for roots and gripping these with his scratched hands. Had she ever regained consciousness through those hours? As the long night progressed he'd felt his pockets emptied and genitals skated over. He had wished for blows as he sobbed.

His father strode forth into the grassy currents in the foreground. Bruno was headed towards the Rifugio Venezia, the only lodge on the climb. This stone building stood far off under the mountain wall. A tide of sunlight would soon envelop its roof. The dog yapped in the wind, plunging through tussocks. As he paced after them he thought of fossilised shells laid to rest in the bedrock, their ivory curlicues now sunken into the rose-hued cliffs above, graffiti from the land's marine epoch. Now the sea was a hundred miles away, a polluted gulf bearing the raft of Venice and sweeping the *bora* over Trieste. Soon enough, his eyes traced Bruno heaving up the steps of the lodge and he saw there would be no solace anywhere.

Inside he found Bruno at the bar dunking a teabag into a mug of hot water, holding the attention of the waitress. It made him sick to see this. The woman was perhaps in her forties, probably Romanian; they were always foreign in the mountain restaurants and lodges now. Her peach shirt scooped low over modest breasts and her eyes stirred as he entered. His father looked up and he knew the pair had been intimate. The woman turned to the machine while his father moved to one of the wooden tables and waved at him to come. He walked over and ordered a coffee, thinking stiffly of Annette. He saw that Bruno's gestures were kinder now, leavened. But when she brought the coffee his father ignored her. Later she spoke to them, asking

Bruno in accented Italian if she could feed the dog. Scottie gobbled morsels from her hands.

When an English maverick first scaled this peak in the mid-19th century, it had been nameless. The locals had lived in combat with the winter from a time beyond memory, when each season the trail south would be blockaded by ice strata the mules skittered over, dropping into ravines. Villagers subsisting on polenta and onions were driven insane by malnutrition and the ceaseless cascade of snow, hardened by crystalline, ebbing days. Summers were a morass of steel rain and landslides, stillbirths, haemorrhage and fever. Annette said only an Englishman would look to the brutal crenulations above the sooty mice-filled hovels, and see a kingdom to conquer. Once this occurred the mountain began its venerable life, no longer an overblown wishing well rising above the catastrophic ranges.

He felt uncomfortable and stood. On the far wall there were photographs of tall men embracing even taller wooden skis, with spring bindings and dangling leather straps. They looked as though they had lived arduous, fleeting lives. He saw stark, familiar images showing the varying moods of the peak. With or without snow it scored the sky, thrusting with violence. He knew that all through the Dolomites there were memorials to the dead. This was one of the things they had talked about: Bruno was seeking a permit for a plaque in Annette's memory, and the exact place had to be located for the rangers of the *corpo forestale*. He knew that Bruno had wrapped up two sticks of chalk from a kitchen drawer and put them in his pocket.

As he paid his father introduced him to the waitress as his son. It was said quickly and the woman's eyes struggled over his face. Outside, Bruno glanced at him as they stood on the wooden deck in a corridor of cold wind. But he bent over his boots and said nothing.

He knew that a man's organ is always there, like the branch of a supple tree.

He fell in with his father's pace along the first trail banking upward. He tried to return to Annette, salvaging an image of her hiking between them. Her faded hat and her cries to Bruno to call Scottie away from her heels. This made him feel a swimming bliss and for a moment he stalled. How was it that they had failed her that afternoon?

Midway down, it had happened on a steady trail no riskier than any other. He saw her body begin to grapple with the air. He'd pushed down the path as she rolled over, shot through with velocity. He saw her eyes were shut tight and the dog was beside itself in circles and *he hadn't looked away*.

He paused to let two other hikers pass by him as he wiped his forehead. He felt the coffee gnawing at his stomach.

The night before they had agreed they would first climb the summit. On the descent, they would revisit the place where she had fallen and mark it for the rangers. The weather was clear and the rangers would pass by early the following day to affix the base for the plaque. He guessed that he and his father might make some sort of homage up there. Neither of them had ever spoken of responsibility. But ever since the accident they both walked as guilty men in the village. It was known that she had fallen like a bird between them.

For years Bruno had been with the *soccorso alpino*, men who dislodged bodies from the rocks or located children lost in the forest below. He brought home stories of madness or tragedy to the kitchen table. An able local had gone off-piste skiing one winter. This man's clothing and equipment were found collected under a tree, but never his body. Before a group of people, including the man's wife, a French journalist had thrown himself off the platform overlooking Marmolada and the pinpricked spread from Civetta to Antelao's prominent cone. They had never found that body either. Or probably the pitch against the rocks had made carrion of him for the crows. He had calculated it would have taken the man's free-falling body a matter of seconds to plummet from that point. Seconds where the journalist's eyes registered colour flashes and his brain might have entered a compressed lull as his clothing whipped. They say that falling is the easiest of deaths, that the body reinstalls its preternatural love of flight; that impact is delivery.

Last night they had fumbled with words that tried to evoke Annette. But it was Annette who had been the head of their triangle, who had illuminated and framed their conversations, who had darted between them and sounded musical. Whatever was said yesterday had been wooden, spoken by two men whose memories had been destroyed: for they were now the two men who had nodded at her bludgeoned face and torn shoulders at the helipad, who had trekked home to separate bedrooms where each wept. In all this time neither had visited her grave, nor had either man thought of putting an anniversary notice in the local newspaper. Annette's jackets remained pegged in the hall; her robe behind the bathroom door. Bruno had pushed across a piece of paper with the text he would have engraved on the plaque. Just her name, just the dates. Both of them stared at the cursive loops that spoke the syllables of her extinction.

Annette H— S—
02-03-1962 – 11-10-2014

One night when he had not been long in London, he awoke. He was shaking and his heart pumped irregularly. He had paced around the flat trying to breathe, wishing he had a woman to hold or more tangible friends in his life. His mother had said his birth had ruined her; they had been too long getting her down the valley and over the pass. She had told him that within him, he held all the souls of the babies she would never have. When he was a boy he had believed her and felt the nestling of these children inside, sisters and brothers who were limbless and mute. He had believed he was their custodian. But that night he had waded into himself and realised his parents were designed to live without him, that he had always existed on the outskirts of their primal fury. He knew he had been banished and felt betrayed.

On occasion he had brought friends from the city on the slow, nauseous climb to his village. They were astonished by the setting. He saw their discomfort before the tumbling dimensions of the landscape and the hyper-reality of the soaring rocks. How they hedged themselves behind books, or got irreparably drunk at the *baita* parties in the woods. Anything to reduce the vastness to an inactive background. Or they hiked at breakneck speed, rolling towards the peak with electrolyte-enhanced drinks and GoPro cameras, telling him they couldn't believe he had come from this. That was when he knew it had been a mistake to reveal his origins. He had seen another girl from his village in a Camden club once; they had looked over each other and said nothing.

He had to concentrate now, his father shouted across. They were crouching along the *cengio*, a natural sleeve dug into the rock, where one bump of a knapsack or shoulder could send you tumbling into the void. Climbers paid the most attention here, but today he slipped through without trepidation. There was liquid along his limbs, behind his knees; his hands pulsed. Bruno waited for him at the Passo del Gatto, where the earth fell away and he had to reach out to the cold cable looped through rivets and half-leap to the other side, his boots anchoring on the rocks.

Beyond the *cengio* they advanced onto the raw flanks of the mountain. At any moment stones could be dislodged by climbers above, but he knew their helmets were hanging behind his father's front door. There had never been any talk of wearing helmets today; death had rendered them careless. Above, the slopes glimmered silver, with yellow trails etched across in slack lines. Bruno veered onto the steepest, most challenging path. As he watched his father's drenched back and the stick he had taken up prodding rocks, he wondered whether this would be a true commemoration, or if some part of his father needed to expunge Annette from his core. Since her death Bruno's moods were darker and he had become foul-mouthed. He lived in that dim, freezing house, feeding Scottie and himself from the same pan. Last year there had been talk of leaving the village, of going down to Belluno to live with his brother. But he had seen his father in the city: his agility rifled around inside of him and the traffic set off his unforgiving moods.

There were *caprioli* watching them now, attracted by Scottie's scent. He could see other climbers in bright clothing with scarves knotted at the backs of their heads; his eyes caught on a woman's gleaming calves. Bruno quickly reached them and the group pulled to one side to let him pass. From the way they were braced against the rock, Bruno must have spoken sternly to them. He was rude to anyone not of the valley. One girl bent down to pat the scampering dog but Scottie rushed on. They turned to watch him ascend in Bruno's wake and he glanced up at their tanned faces and sports sunglasses.

How he wished to be among them! How he wished to be a visitor on the mountain! But even as a boy trailing after his parents, he knew that the history of his being had been written in this place. As they trekked he had peered over the landscape, imagining hunters pursuing prey or the shaman making a sacrifice between boulders, a crouching man with a box jaw and recessed eyes, an animal gutted just above the treeline, blood spilling and hooves ceasing to clack on the stone. Annette used to say that they were never born, so they could never truly die. 'Self' was just an idea, a passing, she had said to him.

Where am I, my child? Where am I, my child?

He greeted the group of climbers and they moved over to let him pass. His father and Scottie had gone into shadow beneath the cliffs and as he paced on he was alone. The highest reaches of the peak lay in ashen planes above and he smelled the mineral warmth the sun drew from the rock. He found himself in an arena of stinging silence and heat. This was the last expanse before the narrow summit climb, a parabola of whiteness. He could make out Bruno and the dog in shapes on the ridge. Soon enough he was there, hoisting his weight up those same powdery steps. He had to measure his balance with every footfall. Millennia ago the great mountain had cracked apart, forming a detached peak now standing in limpid facets across a chasm that ran a mile into the earth. The air funnelled and howled through this shaft, bearing a crop of suspended falcons. As a teenager he had crawled on his belly up to the ledge, watching his white-knuckled fingers clutch the very delineation between ground and space. He had wondered what it was that kept him from hauling his body over.

At the summit he found Bruno eating a panino with salami, the dog resting beneath him. They would not linger here, he knew. He sat down and drank from his flask. That day Annette had been last to arrive; she'd hugged the monumental cross at the top, needing to steady herself. Today the rusted spire rose high into the blue. Bruno muttered to him when the brightly dressed climbers joined them on the platform. As these people marvelled at the spinning panorama and neighbouring mountains surging from green folds, his father stood and brushed his shorts and the dog peered upward, ready to chase his heels. Bruno marched across the uneven surface. His head and taut neck dropped down the trail.

When Bruno was gone he finished his food and made a ball of his rubbish. Two years ago Annette had sat before him feeding salami bits to the dog; he remembered he'd felt bashful noticing her long white thighs. His head fell between his knees. One of the women lowered herself next to him, saying something about his companion being in a rush. He looked up and shrugged. He stepped through the group as they unwrapped food and passed around drinks. He could see Bruno moving at a pace along the lower ridge.

As he set off his legs felt like jelly. Descent required no labour of the heart and lungs, just a sturdy pair of knees with able hinges, and shock-absorbing thighs. But his legs were addled with weakness now that they had to return to that place. Below, his father emerged from the boulders onto the shimmering terrain, half-jogging along the loose spirals over the mountain. Bruno would not wait for him. He tried to hurtle after him, but there were parts where the trail slid over gravel or veered close to the edge and he had to slow down and focus upon his boots. Several times he felt the seduction of gravity. It seemed his body wanted to plummet and he pulled back swaying, his head like a balloon on a string. He saw the mountain in billowing shapes and thought he could guess what dying felt like, the lonely slipknot of its sliding contours.

But when he realised he was approaching the site of Annette's fall he was busy thinking of another thing, a woman he had met in a pub who said she climbed in the French Alps. It had been a good night, not sexual. She had odd, wide-apart breasts and a severe face. Yet when he had called her the next week she said she couldn't go out with him. No reason, she just said she couldn't.

Enraged, he'd wanted to cry that he had never desired her.

That was when he found Bruno standing on the path before him, his eyes culpable screens and his spine slumped. This was where Annette had fallen.

At first he could not reabsorb what had been scorched into his mind so he squatted, leg muscles twitching and the sweat rolling from him in the sun. His vision shifted over the quilt of rock spurs beneath and he noticed the dog patrolling the site and turning on itself. He thought its vivid fretting would make him scream.

Bruno took the chalk from his pocket and began to draw a vicious 'X' on the mountain wall.

He felt a pressure welling in his throat and was afraid he would faint.

When his father began to weep with a busted choking, head bent to his chest, he stood up and stepped away from him. He could not feel Annette anywhere and his recollections were overwhelming. He said nothing, began descending the trail. Bruno remained bowed while the dog skittered around with small yelps.

He ran for a stretch, seeing the version of himself that had scrambled down for help, shaking a mobile phone that could draw no signal from the air. As he raced along he had nursed the hope that she was dead and he knew she had to be; he prayed her eyes had stayed shut and she had never seen the mountain pulling away and the ground charging towards her. An hour later the helicopter had fluttered upwind before steering into the valley where they watched its futile gyrations. He stilled under the rock face. After 10 minutes, Bruno came lumbering down without the dog. He waited, looking for Scottie. For the whole trip the dog had stayed glued to his legs. Then when Bruno pushed past and resumed hiking, he understood. He grabbed his father's upper arm and looked into the man's revolted eyes.

'What did you do to him?' he cried. 'What did you do to Scottie?'

'He wouldn't move,' Bruno answered. 'He wouldn't leave her. He wouldn't leave her.'

Bruno charged like a madman down the trail. In a matter of moments, he had lost sight of him.

He crossed the flats and wandered alone into the forest. He listened to cowherds whistling on another ridge. He pulled off a piece of resin and stuck it behind his front teeth, sat down on pine needles. When it became too cold he walked into the soundless village where cars were parked around the lights of the restaurant. A row of heads sat under the deer antlers and bright television inside Amelia's bar.

The doorway to his family's abandoned palazzo was boarded up but he crawled beneath the plastic sheeting on a low window and moved into its silence. Just over two years ago, the new wooden stairs had been sanded and they bore his weight up to the room where his parents should have grown old side by side. He lay down to sleep on the ruined floor, now a scored surface. His stomach gurgled and his shoulder and hip were frozen. But he slept, he did not dream. Soon after dawn he awoke. He stretched his limbs, pulled his body into line, then climbed outside into the square again. He washed his face with skin-numbing water from the trough. He looked around the piazza where he had played as a child, over the houses whose inhabitants he knew by name and gait and pitch of voice. The facades were clustered one on top of the other, a tight citadel with deer carved into front doors and displays of geraniums. He knew it was time to return to his father.

As he walked up the hill to his uncle's house he knew that he would find them folded together, Bruno and the waitress. The Romanian woman would have made up the bed swiftly; she would have noted the streaky windows and mildew in the shower. He imagined her bare shoulders would be locked within an embrace that felt like stone and fire, that felt like the most defiant embrace she had ever known, and she would know this embrace was stolen.

Yann at Night

After the holiday on the island his father drove them back to their mother in Paris. Yann's father was a tall Venetian who rarely drove cars. He liked to drive at night and he drove fast. Under Mont Blanc he stopped at a rest area and the vehicle took in black mountain air. His father stepped out and Yann saw the giant peak twisted towards the moonlight, that poured downward in a tumble of silver skirts.

'Come and look, Yann. Your father has climbed to the top of that.'

In the round yellow tunnel through the rock underneath, the car sat behind trucks and grew hot inside. Yann watched the recurring emergency exit signs with a running man chased by jagged flames. His sister sat up in the back seat. On one of his father's fingers was a golden ring with a flat blue stone that came from Persia.

Yann knew they were still a long way from Paris when the car hit an animal and his father fought to control the steering wheel. The car skidded left and right before they pulled over to the verge. 'Goddammit, Goddammit!' his father said. He opened the door and dropped his feet onto the road. Yann could hear him breathe in deeply, shoulders fallen and two fingers pinched into his eyes. Yann smelled wet pillows of forest air and Constance was still asleep.

His father stepped around into cones of light, so that Yann could only see his crumpled shirt and his face in brown lowered ridges. There was no sound. His father recoiled, then turned to the roadside, following something that dragged itself into the woods. Yann saw a blur of red and white. His father crouched down by the front of the car and Yann thought back to the island where they had stayed in a warm stone house that he hadn't wanted to leave. Yann and Constance had gone by themselves to the water, and every morning they watched a fat man with rubber rock shoes and a spear gun, who caught a few small fish. They saw his body submerge and the hard kicks he had to make to go under. There were sea urchins on the bottom and Anita told them never to swim in there or they would suffer like crazy. Anita was their father's new girlfriend but she had driven back to Dubrovnik yesterday for work. Anita had bought a basket of blood-red sea urchins and they watched her skin them alive and slice up the pulp for spaghetti.

'Now look who's suffering!' she had said to their grins.

His father came back to the driver's seat and turned the key. The engine started and he changed the gears. They pulled ahead for a few metres then began to move along.

The car stopped. The engine shut down and there was no turning it on again. His father struck the steering wheel with flattened palms.

He took up his phone and called a number, listened to a recording. He rang another number, the phone ringing and ringing until someone answered. Yann heard a crabby voice inside that said, 'Eh? Eh?' so many times. His father threw down the phone, locked the doors, closed his eyes.

'There is a man coming with a tow truck from the village,' he said. 'Tell me a story, Yann. Don't let me sleep.'

Yann made up a story. It was about a mountain climber from Persia, trapped for 10 years on the summit by spirits until an enchanted gold ring appeared in the folds of the rock. Yann studied his father's almost-dark face, the way his lips fell apart as he was taken by sleep; how his eyeballs travelled under their lids, attentive to Yann's voice. Yann thought that his skin would taste salty if it was kissed. By now his father's mouth had lines at the sides and his teeth had grey ridges, but Yann had seen a photo where they might have been twin brothers: his father was a boy in shorts standing by a canal in Venice.

On the island, his father had shouted when Yann and Constance had fought. He had shouted at Anita too, had made the mascara run down her face until he embraced her in her bikini.

Near the end of his story Yann saw bold lights come up behind them. His father straightened, peering in the mirror, and Constance began to cry. The tow truck's grumbling motor shook through the car. Yann's father wiped away a tear of dribble that had come from the side of his mouth. He stepped out, slamming the door. Yann looked across to the sea of trees. He knew the fox they had hit was in there, panting on a patch of freed organs and blood. He knew it was staring into the spiralling branches, hearing these noises come up from the road.

In the morning some crows would start tugging out the plastic straps of its innards. Yann told Constance to be quiet or he would tell her the goriest story in the world.

They were lifted into the truck's cabin carrying their beach bags and sweaters. The ramp was lowered and Yann heard a clanking and the hiss of hydraulics. Their car crawled up behind them with its torn light. Stuck above the cabin window, Yann looked away from a poster of a nude woman. He saw a Holy Mary magnet on the dashboard, and the wrappers and stinking hat the man had pushed across the seat.

His father climbed inside, taking Constance onto his lap. Constance's arm went around his neck and she began to suck her thumb. The driver sat next to Yann. The truck pulled out onto the empty motorway and the engine laboured before it began to pick up speed. The next exit was not so far. The man slotted coins into the toll machine and drove more raggedly than before, given the road was bent and narrow. They came to a village surrounded by fields dotted with large white rocks. Yann saw that these were cows showered in moonlight.

His father had left his phone in the car, which was now sitting upon the rusted truck in the brightly lit garage. Constance locked her arms around his neck even tighter, and his hand cupped her bottom in her shorts. The driver had furrows in his cheeks and dark, berry eyes that stole glances at her. There were two beds in a room off the garage, he said, they should sleep there until daybreak. Yann's tired father nodded. He was too exhausted to care. They took off their shoes and Yann turned over his pillow; he could smell someone else's hair and breath. When he could hear Constance and his father inhaling, he sat up and looked out of a round, barred window. There were buildings and through a cleft between them he saw the cows in white mounds. He rose and put on his shoes and walked into the garage, dragging his fingers along the side of the tow truck, feeling dents and rust flakes and grit. On the island, Anita had disappeared one night and come back bumping into things. Yann had heard her puking in the toilet. Anita had black hair in a sloping line across her forehead and down behind her ear. She squeezed grapefruit juice for them and spooned in curls of smoky honey and rinsed their glasses.

The door was unlocked and Yann went outside.

At the end of the street he saw the square with its war memorial. There was a bar that had a green light inside; he saw that the light was a scrolled green word in the window. He wanted to see the cows but he also wanted to see the word that was written there. He crossed the square and stood before the bar. The word was written in a language he had never seen, with strokes and curves threaded together, then pulling apart. There was a man standing at the window looking at him. Yann turned and ran. He heard a call and tore back across the square and raced down a side street trying to keep his footfalls quiet.

He saw blackness at the end and ran towards this. But it was an unlit park with trees and a spiked fence with a locked gate. He jogged along the fence then turned back. He had lost the garage. He stopped. He thought of the fox listening to the woods, each hour shorter as its body drained. He thought of Anita listening to her rushing music with cymbals and horns. Anita had said that Saint Agnes was the best saint, that she was just a girl when the Romans tortured and beheaded her, then dragged her body through the streets. When Yann was small, their house had been full of African masks and carvings that his parents had collected before he was born, when they were still together. There were voodoo dolls with nails in their heads and boxes inside their stomachs bearing mirrors. This is why Yann told stories and he was never afraid.

He crept along an alleyway and crouched where there were bowls licked clean. Whenever Constance slept her lips would open like their father's, and Yann would put his finger inside her mouth. But on the island when Constance climbed into Yann's bed, their father said Yann was too big for that now and it wasn't allowed any more. Constance had cried that Anita slept in their father's bed and their bottoms touched. Anita took Constance upstairs and Yann's mother phoned and his father didn't take the call. He had thrown himself on the sofa and asked Yann for a long story, absolutely the longest story he had ever told. Yann's father liked his stories to be full of splatter with only the heroes spared. He didn't mind stories with girls but they weren't allowed to win.

Yann stood up and looked out of the alleyway. The road was empty and there were no sounds or footsteps. He could smell the breath of cows on the air. He started to walk down a street after the park, which took him to a wide field with wooden fence posts slotted together. In the corner of the field the cows were a glowing sculpture of rumpled spines and poking horns and curved heads. Yann passed through the fence and walked to them, over tufts of grass and cracked patches of mud. Some of the cows looked up, and he felt the curiosity of their eyes which were brown pinpricks. Others were asleep with vast mauve faces that looked like papier–mâché masks. Yann touched one of the animal's flanks and felt tough bristles as he pressed down his palm. He knew that the red coat of the fox was still now. He knew the stone house on the island was quiet and bare. Soon, some other family would come with their arguing and bags.

Yann found his way back to the garage and slipped through the door into the room where his father and Constance lay asleep, enfolded as they had been before. He unwrapped a toffee he saw on the table, but it tasted sour and he spat it on the ground. He took off his shoes and curled himself up against the wall and knew that you could never go back anywhere, no matter how hard you tried.

Return from Salt Pond

All the way home she talked. Even her suffering silence was dialogue, insinuating itself along the cords of his brain, snaking with his thoughts, coaxing words from him that were unwilling and clotted. That way he often dwelt in defence, and she had become so agile. When they had nearly arrived at his mother's house at the edge of Accra, he took a shortcut behind the new formal streets of the estate, driving through a cuff of blackness under a disused railway bridge. At the exit there was a crump, or a blow, and the windscreen was in tatters over them. Gunning the car as flickers became ragged youths, he glanced at her face in the dark, saw its shredded bloody supplication, saw the rock sitting in her lap like a grinning child.

Kenneth had lived abroad for years but he came back often enough to know the unsealed roads out of here. He accelerated, charging in the dust, hearing cackles surrounding them as the night air entered the ruptured window, sailing over the silver splatter on their clothes. He could not speak. Not even an, 'Are you okay?' could come from him now. And he knew she was just as misshapen, tossed in the same gulf.

He reached the estate with its clean kerbs and glassed-topped walls. Street lamps. He could talk to her now. Decide whether to take her to the dodgy hospital on the far side of town. Better a clinic nearby. But still Erica's mouth stayed closed. He heard a gust of her prattle from five minutes before, the reprimands as echoes on the air. He stopped the car at a junction, reaching for the moist map of her face. He pressed his lips to hers, feeling a fleck of glass between them, and her tongue was cool and unresponsive.

'Erica. Tell me you're okay,' he said to her.

She nodded. They both looked at the substantial rock that had been lobbed through the glass, now in a corona of shards on her jeans.

'Take this off me,' she said.

He wondered if they should go to the police. But then thought of the hours sitting in the hot oil-painted rooms, the officers like cartoon cops, their adhesion to cardboard colonial praxis. Then the unfolding hassles afterwards. He and Erica on trial for not being locals. What were they doing under a railway bridge at night? They were surely committing indecent acts? And finally, the row of stocky thugs from downtown. Thugs who could find out where he lived. Thugs who could hammer a nail into his dog's head and rape his old mother. If he were more righteous, he could put time into this thing, root them out, spit on their faces. He could spend the next year sitting on a grimy court hall bench waiting his turn amidst the punks and uncles, the battered market girls and baby thefts, the crocodile tears and pragmatic stink of pardon, with a judge in a crisp wig waiting for a fatter handout.

He turned to her, lifting the thing from her lap; he opened his door and let it fall to the roadside. 'We'll go to Ibrahim's,' he said. 'We'll clean you up there.'

The rock gone, she clasped herself and began to cry. Slivers fell from her hair to the masses on the seat.

'Oh God, Erica. Look at you, baby.'

It hadn't been such a bad day, but to end it like this. The Salt Pond property had been what they were looking for. The timber of the main building was sound. The mud huts for guests were in fair shape. The trail to the beach was magical, and able to be fenced off. If their dreamy move to Ghana was ever going to be orchestrated, he felt that these could be its initial chords. He envisaged the platform construction on the hillock where the jazz bar would be located, and she had noted the nearby well-respected clinic and proximity to the busy coastal road. The divisions in their thinking hadn't been palpable immediately. She touched his arm as the agent led them from the main building through the messy grounds sloping to the sea, around the parched huts with their weary vegetation and lopsided stools. She kept turning back to him, grinning at him, her eyes wide. But then when the agent was gone she said some bullshit about not wanting to shift all her savings for the deposit and expecting him to cough up – at least 30 per cent. It was said carefully as she sipped her second beer. There had been forethought and he felt played. Then, as they were leaving, she said she wanted to see one of the huts again. They walked down the trail to the dusky sea. Inside he pulled down her pants and fucked her quietly, the door half-closed and children running past and their two faces pushed into the gasping, coarse walls.

It was more money than he had earned in the past five years.

Kenneth curved into his oldest friend Ibrahim's street, hoping that his wife Fifi was at home to see to Erica. He wanted to throw off the shock by discussing it with another man. A part of him even wanted to imagine what the youth had felt – the rock rasping against his shirt as the car entered the short tunnel, lifting its mass into the night air. Then hauling back and volleying with force. Now he saw their shattered car from the outside, the faceless crash dummies and the chitter of the glass. He wanted to tell Ibrahim how the impulse had run through him – Gun it! Gun it! – while Erica was midway through arguing with him, undoing him. And how shit-scared he was that there might have been a dozen of them in the night.

'How you doing there, baby? We'll get you through this. Don't sweat, darling.' He put his hand on her thigh.

He beeped his horn and Ibrahim's ancient watchman slid across a metal peephole in the gate, staring at the vehicle for minutes. Kenneth heard Erica's sobs and reached his arm around her shoulders.

Fifi took Erica to the bathroom where she began to tweeze out the glass. He and Ibrahim sat down with two beers on the porch. He was exhausted, his shoulders were wrought and a rogue pain travelled along one side of his neck. He had a few cuts, but the glass had landed mostly on his jeans. His knuckles were scratched and he had dug a jagged piece out of his forearm. It was now sitting on the coffee table in front of him, blood-free, a piece of today's ghastly jigsaw puzzle.

'It's the fourth or fifth time I've heard about it. I'm amazed someone didn't warn you,' Ibrahim said lazily. 'It's some bunch of thieves from Tudu, they come here in the night. Things will move when they knock out some politician's son in a sweet car and steal his gadgets, you'll see. But small fry like you – bet you didn't have a hundred bucks between the pair of you.'

'Not exactly. But Erica had some dosh.'

'Then here's to you and dosh, bro,' Ibrahim said. 'Did you see that place you were talking about? Where was it? Sekondi?'

Now Kenneth wished he had never told Ibrahim about the Salt Pond place and their impossible hopes. The jazz club. The music school. The cool beach hotel. It seemed as foolish as tonight's crushed glass was coldly tangible.

'We went there. It may well be a rip-off. Ownership stuff. You can never know who you're buying from,' he said.

'Erica's interested?'

'We both are. It needs some thought.'

Kenneth knew Ibrahim was biding his time, waiting for the cracks to widen. Erica was older, she wasn't first-choice material. Divorced, she'd made a mess of her career, changing in her thirties to become a musician, failing, then returning to teaching. They'd hooked up in Guildford outside a pub between sets, both jaded exiles on a landscape of wet buildings and shrouds of rain. Someone had read her cards that afternoon and said she'd fall in love with a dark-skinned musician. He'd thought she was bonkers, but he let her lead him to her flat. The morning after she was all honey and roses in his heavy arms and he couldn't let go of her.

'I had an almighty shag with Adua this afternoon,' said Ibrahim. 'Christ! I've still got blue balls. They're paining me! And now I've got Fifi to look forward to tonight. Dutiful spouse sex, there is nothing sweeter. Ah, my sweet cock-sucking wife! You ought to tie the knot and start having fun again.'

But as Ibrahim talked, Kenneth looked out over the neighbourhood with its stands of satellite dishes raised to the sky. He smacked a mosquito on his neck. 'Thanks for tonight, you know.'

'Don't be foolish, man,' Ibrahim said.

'Erica was pretty shaken up. It all happened out of the blue. I'm sure she thinks it was aimed at her.'

'Don't be thick. Those cunts couldn't see a thing in the dark.'

'The thing is, if they'd got inside the car, I don't know what might have happened. It doesn't bear thinking about.'

'No, it doesn't. Look, you have your woman. You can borrow Fifi's car. Take her home along the main road.'

Ibrahim was smiling at him. This was the smile Erica had said she found unsettling. She said she could feel him beneath her skin, his insatiable sexual navigation. Now Kenneth tried to hear some sound from inside but heard nothing; the women tucked deep within

Ibrahim's house of slick tiles and crooked doors. Ibrahim's fingers were running a riff along the cane armrest.

'Weren't you supposed to be playing tonight?' Ibrahim said.

'Yes. I backed out. I asked the guy who helps out at the Golden Tulip.'

'Adua says you look kinda kinky when you play. Says you get this grungy look that sends a ripple around the room.'

He snorted. 'So who's this Adua?' he asked.

'She's just back from the US. She did a journalism course at Columbia, now she wants to shake things up. Starting with me,' Ibrahim said.

Kenneth shook his head. Winding back, he thought there had been an instant when the windscreen was still intact, when there was a smear or friction on the glass, poised or stilled as they bickered. Had there been time enough for him to whip out his arm to protect her? Hadn't there?

He felt such sorrow now, such grief. For what he knew – though until this moment he had deflected the thought – was that the rock had finally shut her up. All she had spoken of the whole way home was his lack of money. How she couldn't be expected to risk her life savings. What if they split up? What if the business was a failure? He had hardened, breathed in and out, at one point wanted to see her crushed, slapped, mortified. Driving on, he had overturned these thoughts, ashamed, but discovered he found her repellent, and even the warm fuck two hours ago seemed grotesque.

He had to see her. To apologise for this. To hold her, inhale her.

'Shall we go inside?' he asked Ibrahim.

'What's your hurry, man? I can hear them upstairs. Fifi's probably emptying out her whole wardrobe.'

They opened two more beers. A donkey bayed from the scrub surrounding the estate. Then a car horn sounded in the night, headlights slewed one way, then the other. 'See? They're still out there, your stupid thugs. They're most probably bored as hell and high as rafters.'

Kenneth drove Fifi's jeep out onto Ibrahim's road under the lights. It was a compact woman's vehicle, all wheezy and light, tyres that sang on the bitumen.

'You look better now,' he said, touching Erica's cheek. She had on a pair of Fifi's flashy designer jeans, loose on her thin thighs, and a white T-shirt with a parrot on it.

'I had a good hot shower. Fifi's bathroom is like the fifth dimension,' she told him.

He laughed, thank God Fifi had opened a bottle of wine. All he wanted was to go home, commune with her. He saw them slithering on the bare floor.

'You don't want to pass by the club?' she asked.

'No. Why should we?' Now that he had spoken to Ibrahim, Kenneth wanted to tell her. He wanted her to see how he had been bold and, in his way, successful. He wanted to sluice into her, whisper that Ibrahim would lend him fifteen grand. They could buy the Salt Pond place. Next week even. It was all going to happen.

'I thought you'd feel like playing. You know, shake it off.'

'That could be a plan B,' he said, reaching for her thigh.

'I don't want to go to the house.'

'Why? I thought you'd want to wind down.'

'I am wound down,' she said. 'We stayed far too long at Ibrahim's. I don't think I could go home and stare at the four walls. Not after this.'

He backtracked into third gear by mistake and the car threw them forward. Originally, his compulsion had been to be out there every night, his bass creamed to his hip and whatever happened. There had been women. Foreign, local; curvy, slim. He was big and bulky and wore small glasses and he was very dark. They would say yes to him and he would make love over and over to their bodies. But it was Erica who had locked him into the raw, amplified state that now governed him. He would raise his face during a jam, look everywhere for her in a panic discharged only by connection with her eyes, and he would crave her open thighs and the heat of her cunt.

'You don't want to talk about the Salt Pond place?' he asked her.

'I think we're done with that,' Erica replied. 'In every bloody way imaginable.'

'I don't see your point.'

'Kenneth. It seems pretty obvious to me. Someone throws a rock in your face when you're talking with the person who's never going to come to the table for your dream. To the person who doesn't realise it also takes physical commitment to show belief. To me that pretty much means it's over.'

'It's my dream too,' he said. 'And it's not over.'

'Can't you see?' she cried. 'What happened tonight was a sign. It had to be, Kenneth. These things just don't happen. A rock in my bloody lap? And you think we're going to last long enough to have children?'

Kenneth felt the twang in his neck return. He thought of Fifi on her knees, Ibrahim tugging her thick hair and holding her scalp, rolling her over afterwards as she secretly wiped her mouth. He stared at the angry face next to him.

'Whatever this was,' she said. 'It's a blockage. Someone is telling us to halt. This is not the way we are meant to be going. Or me at least.' She turned away from him.

He shifted the gears of Fifi's stupid car, reaching fifth on a short stretch before a bumbling taxi loomed up in front of them. He accelerated around this. He glanced at her pale folded limbs, everything folded against him. At the intersection he made a U-turn back into Ibrahim's neighbourhood and then – as she sat up in alarm – veered onto the dirt road they had taken earlier to escape. The lightweight car rocked down the trail and he knew he wanted to hurt her.

'What the fuck are you doing? Stop the car!' she said.

He skidded on, headlights bouncing as the vehicle jerked their bodies. In an instant they were back where it had started. Beneath the railway bridge entering the cuff of dark. A wall of hefty rocks slid down from the disused track and he saw bottles and cans, a discarded handbag with its entrails in the dirt and a woman's shoe. He cut the engine and they were alone. By now her cries had ceased and her arms had fallen and her whole body trembled.

He sat there in a fury, not believing what he had done, not understanding anything. All he understood was his desire to disprove her, to upend this woman who believed in cards and signs, to discredit and disown her. He stepped out and slammed the car door. He left her there crying and walked away.

He scuffed along the trail, a few times stalling, closing his eyes, drawn to her. She did not call out to him. As the path climbed there was silence and the night air drifted over his skin. He wiped his glasses which had fogged over. He heard Fifi's jeep revving below. It reached the street and Erica had the same problem with the gears. He stood there listening to the sound of the engine disappear.

On the road he caught a taxi to the club and when he arrived asked for one of his old guitars from the back room. He watched the guy from the Golden Tulip play for a while, but when Seth saw him in the audience he finished the piece and lifted his guitar strap over his neck. Kenneth finished a neat whisky he thought he deserved, and stepped onstage to a round of clapping. For years he had played on and off here. There had been an uninterrupted stretch of six months when his father had been dying, when every night he had come to the club from the hospital with stricken hands. Every night he had changed the old man's soiled garments and sheets. Kenneth had a strong suspicion he would end up like him, a marooned vessel other people would have to look after and clean. He hoped he still had time to think about these things. But tonight, as he thought about the burst of shattered glass, he realised that what he wanted more than anything was a companion to see him through. He wanted a wife. And what Erica saw as a sign that they would never stay together and produce a child now made him think of orgasm, and the grappling and piercing and deliverance of sex. He wanted to explain this to her. He imagined her limber body over him and felt weak in his groin. He knew they would never make love again.

He nodded at the band and the Norwegian trumpet player introduced the number they'd planned to do next. He smirked at the tight, enfolded audience: there was a good crowd, faces he knew, old friends and unknown women he knew he could sleep with tonight and every night of the week. He waited for the dizziness he felt when he couldn't hunt down Erica with his eyes. He was surprised this was already weakening.

As he began to play he imagined the group of thieves on their way back to Tudu. For a moment he thought of them as princes, with wiry, anatomically precise bodies. They were warriors and these skirmishes unleashed a hurtling force. He wondered what these young men would say to each other as they crossed the city with pockets full of riches, as they swaggered back into labyrinthine neighbourhoods that stank of goats. He saw the torn foam mattresses where their bodies twitched through the grand chapters of their dreams, the maggot-ridden *kenkey* eaten in tongues of light.

They Came from the East

They came from the east in buses; becalmed men, devoid of propulsion. If you bumped into one on the Underground you would see no forgiving nod of his face, just a trigger, a finger on steel. You'd sense a pulse somewhere, a relic almost bred out of you, the garlic reach of his breath. You'd apologise, aware of the titillation of the word *mercy*, looking for a raft through the percussion of his stare. The train would move on and a brief audience would look at their feet.

These men found jobs and made themselves useful; they had been very useful. Your father who believes in contribution takes one in, saying this man had been thrown out of his windowless squat, saying that these wars had occurred on our doorstep. Saying there had been snipers and bombings and massacres and *we had watched.*

Your mother says she'll have no stranger in the house. Your father makes the back shed comfortable. One evening a man is introduced.

You shake this man's hand. You think of corpses nursed together on stinging summer days.

It is two years since your parents failed to persuade your brother Milo to reside in this world. One autumn night Milo never came back from the park. At home his cut-out is still everywhere, his osmotic reign in doorways, adrift on the stairs. Milo's *danse macabre* takes places every night, an ache of energy from the kitchen to the computer screen, then barefoot through the frosted, mugger-ridden common. Milo's physical health was always inviolate, merely brushed.

Your parents remain distraught with mourning. Most nights you come home to find your mother banked against your father, who is fastened around her body.

Tonight, the foreign guest steps into the kitchen from the dark garden. For a moment his back, entrapped on the glass door, braces. The man's eyes are strange and gel-like.

Boiling water rolls in a pot.

Your father releases your mother, whose tears mark her shirt.

Except for Milo, who had a labourer's job and grew thick, pulsating digits, you are all musicians in this house.

The foreign guest is a voiceless man who observes. On a Sunday, he sits on the step outside the back shed. His not-home. You look down at him from your window, the way the war has cast this man into a script of fenced-off yards and the undulations of a new city.

You step back when his eyes shoot up to your eyes.

You are a tenor. You return to your exercise. But as you sing you realise the house is empty and the back door is not locked. You listen for creaks on the stairs.

You begin a more complex vocalise – Rachmaninoff's – yet beneath the ascension you hear a firm knock. You stand there, chin rising, score gliding to the floor. Your armpits prickle. You think that terror is the intrinsic, bowel-trembling note aligning all beings. You think of nocturnal rapping on apartment doors and men being dragged off, ankles bumping down stairs.

You start again, expelling the notes, riding the upward carriage of the music. But hear a capable voice mirroring your own. You stop, the singing stops. You have heard the largeness of the foreigner's voice on the other side of the door; its airy lift, portions of its unschooled embracing. This is a travesty.

You are furious. Are you being mocked?

Your father says that the foreigner calls himself Peter. Peter has found a job on a building site a few suburbs away. He catches the train in the morning, at night he walks home. Your mother has not warmed to him. She has followed the war trials on the news. She says, 'What if?' But she cooks for him, sets a place for him at the table. Peter washes the dishes and your mother goes outside to smoke a cigarette. Then she drives into the city to rehearse. Other evenings your mother and father watch a film in the front room with the door ajar. You enter and they are entangled on the couch. They stretch out with fronts together, fingers in hair.

Peter reads a tabloid newspaper on the cleared table under the kitchen light.

You go into Milo's room which remains a lair, a loophole. Sit at Milo's desk staring at the dead cells of the computer screen. You think of young men your own age, promised safety but pushed off buses and led in single file through the woods. You think that Milo, had he been raised in Peter's country, would have worn a uniform and slaughtered men. You are not sure how this skill is devised but you know that your brother would have given captives water, pronounced their names; absorbed duty.

Shot them.

You disconnect that thought, but it stays awash in you.

Your father travels to Devon to see to works on your grandfather's house. Your mother is at college teaching. Peter has long departed across the suburbs on a dawn train. You have a recital tonight outdoors; your throat is dry. You swallow honey and make herbal tea. You do not possess Milo's exuberant organism. When Milo finally hanged himself in the park, the doctors wished to dissect his brain. You don't know why your parents agreed to surrender this immense portal, but then they never thought to ask you.

In slippers, you tread across to the back shed where Peter has now lived for three months. You have your mother's extra set of keys. Since your father swept up the wood-planked floor and cut a carpet piece to fit the room, no one else has been in here. Inside there is a bed, neatly made, a chest with a lamp. There is a desk and a buckled landscape hanging under glass. You begin to ransack. You strip off the bed, pull away the furniture from the walls, lift up the carpet corners and peer as far as you can see. You are looking for trophies. You remember the tooth that a Belgian soldier kept for decades, shown in his palm on a current affairs programme on TV. The tooth had been taken from Patrice Lumumba's dissolved head.

You pull out the drawer of the desk and in the cavity underneath there are two things. A gold chain, bloodied or rusted, with a crucifix. And a blurred photograph of your mother. Now you are satisfied.

You shred the photo into minute, unbearable pieces. When you look at these morsels at your feet, you realise the woman was not your mother at all.

The performance goes well. Afterwards you go out with the group and drink a whisky, not your usual drop. Your heartbeat has quickened; there is a girl who seems to admire you standing at your side. She looks at you with slow enquiry. She also sings. The girl drinks white wine, glass after glass, bumping into you. Your flanks graft together, you separate from the others. A voice travels around with the name of the restaurant where the group will go next, but you've told your mother you'll be home early. She's not comfortable alone with Peter in the house.

You're single, you haven't had sex in months. You can feel your loins begging, churning. You're ashamed, looking at this girl, at the force your body has compiled from nothing. A glass of whisky and a few scrapes along your thigh. You're ashamed at how you've ceded to rough thoughts. Where before, while singing, you felt a holy surge, a climb towards a communal sense of articulation, you now feel demoted, belonging to a species at its vulgar, grappling genesis.

You turn away from her, leave the group and catch the Tube home.

Milo used to run through the park with fierce love. It is where you go now. Your throat is hoarse again as night air roves over you. The trees are scarcely visible, then loom up with their architecture, buttresses sliding into the ground. Your mother calls, worried that you have gone out with friends. She asks you to come home, 'Please'. You don't tell her you are around the corner on the common.

You sit on a park bench. You hear druggies up on the hill and wait a while, listening to their cracks and calls. You wonder if that would be an easier way than this.

Twenty minutes later when you walk into the kitchen, you know a physical force has passed through here, you feel it jarring the air. Your mother is immobile at the back window. When she turns, you see her face has been employed in a frantic way; it looks lopsided. You ask her what has happened, what's wrong. She says, 'Where were you?' As if those lost moments have been critical. Food steams on the stove.

Peter is absent.

In the night you hear your father's keys in the front door. He bounds up the stairs.

After rain, your hands dig into the earth where you buried Peter's shredded photograph. The pieces are half-dry, stuck together. You take out the mass and put it in a bowl on the radiator in your bedroom. When the bits are dry, you rub off the dirt and spread them on your desk. You separate the lower, darker tones from the aura of daylight cast down from above. You gather pieces of the woman's olive green sweater, locating the contours of her body. You identify her breasts, her belly, her shoulders. You discover a row of stitching around the neckline and link this up. Her neck presents itself, smooth and broad. Next to the border of her skin there is a creamy wall in the background, perhaps a cottage. You didn't notice it before. You look for her curly reddish hair, identical to your mother's, you certainly remember that. You lay out this halo and her face looks like a devoured saint, an empty reliquary. You search for her features in the pile. You separate her brows and nose, her eyes that are unlike your mother's, smaller and without beauty, her mouth, which is colourless and compressed. You flatten these overlapping pieces and are surprised. This woman is nothing like your mother. And yet in that horrible moment you had thought. You sit there, observing. She wears no expression, even though her eyes are breached by the camera's gaze. Her hands are wrapped together beneath her waist and she wears tight jeans; she is a heavy-hipped woman. To the left of the cottage there is long grass, a wooden fence, pines.

A chain disappears beneath her sweater and you know there is a crucifix resting on her skin.

You scan the photograph. You print it.

Your mother drops out of her production and your father takes time off work. They leave for a week in Brittany, taking their instruments. You wave them down the road that skirts the common, seeing the bench where you sat the other night. You watch the car take the bend out of the neighbourhood towards the thoroughfares leading from the city. You are standing on the footpath with a cup of cold tea.

For the past few days inertia has driven you into your bed. You know that it is your doing, whatever Peter inflicted upon your mother. You were told no details. You know there were visits to the clinic. To your parents you said nothing about ransacking the man's room, or ripping up the photograph of the woman with red hair. At night your limbs jerk you awake and you hear Milo moaning, Milo scratching the walls. You see the schoolboy who you know discovered Milo's body swinging in the park. That kid's life now has a rotten thing inside.

It is not hard to find Peter. You catch the train to the suburb where he works. You begin to wander along streets. It is windy, gritty, and you think of your parents driving through France, windshield wipers crossing to and fro, French road signs diminishing in their wake. How, in lumpy beds before the glow of dawn, they will refuel their love from these embers. You approach a building site with a skip on the roadside and white-dusted men ferrying detritus from the house, an orange funnel releasing a cloudy ziggurat of material. You glimpse Peter. At first you think he is going to do a runner, but he walks over to you calmly. You see how he is robust among other men, how his damp hair spiders over his temples. You see it in his spine now: he is a soldier, he has executed men. He has never known capitulation.

You hand him the printout of the woman's photo. He takes the corner, eyes dropping, an infinitesimal slippage. He gives you a turbulent look, folds the image into his pocket, rejoins the other labourers. You stand there watching their cohesion among the rubble.

Astragàl

It was still early when they called him. Not long after lunch, as the day began to turn. From his window he had seen them sunning themselves and smoking on the terrace, and the procession of children pulling sleds, with the ski slope thrust through lofty pines at the rear. He had gone back to his manuscript. But when they found him he was stretched on the bed in a milky doze. His wife and daughter were in the room shouting and shaking him, asking him, had he seen her? Had he seen where she had gone? Hadn't he been looking from the window earlier? His granddaughter had disappeared from the playing area and they were conducting a search. It had happened, Magda sobbed, before their very eyes.

He had not seen the girl, he said. It was sharpening before him, this scene. He looked at the two women with their fraught faces. It was true he had watched over the terrace and playing area before, and he thought he had seen his granddaughter's blue hat. But how could he be certain? He stood and paced to the window.

They were saying it had happened so quickly. She had been there one minute, tramping with her sled up the rise, then gone the next. The women spoke over each other in a contrapuntal way, almost a sing-song that made his heart go ragged. The girl had never socialised well, his daughter said; there'd been a kidnapping the other year, added his wife, aghast, a businessman's son from Turin. He sat down on his chair where the child had crawled into his lap this morning, such a minuscule, downy being.

They said her sled was not to be found and the *carabinieri* were already halting cars and checking the village. Alpine rescuers had been called in. They would soon arrive from their station in the next valley. Children were usually found in the first few hours, said his daughter, heaving, as though the chatter helped. The hotel manager had sent them upstairs and told them to wait for news.

'If she hasn't been kidnapped—' repeated his wife in an outburst. 'There is always that chance.'

'Mother, don't be stupid! Why on earth?'

He pressed his palms to his temples. He looked at his notebook and pen on the desk, his text still innocent of these instants. He watched a skier zigzag down the run. The view of the mountain above was severed by the window frame. A group of men dressed in red and black were in a circle on the snow now, with a dog on a lead. The dog looked playful, the men firm. He saw his son-in-law among them wearing a quilted jacket. They all looked over to where the sun was dropping behind the ridge, diminishing all aspects of detail and light.

His wife and daughter joined him at the window.

For a moment he forgot why they were standing here in such silence: there were fewer children playing, and Luna was not among them. Where was she now? Last night outside the *osteria* at Astragàl she had hurtled into him with her silver moonboots full of crystals and her face so fresh. She'd thrown down her woollen hat and her fine hair had been flattened to her scalp, a doughy smell rising up to him.

'I've got to go down there,' said his daughter. 'Look at Stefano. I have to at least be with him.'

They took the elevator and walked through the lobby with its deer trophies and vases of dried wildflowers and women in scalloped pinafores. Everything moved past them. He felt the hardware of his hip and he noted extravagant joints of wood supporting the ceiling that were weighted and veined. He followed the two women onto the broad deck behind the hotel. The manager's wife appeared, offering coffee and Tyrolese cakes. There were groups of people at a distance: clearly, they were felt for and observed. Children played on the snow in a restricted area near the steps and the hotel manager came out in shirtsleeves, eyes raised to the dimming sky. The coffee arrived and the manager's wife swept back inside. The building's facade had become a dense grey while far off, in spears of light, the opposite peaks still burned above the village of Astragàl where Stefano had driven them for dinner last night. But down here it was the bruised cold of the afternoon, a coverlet before nightfall.

They watched the playful dog heading towards the ring of trees, the men in a solid hike behind, one man turning around with a radio in hand. His son-in-law stood alone on the snow as the line of men shrank and their red jackets disappeared one by one into the dark strip beneath the forest. His daughter went over to a bench by the wall. He and his old wife stood there.

'How has it come to this,' she said. 'How can such a thing happen? Here, in this expensive place?'

He looked at the woman he had married, her breasts above her middle and her crisp curls. A pair of *carabinieri* stepped outside onto the terrace with the hotel manager, who indicated his daughter. He and his wife were ignored. One officer took out a notebook. His daughter's husband turned around and began moving towards them, his steps awkward in city shoes. The young man tried to half-jog but his feet caught in the snow, at times perforating the surface and sinking as far as his shins. They watched him struggling. His wife beside him began a gruff crying.

'What if they never find her?' she said. 'We were all there. What was the child thinking? Who could have taken her?'

'No one has taken her,' he said.

'Then why, why would a child wander into the woods? Just tell me that. Into the cold with all of this fresh snow?'

His daughter had taken Luna to see many doctors. It had been suggested that there was a slowness, a slight disability. She rarely spoke; her mouth was so clipped and reticent.

'We were sitting there,' his wife went on. 'The three of us. If Stefano had just put away his phone for a moment. If Frieda hadn't been talking all along to that woman in the fur coat. We would have seen her walking away. We would have seen what happened to her before our very eyes.'

He poured an entire sachet of sugar into the tepid coffee, felt it pool within him as he drank. Magda wiped her face. His granddaughter's hands were fledgling pink birds that liked to pluck the long hairs on his arm, brush over his cheeks and mask his eyes in a panel of darkness.

What do you see, Grandfather darling? Tell me the colours that you see.

He had held her when she had been hours old, with her insect-like unreeling and the throbbing apricot in her chest. Then they had taken the bundle away, and he'd felt a holiness removed from him. Luna and her minuet of love had come after his daughter's long years of singlehood. Frieda had been left by a handful of men and she'd met Stefano on a holiday in Tanzania. She had returned to Milan wearing noisy earrings carved out of stained teak. She had told them she was engaged to be married.

They watched Stefano reach the timber steps, sweating and his glasses fogged. The young man stood there breathing in white shreds. He saw that Magda wished to go to him. He saw the very instant Magda's thoughts branched into her body. His wife was never wordless for long.

'Did they see anything? Do they think she is in there? When will they be back?'

Stefano wiped his forehead and upper lip with the back of his hand. His trousers were wet to the knees and his leather shoes soaked. He looked over to Frieda speaking with the carabinieri.

'They think there might be tracks,' he said. 'That's what they were saying. They were following them.'

'Into the woods? In there?' Magda went on. 'What possessed her? What got into the child's head? Who could imagine any of this? We just drove up here for a simple holiday.'

Stefano looked up at him. 'You didn't see anything from the window, Sir? Frieda said she saw you looking earlier. They think she might have wandered off on her own.'

He shook his head.

'Oh, him,' Magda said. 'A fine writer he is. He was asleep when we found him. No chance he saw a thing.'

Stefano stared down at his soaked shoes, bracing himself on the stair rail. They heard a dog barking and all three looked across. The few remaining voices on the terrace grew quiet. The forest trees flowed together, their tips a blue stubble.

'You should get out of those wet things,' Magda said. 'I can't understand this. I can't understand what is happening to us today. Yesterday we were all together eating dinner, it was so simple. And now this.' She turned away and walked inside.

He saw his son-in-law still had something to say to him. The hotel manager appeared in the doorway again. He advanced a few steps, glanced at them and then across to the trees before retreating.

'They were angry we didn't call earlier. The *soccorso alpino,*' Stefano went on. 'They said there wasn't much light left now. There was one who was quite vocal. I didn't think it was necessary. I don't want Frieda to know this.'

The young man bent down as he spoke, eyes fixed on the timber. 'They said we should have alerted them first. Not the *carabinieri.* They said we were stupid for thinking she might have been kidnapped. Stupid, the guy said. It was your wife's first thought – I'm sorry. Frieda and I just went along with it. They said we should have called them straight away. Then there might have been more time to find her.'

He listened to his son-in-law, but found he couldn't talk. He'd been dozing when the child had ceased playing, when her gaze had drifted away. What had called her from beyond the border of pine trees, down the savage incline? Her little steps, one after the other, her passage into the shadows, under the branches with their green twirling skirts and spiralling arms. All of this would have been visible from his window if only he had not fallen asleep. He looked up in a rage to the first folds of the peak and the summit in a crust of white pleats.

'I need to join Frieda now,' Stefano continued. 'And speak with the officers. Though it seems clear we did the wrong thing by her. Sir, I'm infinitely sorry. They didn't seem to hold much hope.'

His son-in-law hoisted himself onto the deck and walked over to his daughter, who was speaking with the two uniformed men. The group moved inside to the restaurant and he could see them arrange themselves at one of the windows. Frieda looked pale and dumbstruck. A waitress brought him out a glass of grappa on a wooden tray painted with alpine flowers. He threw its caustic tang into his body. Suspended above the ski run, the chairlift lay idle for the night. Its cable drew upward with each double seat deathly still, pressed against the dirty white, pylons riveted to the bedrock in steep ascension. Each one was open-armed, imploring.

Now his eyes dragged over the immense compartments of the mountain's structure and the shadow deepening between these in plunging cracks. The mass reared into the sky's blue palette, its tip an incandescent flare as the sun sank downward and the planet revolved. It was a terrible cycle, he thought, each day symphonic yet the hours so meagre and convulsed. He had thought that there might be a Oneness up here, far from the city, a few words of grace written at every man's core. But he stared over the callous geology of the mountain as his eyes followed the ravine that knifed through the trees.

Magda came outside in her heavy coat.

'You're not going to make yourself ill standing out here?' She had brought him his big jacket. 'The child wouldn't want that either.'

He put on his jacket and they stood together.

'I've had a couple of drinks,' she said. 'Are you ready for this?'

She walked stiffly over to the railing and spoke back to him. 'I'd rather it was one of us, you know. I've been sitting upstairs thinking it should have been one of us. Either of us. You could go on without me.'

He thought of Magda's body on the rocks, tugged out of icy water, her purple flesh and rolled-back eyes. It was true, the image was easier. He was ashamed. With Luna, the idea would not come to him and his mouth ran dry.

'Do you remember how we were?' Magda asked him. 'You do, don't you?'

He did. He remembered her waist, encircling it; consecrating himself to her mound.

'It was not so terrible,' she said. 'In my way I felt loved by you.'

He listened to her surrendering her thoughts. For decades he had never troubled himself over her, and he knew the way he cared for her had been indistinct. But back in those middle years he had loved her with a bestial desire, she had been a raft to topple and grind to the floor. Then, for an age, he had ignored her body; it had grown florid and creased as it stood before him.

They heard a sound from the other end of the valley. At first it was muffled and might have been a low aeroplane, but soon enough they saw it was a helicopter approaching. The craft dropped steeply over the hotel and agitated above the arena of snow before them. The hotel manager rushed onto the terrace, now wearing a gold-buttoned waistcoat, nodding to the pair of them. Frieda and Stefano drew together at the window.

The tail cocked upward then the blades levelled and two long skis touched the snow and bore the weight of the machine. The hatch swung open and a man advanced in a crouch. The rescue men in red jackets had appeared at the rim of trees carrying a silver-wrapped package on a stretcher. His heart was thrown about. Stefano careered out onto the deck. Frieda followed with dizzy paces.

'They radioed in,' Stefano said to him. 'Someone just let them know at the hotel. She's fallen quite a way, but they've found a pulse. It's very weak.'

Stefano and Frieda staggered across the snow which was icy and hardened now. The men parcelled the stretcher inside the helicopter and one of them motioned to the pair to keep their heads down. He saw his daughter climb on board, but Stefano was absorbed by the group as they fastened the door. Instantly the craft was airborne and cutting across the valley, lifting towards the ridges, buzzing into the dusk. One of the men was rewarding the dog while the others began trudging back to the car park. Stefano stood there, wiping his eyes. The hotel manager went down the steps.

Magda returned to him. Her face was wet.

'We have no time left, do we? You or I. We do not.'

He was frozen now. His fingers had no feeling left in them, his feet were burning, each toe hammered in his shoes. The last cusp of the mountain peak had gone purple and the crests circling the valley were drenched in red.

'There is a chapel at Santa Fosca, on the road back up to Astragàl,' his wife said. 'It is a tiny, unadorned place. Let us go there and pray for this child.'

The Architecture of Humans

I realise I was never wired to say 'no' when my hippy aunt Merle is levelling me with two beer-bottle-green eyes, asking for an egg donation. I say 'yes', retreating to 'maybe', and Merle's face brightens with a joy I have just relinquished the right to tamper with. Merle has turned up in London at the pub where I am working part-time, big and big-featured and looking African after so many years there, even though her skin is freckly porcelain with broken red lines. She says, 'Fern, you're the only one I can count on!' Merle only calls when you can hear she's on a bus to Mali, on a windblown beach front, in the teary corner of a bar. She slams over the counter and pulls me into her embrace.

I fly out. This is the first time I've been back to Ghana since I was a child. Merle is a sax player who teaches music at an international school here. She's had affairs with politicians and wears headscarves around her flossy red hair. We give each other swamping hugs. In common, we have the steel pin of her sister, my mother, a woman who refracts all light and touch. Merle is my mother Fabienne's younger, startling sibling, whose life is a cavalcade of summer returns and resumed kitchen bickering and flip-flops at the airport; a cradle of tropicana that makes Fabienne roll her eyes. The egg donation is a colossal secret. Merle already has one child, her mixed-race daughter Victoria, conceived eleven years ago with a francophone guy in her band. Victoria is prim and tubby, which hits you afresh every time Merle repeats she can't understand where Victoria comes from, and she feels that I am hers.

Ghana is hotter than I remember and Merle doesn't have air conditioning. I sleep on the bed in Victoria's narrow room; my cousin sleeps on a rolled-out mattress on the floor. When it is time to get ready for school, Victoria sits up sleepily and looks at me in fright. She takes her clothes into the bathroom and locks the door. She comes out in her uniform with buttons about to burst all the way down her middle. In the kitchen there are shouts, and a slap that cuts off Victoria's whines. I think about these insoluble markers along my cousin's childhood, wishing I'd guessed Merle would be such a crappy mum. When Victoria leaves with the driver in Merle's boxy olive-green Lada, I wait ten minutes before I walk into the kitchen. Merle is putting mugs and half-burned toast out on the porch and the screen door whacks each time she enters. Noise doesn't seem to bother her. Today she has taken the morning off school and we are going to the clinic for my first tests.

'Sleep okay?' she says.

'I'm not used to the heat yet. I'll get used to it.'

'Do you want a fan? Sorry, I never thought.'

'Yeah, maybe. It was hot.'

She pours me some filter coffee and pushes across a can of creamed milk and a stainless-steel pot of grey sugar.

'Here's a spoon for that,' Merle says. 'Do you want eggs?'

'No thanks. No eggs.'

We both smile.

'I'm not really sure what you eat, Fern. You just tell me. You just tell me everything.' She sits back, drinking her coffee, her broad shoulders scattered with freckles. She's wearing a sarong that pushes down her boobs, which were uplifted blossoms once. Each summer when Merle came back I learned things about my womanhood that my mother never told me. Merle went braless and her spine dug deep into her back and her rump kicked out and I understood what men wanted from a woman's body just by looking at her. Now she is 43 and she's been trying for this baby for over a year. She told me she's done everything. Local herbal doctors, tests in a big clinic in Abidjan, a check-up with a Swedish gynaecologist friend. I'm not exactly sure what's going to happen next. I've taken eight weeks off university, supposedly to work on my thesis, and given up the pub job. Merle paid for my ticket. I don't ask Merle how her boyfriend feels about this, but I know that once they take my eggs, they'll mix them with his sperm in a petri dish. Merle told me on the phone they'd implant her with a long needle, and hopefully the embryo would stick. Her uterus was good, she said to me, *if bloody Victoria could cling to her uterus wall, then any baby can.*

Merle's yard is mostly dirt. There is a tan dog. She has house-help, a young girl with dark rings under her eyes. The girl walks behind the house with a chewing stick at the side of her mouth and a worn towel wrapped around her.

The clinic is a short way out of the city along the coastal road. I don't remember ever coming to this end of town. The blocks are a cram of old and new and the clinic is on the lower floor of a refurbished colonial building. There is a painted sign in front expressing some doubt:

Doctor Henry Danquah, Questions of Fertility

Inside, an older nurse sitting at the desk observes our entrance. She has glazed black hair and full cheeks. The nurse greets Merle and her smile moves over me. I am the promised one. The bearer of eggs. It is icy cold in here and there are bars on the windows and a terrazzo floor of shattered marble. As we sit waiting for the doctor I think of Victoria as a tiny emblem, descending Merle's lightless fallopian tubes, now probably blocked or stuffed from disuse. Merle puts her hand on my knee and I feel we are unlawful. This is not about fertility, this is about creation. We are here to mix up a being that does not yet exist. I want her hand off me. I smell her breath.

'Are you okay there?' she asks.

'Sure.'

We hear chairs shifting behind the doctor's door. Before there were no voices, and now we hear undulations of conversation.

'We'll meet up with Kwaku when we're done,' Merle says. 'We'll pass by the building site on the way home. He's waiting for us there.'

'Building site?' I ask.

'It's my dream house. You'll see. It's our secret. It's where this baby's life will begin.'

A stocky pregnant woman ambles out of the doctor's surgery and we are called inside.

Merle is elated. She's brought a special cool box to chill the vials of hormones for my injections, and organises my syringes into a separate plastic container, which she rolls up in a canvas tote bag that I know is dear to her. She tucks both of these on the floor behind our seats as though they are precious cargo, not to be stolen or touched. She drives into the stream of traffic, talking, asking me when the last time I had sex was and what drugs I think might still be in my system. I tell her René and I had dawn sex before I flew out, and he doesn't really like what this is all about. She wants to know if René might turn up here on a whim and expect to get laid. I tell her he won't. I tell her we took stuff at the festival we went to last weekend and she bites her lip.

'I'm sure it's okay,' she says. 'It's not as though Kwaku isn't smoking dope.'

Last night on the porch Merle told me about the first time she and Kwaku went to bed. Merle said he dropped his jeans and she saw his thighs. His thighs! And she was smitten. It makes me think of René who is French and burly and quite reluctant to undress. I don't want to meet Kwaku, who is somewhere between my age and Merle's. It feels awkward now, being the conduit between two lovers. I thought I would feel happily involved – and Merle did put an unnecessary cheque in my account – but I feel like a piece of plumbing, my ovaries a pair of helpful pods. I wonder what Kwaku thinks about the child they couldn't manufacture through sex, now being partially extracted from my body which is twenty years younger than Merle's speckled limbs. I wonder if I will feel attracted to him, and what I would do with this hard fact if I am.

'You just wait till you see the place,' she says. 'We're right on the water's edge. It took an age to get all the permits and then James – that's our architect – had to go back to London for two months. But we're up and running now. I mean, it won't look like that to you, but the basics are all done. Kwaku's always out there taking care of things. God, Fern, I must have Witless-Woman-in-Love stamped on my forehead.'

'No, you don't,' I say. 'I can't see it anywhere.'

Merle smiles. 'We were hoping the first rooms would be ready for you to stay when you got here. You'd be closer to the clinic to have your ultrasounds and check-ups. But it didn't happen. There aren't really any pipes out here so we had to build a big septic tank and bring electricity down from the village. Neither of us has built a house before, and James does get a bit up Kwaku's nose. James spent years abroad, only came back here when his mother died. He tends to treat Kwaku like a bush boy.'

We branch off and take a withered road heading to the coast. We pass a couple of villages grafted onto the dust, both with rundown colonial villas whose columns and scrolls are sketched with rich orange. I see two barrels of water tied either side of a donkey whose eyes are trained on the ground, and a jet-black cannon sitting on a white concrete pedestal. The cannon and the pedestal have been recently repainted. I wonder what type of thinking makes an ex-colonised people want to parade this trophy. It must be some sort of gravitational pull, an old subservience flickering. I think of my mother Fabienne, who would have stood under the sun reminding the man with the paintbrush that his people had been blasted, chained and trafficked by the owners of the tilted iron cannon with its pyramid of gleaming balls.

But not Merle. Merle's russet hair whips with delight and I hear the glass vials jostling under my seat and she takes the next potholes carefully. My hand flattens on my belly as though this is the starting point, this furrowed patch of terrain. But there is nothing in there. Just a set of young woman's organs, possibly a slick of René's sperm as we didn't use a condom before I left. (I'm not telling Merle this.) On the phone, she never said a thing about her dream house.

'Kwaku grew up out here,' Merle says. 'He's the one who got us the property. There's a polo club further on where the Lebanese hang out. Our band did a month of Fridays there and Kwaku had a job on the grounds.'

'Instant attraction?' I ask.

'Are you joking? I had my eye on a Lebanese guy with digs in Knightsbridge. This is the last thing that was meant to happen. Kwaku turned up every time we played and just stared at me.'

A final dusty hill then the seafront spreads out ahead, its curves crushed by a forest of coconut palms. Out on a rock shelf there is a construction of cast concrete beams like an empty shoebox.

There is only one word left in my mind right now. It is *folly*.

In the evening I give myself my first hormone injection. I load the syringe, pull down my trousers and shoot it into a roll of flesh I gather on my abdomen. Victoria lies on the bed watching me. Merle was surly at dinner and spooned reheated rice and stew onto our plates. She has just driven out to meet Kwaku in a bar. Victoria has plugged in the fan and the air frees itself over both of us, but the metal basket makes a tinny noise I know will drive me crazy in the night. Victoria turns over onto her tummy and ignores me. I disinfect the pinprick and wonder how many pinpricks it will take to produce a viable cluster of eggs. The doctor wants to do an ultrasound in a couple of days. René kept asking me if the setup was legal, or monitored, or even safe for my health. He thinks I am doing this because nothing I have ever done in my life has produced a consequence.

René said he wouldn't give these people a kitten.

Victoria is not asleep. I'd like to ask her what she thinks about Kwaku, who wasn't at the dramatic building site this afternoon, who called up Merle in the middle of our tight-lipped meal. Victoria is wearing pyjamas I suspect my mother has sent her from home. Her hair spills onto the pillow, the wall above her is blank.

I boil up some citronella stalks and strain the scented water into one of Merle's mugs.

Merle looks in on me in the morning. She's parcelled Victoria into the car and sits down on the bed. I feel shitty; my intestines feel like there is water running through them.

'How did the injection go, darling?' Merle says.

'Fine. It was okay.'

'Kwaku's here. He's not up yet but he'll make you breakfast. I have to fly.' She kisses my forehead. 'Got to look after you. You're our little incubator.'

I stay in bed as long as I can, until my bowels are knotted and I am bursting with piss. I can't hear Kwaku in the kitchen. I sit down on the loo, expel everything then quickly shower. Light-headed, I think of digging myself into René's arms. We have agreed to call once a week, no emails. By the time I call him on Friday I will have had five injections of hormones in my belly, and at least two ultrasounds; perhaps there will be a batch of microscopic eggs trapped in the wavy turbines of my ovarian follicles. René is going back to Paris next weekend. He said he needed to catch up with a few people. I worry that means an ex-girlfriend called Sabine.

In Victoria's room I fold up my clothes in my suitcase on the floor, roll away the mattress, and stand in front of my cousin's crooked wardrobe with its chipped brown paint. I hear nothing from Merle's bedroom. But Merle's door is ajar and I see the long, rippled extension of Kwaku's spine on the sheets. His shoulders are turned inward and arms collected beneath his chest, the back of his shaven skull is square. Seeing this faceless outstretched body makes me struggle with Kwaku already. I wonder if Merle has ever gazed upon him like this. Of course she has. A woman always watches her man cruising through sleep. I want to stretch along that back and inhale the column of his neck.

He comes out when I am sipping tea on Merle's porch. He looks embarrassed, eyes narrow with sleep. I see he doesn't want to spend time alone with me either. We make small talk about how early they traipse off for school, about how he tried to get to the site yesterday but was held up in Ada, a town on the river towards Togo. He apologises for that. The young house-help crosses the yard with a tub of wet clothing, chewing stick in her mouth. She shouts something to Kwaku in Twi which makes him frown. I see the smile doesn't leave her face as she rounds the house. For some reason, I am certain this woman can intuit our baby plan. She would have heard Merle and Kwaku over and over at night: the lovemaking turned into laceration and shouts.

I wonder how Merle put it to him: *My niece Fern is coming out from London, they'll bump up her egg production, remove her eggs and mix them with your seed when you jerk off at the clinic one morning, then vroom!, they'll plant little embryos inside of me. That's our child, Kwaku, that's what we'll do for our lovebaby. See?*

Kwaku balls his hands between his knees. He looks about the yard as though there are things to be done. He shovels sugar into his coffee. You can't tell me Kwaku's carnal aims included producing a baby with her. Not this lean, restless youth Merle could engulf with her limbs, who could go out there and impregnate a whole nubile village.

It's possible that we could talk about Merle's dream house, though I'm worried my consternation will come out fast. And I'm even more afraid of seeing through to Kwaku's unsteady feelings. I watch his fingers roving over each other. They have very lengthy joints. I can't believe this man and I are providing the raw material to create a child. Would it be ours, in anything but the language of souls? Should it be?

Kwaku lifts himself out of the rattan chair and runs a palm over his head. His eyeballs are slightly protruding; I'm hoping Merle's new child won't have these. Kwaku says he has an 'errand' to run. It sounds like a line from an American film. He walks off the porch and across the yard, up to the gate which he hooks shut. I hear a dog barking along the road.

Though I said I would, I cannot get used to the heat during the night. I lie awake, listening to Victoria half-snoring and the night birds outside. Kwaku rarely comes to the house. Merle says he likes to keep an eye on the building site. But when he does pass by I hear them talking in the dark and I know her urging him to stay goes unheeded. I listen to them make love and it makes me miss René, who on the phone has a flat, defiant voice. René asks nothing of the procedure. In three weeks I have produced a worthy clutch of eggs according to the doctor's ultrasound screen, a harvest I cannot decipher within the topography of my abdomen. Merle is enthralled but I see a tiny galaxy of consequences. Dates are fixed for the egg extraction and embryo transfer. Merle takes me out a few nights before, to a windswept bar in the grounds of a luxury hotel. We meet a friend of hers called Tina, from Barbados, who arrives dressed in parrots and flowers. Tina has a local husband and runs a guesthouse on the coast, but Merle warns me in the car Tina knows nothing of our arrangement so I should keep my mouth zipped. We drink non-alcoholic cocktails. Tina is an easy talker until she points out that Merle's architect James was once held in a cell overnight for beating up his wife. I see Merle's eyes scramble. Merle says she knew about it, but it's obvious she's been stung. Tina tries to recover the conversation, before her daughter calls from downtown with car problems. She hurries off through the floodlit garden and we are left alone.

'I'm sorry, I don't know why I asked her to come,' Merle says to me. 'Fucking nosy.'

'Yeah, she was. She had a parrot thing going.'

'Yeah,' she says. 'Thanks Fern, love. You must be bored silly out here.'

'Pretty close to it.'

'I don't think it's going to work.'

'Say again?'

'Oh, fuck it. The transfer. This baby,' Merle says, staring at Tina's abandoned glass. 'You know, Tina's right about James. He took ten thousand pounds and disappeared. I had to pay people – thugs, dammit – to get him back here. He'd gone and set himself up in Hackney with a girlfriend. He's an overeducated prat.'

'I hear you.'

'He sold off a lot of our building supplies too. Now Kwaku keeps an eye on him. He's back with his wife at McCarthy Hill. She took him back in.'

That first week we drove along the sandy trail with the car panting, Merle's incomplete villa revealing its nave and struts between the palms. It was further back from the sea edge than I'd thought, but its static structures already looked like ruins. We walked out onto the platform where the glass window panes should have been, above rocks where the sea fluxed. We imagined sipping tea and watching the sky draw away. Our dreams were elegant. We walked upstairs to the empty first floor where four bedrooms and a studio would be installed. My aunt stood on the cement, hair in red strands like a mermaid on a plunging clipper.

The day before my doctor's appointment Victoria isn't feeling well and won't get up to go to school. Merle comes in, tries to shake her whining daughter, who she concedes has a temperature. I tell Merle to get going, that I'll look after Victoria today.

'Stay away from her,' she says. 'You don't want to pick up anything.'

Merle storms out and the car revs off.

Victoria turns away from me on the mattress on the floor. Merle told me her father was an older, agile guitar player from Mali who returned to wherever he had come from. She said he had a big bun of Rastafarian snakes coiled on his head, and the day Victoria was born he'd had them all cut off and come to her as a dignified man she barely recognised. He had land and wives and he didn't need the music. He had wanted to bring her and the baby up north, Merle laughed. They parted ways and Victoria was fatherless. When Merle came to London in the summer she used to dress Victoria in exquisite pinafores sewn out of wax prints. The little girl would hide under the table in pub gardens; any number of people would try to entice her out. Merle would drink pint after pint and it wouldn't show for a long time.

I ask Victoria if she wants a cup of tea or some water from the fridge. She doesn't answer. In the kitchen, I boil up some water in a pan and drag a teabag through it. I pour the tea into two mugs, adding clumps of sugar and the only piece of lime I can find. When I come back into the room Victoria is sitting up in bed, staring out of the window louvers at the dog pawing the ground.

'Are you leaving soon?' Victoria says.

'Not yet. I'm not sure when. You know why I'm here, don't you?'

'Merle's too old to make a baby, so you and Kwaku are doing it together.'

'That's not exactly true.'

I give her the cup of tea and sit down next to her on the bed.

'I saw Kwaku's thing,' she says. 'He was in the bathroom.'

I try to think of a way to decriminalise this instrument, to make it into something generic, a common tool. But I don't want to be the one to explain Kwaku's penis or Merle's frail cosmos. There must be a seam I could mine to tell her that her life is more than this airless room, and the cries she's heard for a year on the other side of the wall.

I wonder what a grown-up Victoria will say to me about the stash of eggs not far from where I am resting my hand. She'll figure it out one day, when Merle's new toddler is running around another poky house with fingerprinted walls, when she is doing homework and yelling at him to shut up. She'll read an article somewhere and remember the nightly injections in my belly, and Kwaku's weirdness around me, and it'll all make sense.

We drink our tea. Victoria watches the dusty yard. I open my hand over where Merle's borrowed eggs are stored, waiting to be siphoned out tomorrow. One day, perhaps when Merle's new baby is a young jobless man and Victoria herself is a slim chain-smoker living in London, I will tell my niece a story. It is the story I am not brave enough to tell her now. I will tell her that on the day she was born, a man sat down in a barbershop in Accra and had his high, crowning hair cut off. Our eyes will connect and hers will be alert. I will tell Victoria that this man watched as these grey woven cords dropped to the floor and he saw his bare scalp for the first time in decades. I will tell her that this man rejoiced for his newborn daughter and he felt jubilant and blessed.

The Bamboo Furnace

For my father, Kevin McNamara

He was sent back with a tropical bug eating through the flesh of his leg. They had tried treating the advancing wound with dry ice, but it hadn't worked. Further doctors came over from the Spanish mission where one local man had had the skin cut away from his cheek, and his jaws now worked like a moist robot. When the limb began to putrefy, he was airlifted out to Singapore. They had to prise Sybil away from him: first from his chest, then the bedpost; there was grappling and she was dragged screaming across the floor. In Singapore they did the job. He found himself back in Brisbane, sitting opposite his sister Martine at the yellow Formica kitchen table.

Martine had tried to set up the house as best as she could. She had taken out unwanted chairs from the years when the family had run riot, and given him their parents' double bed with its isolated hollows. She had put an extra chair in the bathroom, thinking it might serve for balance, or to lean the crutches on when he was relieving himself, so they wouldn't rattle to the floor. Lionel had shrunk while in the hospitals, though she could tell that until recently he had been robust. Much had been robbed from him, and now he had been felled.

After their tea she poured two glasses of beer, watching his sun-ravaged forearms and the shaven mould of his chin. He had come to her in civilian clothing, a shirt with small arabesques. Thirty-one years ago, his cheekbones had been concealed in a puffy boy's face, but now they seemed crafted with ceramic grace. His ears had grown into fleshy rinds below his crew cut. She was certain they had heard night sounds from bamboo forests, and babbling voices from villages of half-dressed women.

Lionel looked around the unchanged kitchen remembering what was in the drawers, knowing that Martine would keep her bills clamped by a wooden clothes peg as their mother had, with the fabric-covered shirt box full of photographs underneath. She would have followed her ways with little modulation. Martine's whole aspect had broadened, where a woman like Sybil would spend her life becoming fine-boned and minute. He had forgotten how white women aged with such symphonic slowness.

On the sideboard behind his sister's attentive curls were cedar wood framed photographs of the clan who had driven him to the port. Their faces had stayed creased with pride these long years, a vigil in serge suits as the cancers and heart failure had pulled them down one by one. He saw himself in their midst. Just six months after being ordained, a shiny-faced buck gripping the rail. He remembered how they had posed along the ramp up to the rusty ship, squeezing his hands and their tipsy embracing. How they had touched him that day! Daubing his new clothes, anointing him. He could still feel his father's hand grasping his shoulder and its repugnant demand for salvation. He had ridden the old man's pride like a show pony. His mother could not be convinced to make the trip that day: she'd known she would never lay eyes upon him again.

A week into the voyage he had caught typhus and landed in Manila a ruin, his gut and whole equilibrium off balance for years. He had suffered the boat south to the islands. Mules were ridden, he no longer remembered much. Two black-haired brothers in cassocks had left him at the outpost that would become his contracted world.

'Would you like some more beer?' Martine asked.

'Of course, yes. Thanks.'

Martine went to the fridge and Lionel envied the way she had stayed close to this earth. He could see how the shape of her life had drawn down her shoulders and made a dense slab of her back, a broad swimming bundle of her rear. In all these years, he had rarely thought of his sister or her placid tragedies.

Martine noticed how he no longer wore the silver ring they had given him at the seminary. In the past she had studied this ring on his fourth finger. Inscriptionless and rounded, a talisman that said he was bound to *them*. As children, she and Lionel had run off from a picnic and followed a trail to the river where willows swung and a boy had drowned, trapped in their roots. Lionel had gained the knowledge that their mother would produce no more babies. Martine had watched his arc of piss against a tree. They saw the upriver ferry pass homesteads on the other bank and the wash pleating murky water. A great-aunt of theirs had lived in one of those homesteads. Martine knew this aunt had been rich and vibrant once; she'd seen sepia photographs of a striding woman in fur collars and button-down shoes. But Lionel had told her that as soon as she died their father would buy a new motor car.

After the operation there had never been any question of Lionel going back to the seminary on the coast. Deirdre had said more than once she couldn't understand how Martine could take a stranger into her house after thirty-one years, even if he was her amputee brother and a priest. It was Deirdre who had made the largest inroad into her life. Deirdre's kids were her godchildren. At eighteen, straight after Lionel left for the Philippines, she'd started going into the city to work. Deirdre Sheldon was in her typing pool and Deirdre's sandy-haired fiancé Sten was a building contractor who'd come out from Hungary and learned the language. They would go out with Sten's friend Tito and it was jolly. Tito soon unravelled the first confines of Martine's womanhood, but then disappeared from their quartet. By that time Deirdre was already throwing up and one evening in the car Sten apologetically ran his heated, level hands over Martine's breasts, and through the gestation of each of her godchildren he had booked a room for them by the river. When Deirdre's third child – Christopher – was born, Sten had paid to extinguish the embryo in Martine's womb.

'Could there be a little food later on?' her brother asked as he closed the newspaper. 'I think my appetite may be returning.'

Martine knew how he relished peas and lamb chops.

Lionel often became aware of the tingling moistness of the wound and felt razors of fear. If the cells reignited in his body – to whom in this tight-lipped, fair-eyed country could he release his cries? The Spanish priests had understood him, with their clipped beards and their hollering offspring in the compound. One had wiped his face and heard his mutinous confession. When the cut had first begun to fester, Lionel couldn't believe the jungle had turned on him. He had seen these open wounds char the life of a man. Yet he knew what he had done. He knew it was his years of fondling Sybil under the netting, and the children he had seeded in the low sling of her belly. All but one of them had been taken back, pulseless remains Sybil had buried while he raised leaden arms to his God. Even the fifth child –

he'd had no faith in the thriving creature until he recognised Martine's hardy genes.

The day the baby girl reached six months a wrinkled letter was spat out of the jungle. It told of his father's long–ago death and burial at Saint Anne's. Reading and re–reading his uncle's letter, Lionel thought of the rank casket at rest within the earth, and blind worms weaving through the old man's flesh. It was a shock to discover his daughter, Candide, had been born the very evening his father had passed away. With that knowledge Lionel had gone on a bender for days. He had thrashed through the bamboo furnace beyond the village, tormented by the passage of their two souls in the underworld.

Sybil, feeding the voluptuous baby, did not stir when Lionel stumbled back into the compound three days later. She knew Lionel had glanced at her through the eyes of the buried cadaver, she knew he had seen her as a cheap yellow–belly holding a half-caste child.

Lionel was sitting out on the veranda reading *The Courier Mail* with his head tilted back and his stump on the side table. It was the first time she had seen the tortured limb with its cranky purple sutures. Lionel brushed away a fly. She saw this was an introduction he had planned. He cast over another page of the newspaper.

'You don't think you should cover that?'

'Cover what?'

Oh Lord, and now to name it. 'Your leg, Lionel. It looks as though it might still be weeping.'

'Yes, perhaps you're right. There are bandages next to my bed.'

He watched the skirmish on her face. Heard her steps along the linoleum strip through the house, heard the squeaky wood strut nailing down the carpet in his room. She was searching through his drawers now. One day she would find the photograph of him with Sybil and Candide standing in front of the cooking sheds. She would sit across from him, holding the quavering photograph, and she would have to be told.

But Lionel had never been able to name what he felt for the fine-boned woman. Even as the plum babies died and he held Sybil's deflated body, he had felt a coreless alarm that was outside of his understanding.

Martine came onto the veranda with the bandages. Lionel looked at her unrolling the white cloth. Until it happened she would be his foot soldier, his unknowing Magdalene.

'Is this comfortable?'

He winked and she brought him tea.

Martine lay awake, worrying about her visitor and this coda to their lives. He floundered along the hallway but his face was a resilient bronze and his eyes, equipped with untold visions, would close their soft shutters. She knew the same blood ran through them and it was unalloyed. At night, this duality bobbed through her. Deirdre was right when she said that Martine didn't have a clue who Lionel was any more, and Martine had never considered that there might be good priests and bad. Deirdre had said flat out she wanted to meet Lionel, said she'd shake him down in an instant. But even after all these years of depleting discretion Martine never admitted Deirdre too long into her house.

She found the photograph. She came out one afternoon with the image of the Filipino woman tucked under Lionel's arm. A solid, barefoot child between them.

'Who are these people?'

'This is my common-law wife Sybil. And our daughter Candide.'

'A daughter?'

'Candide is now fourteen years old. She was born the day Father died.'

'You've got to be bloody joking.'

Martine stormed back inside and stayed there an hour. She sat at the kitchen table, her shock rolling over and rising in twists.

She returned to the veranda with a dark brown bottle of beer, filled their glasses in a disorderly way.

'We thought you were pious,' she said.

Lionel looked out over the patch of ground he had sprung from, the gormless youth grown into a deplorable messiah. In the middle of the grass stood a thick-limbed frangipani tree and his eyes exalted in the blossoms.

'I am glad that you now know of them,' he said.

She picked up the photograph again. Looked at the woman wearing a gaping cotton shift. Skin as yellow as rubber, tight over her face. Eyes that flickered. All those years her brother had lived among them, she had never pictured their individual faces. They were a submissive mass, she'd thought, chanting and weaving. And yet here was Lionel on an ill-lit day in front of sheds somewhere, and stripes of bamboo forest gushing from one side, with a woman who looked like she belonged to him, and he to her. Martine traced the line where their clothing melded and saw that Lionel's enveloping arm promised loyalty, and the treasured child bore their own family bulk and possibly Lionel's torment. She wished he had not given them names, wished they had never come here with him.

'You're just going to leave them there?'

'I don't know, currently.'

'This house is large enough.' Martine didn't know what she was saying now. She didn't want a pair of Filipinos in this house.

It struck her then that her brother had not given her a thought in decades. He had left her a woolly-headed girl over the washing tubs, steam wetting her face. The years had poured over her and her letters to him had been unwanted vials of news. A cyclone along the coast; their school burned to the ground; three friends in a car wreck. Martine looked at the stump again and wondered what implement modern doctors had used to carry out their barbarism.

Those three times Deirdre was with child, Martine's life had become gilded. Sten would collect her at the corner after work, then they would drive to the guesthouse by the river. In accented child-speak that collected along his throat, Sten said the house belonged to another Hungarian. Martine never saw anyone else but when he washed afterwards she would hear door latches or wood sighing. By the open window Sten told Martine she reminded him of someone and she felt a lyrical, feminine pleasure. When he mounted her Martine would strive to vacate herself, leaving the cast of her body on the sheets, allowing him to heave into this lost woman.

Deirdre had met Sten at the German Club when he was just off the ship, and two years later she finished his obtuse sentences and told Martine in the kitchen she wished to God she had married an Australian. After Christopher's birth Deirdre had her tubes tied, so there was no need for Sten to take Martine to the river any more. Besides, for months after the abortion, Martine felt unfit. She would drive across the suburbs to Deirdre's and take boisterous Christopher into her arms, shedding gulps. Sten no longer addressed her and seemed ashamed those afternoons had ever occurred.

They sat drinking whisky under the awning after rain showers. Martine had returned the photograph to his drawer, but Lionel knew that Sybil and Candide now stood in silence behind his chair. He could see Martine observing their trio. Barefoot, Martine scratched bites on her long sturdy legs with stray blonde hairs. Her calves were a splatter of scabs. They stared out over the back garden with its radiant yellow frangipani blossoms and beds of tossed, wet flowers. Beyond the fence there were rowdy neighbours who kept a crop of car hulks in the unkempt grass. At times the youngest son would rap tools on metal with a deranged ferocity. A bank of Norfolk Island pines released needles into both gardens. Lionel hadn't thought of their lives ahead except to assume that staying with Martine would be bland and safe. It was critical now that he understood motion, and how he would newly walk. His cropped nerves and arteries had barely learned that the leg was no longer there to be nourished. His removed foot: how its absent articulation pulsated at night.

Each dense day that passed Lionel could feel the humid jungle slipping behind him. Sybil had always known that he would be reclaimed. She had spoken these words in corrosive bells over his sun–beaten hide, her tiny body mauling him. As Candide grew tall Lionel had seen the Irish grit that lay under her face, beneath the fine Asian planes. He knew the young woman would lumber through the village with her skewed features to stare at fading photographs in the community church. She would see her father in his worn vestments; she would imagine her parents rutting in the leaky shack. Nothing could shame Lionel more than Candide's harrowed being. Martine had suggested bringing the pair of them out here, but he could never have them where they would become shadowy, disregarded chattels.

When Martine went to the shops he limped over and took up the framed pictures of the young priest. His eyes studied that fair, fatty face. He recalled reverberations of prayer in his skull, yet as soon as they departed his belief had yielded to the sea's rocking template and the explosions of his bowels. None of them had had an inkling where they were sending him. Into what morass. Into what inferno. He was simply left there, banished, all those years extricated from him. He recalled the first infants he had buried in rice sacks, the men slung into pits. The villagers had always known that he was no more than a quaking servant before the great beams of the forest. Sybil, a young widow designated for the white priest by the village, had crawled into his bed one night.

'I'd like to understand,' Lionel said as they had drinks on the veranda. 'Why I was sent away from here.'

'Why you were sent away?' replied Martine.

'It was Father's idea, mostly.'

'You seemed so almighty then,' she said. 'That is what we thought of you.'

'If I think back I felt no particular calling. And I was sent to the most degraded outpost.'

'Even so, I don't know why it had to come to that, Lionel. A woman and a child.'

'You know I nearly died on that passage,' he told her.

'We were not informed. We prayed for you.'

Martine remembered she had cried a river when he left. Then there were Deirdre and Sten and Tito. Her own ghastliness had begun.

'And now it seems I have returned like a man from battle. And what war was this?'

'Lionel, they are all dead now. All of them.'

'Yes.'

'I believe I have done worse,' she said loosely.

He found his eyes had gone to her cotton-clad thighs. Martine assumed a rare, billowing nakedness in his thoughts that he shunned.

'You might wish to confess.'

'To you? I could never.'

But he would always be detained by this point. 'What crime did you commit?' he asked. 'Tell me.' As Lionel stared, he saw her face become a pale enamel.

'I aborted a child.'

Lionel's eyes blazed. 'The father was married.'

'Yes.'

'Then we are not equal.'

He stood up on one leg, hand bulging upon the armrest, and slapped her face. Fell back into his chair and pinched his eyes.

'Please go inside,' Lionel said.

He apologised to her. He said it was the alcohol, and the sense of wrongdoing that had burst through him. His words drifted through her head, they entered and flew about. But after Sten's years of silence Lionel's slap had not been an injury. She had walked up to her room and sat down on the bed, palm to the burning cheek. In circles, she heard their words on the veranda, 'I aborted a child... Then we are not equal...' She saw Lionel's torso rise over her as the decades snapped and the atrocious truth crawled back into her being with its bloody fist. All these years she had heard Deirdre complain about her kids as these joyful children ran around the wooden house on stilts and swung from trees; all these years she had watched Sten go to the tool shed underneath as soon as she arrived. And Lionel hadn't even had to ask twice because she had wanted to feel her soul scalded. Her admission had been waiting for him.

She gave Lionel his tea. She cooked his bacon. She glanced at the stump on the small table. It looked dry, it was healing. Lionel's odyssey was perhaps coming to a close.

They sat in the heat of the morning. He handed her the newspaper and she read it through. There was a murder in the north. A woman's body parts had been found along an estuary. A ship had run aground on the sandbar off Stradbroke Island. The neighbourhood was soundless except for cars up on Wellers Hill Road. She brought more tea, then a beer for them both. In the afternoon she said she'd like to drive him into the city for a look around and he agreed.

The car wove through suburban streets of more wooden homes on stilts, cages of shade beneath; gardens with electric flowers. Further bushland had been colonised and there were new thoroughfares busier than before, and bricked buildings on corners with loud signs she didn't care to point out. He attempted a walk along the block near the Town Hall, but after a few hundred yards his armpits with the crutches driven into them were soaked, and she could smell his sweat. His stump swung between the crutches and his healthy leg, a pendulum attracting stares. The sun beat on their faces and the cafeteria she had wanted to visit was still far off. They returned to the car. He threw his head back on the seat and was silent.

'Shall we go to the river? To the place we used to?'

He nodded. Martine drove through traffic over the new bridge, finding the municipal park which had been cleared of undergrowth after some riverbank murder. The homesteads fronted up on the other side along the brown water, iron fretwork and corrugated roofs soon to be bulldozed away.

But as she pulled on the handbrake Lionel shook his head and said he wouldn't be getting down. He gazed at the river. Martine stepped out and walked a few paces; the air was loamy. She turned back to her brother's face in the windscreen and the sky with its thunderous contours pushed upon the car.

Lionel smelled the eddying water. He saw a mudslide interring a school hut, a father dragging out a child by the leg. He saw a woman pouring water into a son's eyes, the boy's face illuminated.

She came around to him and said, 'Do you remember great-aunt Joan who lived on the other side of the river?'

'I do.'

'You told me that Father bought a new car with her money. That he'd been waiting for her to pass away.'

'I recall.'

He looked at Martine's arms crossed over her dress. He found he did not regret slapping her cheek, for in her culpable eyes he had seen two paradigms of consent. Through Martine and the years cast between them, and the idols both had coveted and smashed, Lionel would understand whether he had ever been a priest.

She drove him home, handed him his crutches lying on the back seat of the car, followed his exhausted catapulting down the side path by the fishbone ferns. She unpinned her hat in the hallway.

Martine brought him a mould-spotted letter with stamps from the Philippines. Lionel recognised his daughter Candide's handwriting. Martine left him alone on the veranda, launching back through the house where she went into Lionel's room and took the photograph of his family into her hands. She wondered if she could induce some supply of sentiment towards the Filipino woman and her daughter, but no new emotion presented itself. Lionel's wife looked out from her triangular face as though she could foresee Martine sitting disrupted on her lover's bed. The woman's shoulder and black hair were eased into Lionel's shirt, a coastline against his shores. Martine trembled to think of the wedding of landscapes.

Lionel read through Candide's poor, devastating English. Sybil had taken ill. He hurtled through the tenses he had taught his daughter in the shack. *She is very bad sick… Close to die…* But almost immediately he understood that Sybil had been restored to good health; that this was just an aggrieved call sent out by his daughter. The page fell to his incomplete thigh. For years that he groped towards now, on nights that were summits, another man had propelled his body. But after the heft of fornication this man would desert him. Then Lionel would see Sybil's slight hands flitting over utensils, her bottom and the purse between her legs. He would call out to her to cover her body, while she would just as easily come over and coil into him.

Lionel shouted all the way through the house to Martine's room where she lay turned to the wall. The youth next door was hitting metal against metal among the derelict cars, and this as well as the memory of his rugged wanting had made him enraged. Martine's bare feet thudded outside ready to hear of some crisis.

'Everything as it should be?'

'Your neighbours.'

'Yes, that's the young son.'

'It should be stopped.'

'It will stop soon enough.'

Martine glanced at the nub of his leg dressed in scribbled pages, a distant frontier. Over and over she saw the word *She… she…* The metallic noise stopped, resumed. Then ceased. A back door swung shut.

She brought out refreshments but saw that Lionel would not confide in her and drag her to his depths.

'You used to have your music,' he said.

'I sold the piano.'

'They are difficult to keep in tune.'

Martine stood, hands loose at her sides. She reached for her pruning scissors and went to cut flowers.

In the evening she heard Lionel showering as she held the telephone receiver to her ear. It was Deirdre, marching through the conversation. But Martine heard protective tones in her own voice.

'He's in shock. He's hardly present.'

'He hasn't said anything?' Deirdre's voice came through a warp.

'No.'

'Do you think there was a woman? For goodness' sake, he was in the jungle for thirty years. There must have been a woman.'

'There was no woman.'

'So, the man is a saint? I don't believe for a minute–'

'He is not a saint.'

Deirdre wished to visit them and Martine was terrified her statuesque Holden would roll up their drive. She told Deirdre they were leaving on a trip to Bribie Island, for a week or so, as Lionel's wound required the sea air. But Deirdre had already tired of the conversation and was lamenting her husband Sten's fanciful yearning for a boat.

Lionel looked for his face in the steamed mirror, wiped away cloud, saw eyes and bones. If the disease were to return he would welcome its advance. He would beg Martine to bury him as a pagan with coins on his eyes.

Sitting outside, Martine listened to his clopping through the house. She sipped her whisky, legs outstretched, ankles crossed. The smell of frangipani was a low sweet stench. All along the neighbourhood a line of Norfolk Island pines had been planted and these now thrust beyond the roofs. They were brooding, dark-willed trees that other householders had taken to with saws. Lionel appeared in the doorway. He lay down the crutches, lowered himself into the chair, propped his stump on the table. He poured whisky into his glass.

'This is where our lives began,' he said.

'Yes.'

Martine looked at the glowing tree in the middle of the garden, the beds of gerberas and hibiscus and zinnias muted by the night, their sorrowful Eden.

The Sneeze

Karen Dessange has been feeling testy. The thought of hhat Gaetano has just done with her credit card account. Vaporising it, in a word. Shifting what used to be joint to a slim flow into her muddy domestic account and saying, What does she need to nourish the banks for? She roars along Chaussée de Vleurgat and feels an angry, head-throwing-back sneeze coming on, fissures through her nostrils along the hot catchment behind her eyes. She slams into the rear of a Fiat Panda and sees three people stumble out as she wipes snot from her cheek. Fuck. A North African man. A fully pregnant woman. A boy with a block of iron-coloured hair.

She steps out onto the footpath. Says in French, 'What were you doing stopping here? What do you think this is?'

Before realising the woman is braced against a parked car, holding her belly, the sobbing boy hammered into her hip. The father explains that a vehicle came flying out from the right and he had to give way. Karen swears at the idiotic Belgian road rules.

She asks if the woman is injured.

The woman's face is dragged downward, steeped in yellow pallor. The little boy's hands are fanned out, one clasping her thigh, the other the seat of her jeans. Why do women let their sons touch them like this? She nods several times, looking to the husband who stares at the beaten rear of their car, which Karen's Gaetano-sponsored insurance will pay for. The woman takes a few steps along the footpath and straightens her back, the son still stuck to her. Both the father and Karen watch her steps, her swollen feet spilling out of her sandals. The right thing would be to take them to the hospital. Karen offers to do this, as she checks her own undamaged vehicle. It's a large Audi she won't be able to run for much longer. She sees shopping bags in the back of the family's Fiat, spinach leaves sitting brightly. She clutches her handbag, feels prickling along the canals of her nose.

'Shall we fill out the forms?' she says.

She is certain something will be amiss. No insurance, no licence, dud working visas. She retrieves the documents from her car. When she opens the forms on the roof of the Fiat she turns aside and sees the man's eyes are full of water. Karen hands him the pen and he writes with difficulty, sometimes wiping his face. His hands, she notices, are of a stone-like beauty, hewn or carved with many shallow creases. The woman now holds the boy on a hip, his face in her neck. She wears a loose shirt which has a jagged, diagonal design; her breasts are prominent pouches.

Karen takes back her pen, fills out her declaration and signs. She hands the man his copy, hears herself again offering to take them to the hospital. Now they stand facing each other on the footpath and the man's eyes are dry. He takes a step away from her. Karen is tall and knows that people often step back because she is looking over their heads. The man's wife removes the clinging child and settles him in the car, then eases her body into the front seat. For the first time, Karen hears the woman speak to her husband in a high-pitched Arabic spatter of sounds. The dented car pulls into the traffic.

Karen goes back to her vehicle, turns off the hazard lights and drives into an empty parking space. She blows her nose and feels lightheaded. She had been going out to lunch. When her phone rings, she sees it is her sister Melanie, who has been calling ever since Gaetano left. Karen does not answer. She sits there breathing, watching another North African woman pushing a stroller. When this woman passes, Karen turns on the ignition. She drives through the city and on to the forest.

It is a clear, ink-filled day with all colour saturated and distinct. The trees embrace over her car. She looks at her rings on the steering wheel and the toneless skin of her hands. She is not wearing varnish and her nails are weak and split. When she was a child, these hands had sat in her lap, had played scales and mastered a Liszt duet. She used to scratch her sister's bare back in fights. Karen has not taken a warm, living thing into her hands in months. She has not touched skin. The avenues twist further into the forest. Lean men are jogging past. She feels prickles in her nose again and holds a tissue to her face, and the stinging impulse fractures behind her eyes. She blinks away the hot light, she thinks of insertion, cavity. She sees a man whose back and bottom look like Gaetano's and she slows the car, staring at this man's buttocks.

She accelerates down the avenue.

Further on there is a grand dilapidated museum she has not visited since she was a schoolgirl. She follows signs to the parking area. She puts her handbag strap over her shoulder and strides along the facade. The stonework feels vivid and heated even though the day is cool. Karen looks up over the building, then down to the lake where swans squat on the grass or dock together some way offshore. She walks up the steps and into the museum. She buys a ticket.

She wanders from collection to collection, from the taxidermied mammals with their wet obsidian eyes, to the pygmies installed behind glass panes. She moves through the Congolese masks and sculpted stools, headrests and bowls, seeing where hands have moved with fondness over wood. After a while the objects feel voiceless and mournful, and she has seen enough. She is alone in the room. She walks over to a row of sepia colonial photographs.

In the gift shop she buys a bracelet of coral and brass beads and sits down for a coffee, watching two brown-skinned girls rinsing cups. She goes outside, towards the fluttering lake now bereft of swans. For a long while she sits on a bench by the water, the swollen day upon her. Among the photographs there was a village girl, a grinning naked young woman whose teeth had been filed into white points. Karen's eyes had travelled over the girl's body like a dark caryatid, full of weight, the skin mapped with scarification textured as wallpaper, a string of beads around her hips, across her sex. Who had she been, this young woman? She laughs, standing against a drawn sheet before a European man with his hooded camera, a man in pitiless boots. One hand on her hip, the other arm bent behind her head with a shadow of hair in the armpit, her breasts in glowing points.

Watching her, Karen's heart thudded in her chest. She has never seen such quivering life. She sits up straight on the bench, a thousand needles along her thighs and a gust of fingertips over her face.

Do thou, O Dica, set garlands upon thy lovely hair,
weaving sprigs of dill with thy delicate hands;
for those who wear fair blossoms may surely stand first,
even in the presence of Goddesses who look without favour
upon those who come ungarlanded.

Hôtel de Californie

They left in separate cars, each with his driver. They took different routes out of the hilly town, one back up to Koforidua where he was working with the plant, the other back to the smouldering city on a winding single lane road. From here the West African coast was a blur of grainy colour, a discontinuation. He breathed easier now that it was over. In another place it would never have been done like this, so furtive and fucked up. Two men in a hotel room on a quiet afternoon, girls swaying past with buckets on their heads.

He glanced at the driver whose eyes were dark screens. The young man had dozed in the car park the whole time, bare feet tossed out of the passenger window.

Now he breathed in deeply, sweating more. When they were inside his skin had been dry and silken, an endless terrain. He had bitten the other's lip, drawn blood, licked the wound, felt unquestioned. He wondered what the other man was thinking now as his pickup negotiated curves, sped beneath boughs reaching over the frayed road, women in chop bars glimpsing his profile. He had watched his lover dress: old printed boxers stitched once or twice, jeans from the second–hand market, a Lacoste shirt washed many times.

Clothed again, they had simply stood in the room, organised nothing further.

He glanced again at the driver, a northerner who had sharp, wide features. Probably it had been unwise to bring him up here today, but he had no way of knowing the roads out of town, the exact location of the hotel, and the pluck of his seasoned vehicle. What if the jeep had petered out on the ascent, or the engine failed to turn over in the parking lot afterwards? How to explain this out-of-town excursion to colleagues at work, or rely on local goodwill?

The jeep drifted down to the coast, tall grass and stunted trees whipping past. At the city edge there was a roadblock where a group of soldiers sprawled under a broad tree. They were thrown back on benches, khaki trousers tucked into polished boots, slick berets on shaven heads, hands holding rifles. One of them stood to wave the car through the busted gate. He had a thick blue belt snug around his waist, temples giving off flints of light.

At the house he showered. His lover's smell was raw over him and now he wished he had washed at the hotel and not brought the strong odour of their skins inside the vehicle. Had the driver seen the other man saunter up to the reception, carrying the folders as he had suggested? He pulled on a pair of shorts. He sat on the bed, looking at the wood grain of the parquet floor.

The driver said an envelope had arrived at the office when the secretaries had all gone. It had his name on it in slanted capital letters. Uncertain, wavering letters. It made him think of a classroom with sixty beaming kids, windowless frames over a dusty clearing, hours of football under the sun. His lover had told him that had been the sum of his schooling here.

HÔTEL DE CALIFORNIE
SATURDAY 4PM

He looked hard at the driver, made sure he didn't show him the page.

'Who gave you this?'

'A woman,' the driver said, hands clasped.

He could have folded over with relief. That afternoon he sent the driver home and stayed in the office, working on for hours. The sun fell and the cleaners mopped. In the evening he walked outside and joined the flux of shadows moving along the trafficked road to the fast-food shops at the junction. Open gutters gaped beside him; girls tittered in his wake but mostly he was ignored, his fair skin a velour of perspiration. At the junction he fell onto a plastic chair by the street and ordered a beer, guzzled it. A smooth girl caught his eye and he smiled at her. She came over to flaunt her rich figure, draping herself over him.

'Sista,' he said, touching her fine plaits. 'Tell me, where is the Hôtel de Californie?'

She told him and he drew a map in his mind.

'You want to take me there?'

'No.'

He bought her a beer, he was finished with her. There were other things to work out. Where to go from here. How to steal him away, luxuriate in him. Perhaps to employ him?

It was punishable by law in this country.

As people coursed past he was surprised to see his driver walking along, his arm around a young woman, both wearing light smiles. He shied back in his seat, half-covered his *obroni* face, watched their backs recede. His lack of safety disarmed him, his exposure.

He was sleepless in the night. He turned off the air conditioning, opened the window louvers. He saw the night watchman shuffle to the front gate and lower himself onto the bench under the strip light, open a Bible and begin to read. Now his skin flushed with sweat. He went to the kitchen for water, pushed his face under the tap, felt the cold stream fill his nostrils and eyes. He stretched on the tiles, rolled his shoulders. Thought of his lover in a prefab house in the hills, a woman by his side, a baby in a cot at the end of the bed.

The jeep refused to start. He sat sweating at the wheel, turning the key on and off, hearing a clicking coming from somewhere in the engine. He lifted up the bonnet, clueless. It was three o'clock and he was early; he'd been certain he would lose his way in the warren downtown. But a taxi? He needed the shelter of his own vehicle in that dodgy zone. A quick getaway and no wandering in the streets. He swore, skin blistering all over. Fuck.

He called and the driver sounded drowsy, put out. But he knew the young man was obedient. The driver said he could catch the *trotro*, he'd be at the house in a half hour.

He kicked a cactus in a pot, which toppled over in a pile of soil and roots. He bent down, gathered up dirt and pebbles in his hand, righted the plant. He walked to the end of the yard, saw that children were watching him through the patchy hedge.

The driver pushed open the gate and walked over to the jeep. He peered under the bonnet. Picked up a rock, hit the two bolts on the battery, gave them a really good whack. Told his boss to try the ignition again.

The engine turned over and the jeep started.

They reached the Hôtel de Californie at 4.20. He was nervy now, he could sense that it was all going pear-shaped. *He won't be here. This is the wrong place. This is a hoax.* He thought of being discovered, being thrown into a cell, strung up, pummelled. He almost asked the driver to reverse out of the car park.

But then he saw a face leaning out of a window, elbows on the sill, smoking calmly. Oh, the rush. He grabbed the briefcase he had thrown in the back, left the driver a roll of bills.

The driver gave him another envelope. He read his name in slanted capitals again.

It had been a while now. The last time there had been a knock on the hotel room door, someone trying the locked handle. Everything had been suspended – all fondling, all love – in that moment. They both stared at the agitating curve of metal. He'd felt a current travel through the body of the other man, saw him draw back destroyed, haunted, their coupling a noxious stain upon the baby and wife. They had solemnly resumed lovemaking. He had watched the other man dress and leave, a different shirt this time, treasured and washed. He'd opened up his laptop and covered his face.

He stood before the driver and opened the envelope.

NUNGUA BEACH
HOUSE 37
SATURDAY 4PM

How on earth to find it? Why couldn't he just have him at his own place? A beer on the veranda, a snack inside. Then the discovery of his rooms, the air tightening as their mouths locked together.

'Who gave you this?'

'A boy, sir,' the driver said.

Was this a game or a trap? Was someone watching him? He worked late into the evening. He addressed a backlog of emails. Emails from old university friends, emails from ex-colleagues back in Europe, from a sometime lover in Berlin, from his sister travelling through Australia. He told her about him.

I've met this guy. He's not free but it's really something. It's going to be another agony thing, I can tell you. I feel like a dog on a chain, on a stake hammered into the ground. There is so much beauty here and I can't run from it. Hot, tropical beauty. Huge thunderclouds and red dirt that steams under your feet. I've read the book you gave me. I really loved it, you know.

He sat back. It wasn't true. He hadn't even opened her book. But it would make her happy. He wished he had a photo of him, even a shot on his phone. Something to stare into, something to examine with intimate recollection. A metal bucket clattered outside in the hall and he listened to the slow sweeps of the mop.

This time when they set out he was calmer. He'd told the driver he was buying some glass beads to take home to his sister, that one of the girls in the office was sending him to a guy at the beach who brought them from upcountry. They'd given him the house number, did he know where it was? He didn't show him the paper, just told him the address. The driver thought for a minute, then nodded. They drove out of the city along the coastal road. Today he had a feeling it would be fundamental, eclipsing. He had wanted to bring some sort of gift but couldn't think what a man would give to another man here, in this country. In the end he brought his sister's book, but knew the other would never read it.

They passed a group of soldiers on the roadside. There was no real checkpoint, just an open-backed military jeep parked in the sun, five men holding guns sitting in the back, heads leaning on the struts of the vehicle. Down an incline to the sea were the hillocks where former ministers had been dragged out at dawn and executed after a *coup d'état*. It had happened years ago and the place bore no new growth, just sand and weeds, the ocean a blue cloth hanging beyond them.

He looked over that scarred cemetery of souls. To think of the thrashing waves as the firing squad took aim, crosswinds entering a pasty mouth, then a bloodless falling.

Deep inside Nungua they pulled up in front of a tin-roofed house with a narrow veranda. His lover was sitting outside with a young woman in a patterned dress and headscarf. She was wearing purple plastic sandals. Two half-empty bottles of Fanta sat on the table between them. The girl had high cheekbones pressed to the top of her face; her skin was glossy.

At first he pulled back, recognition flooring him, and the woman was something he did not comprehend.

Then his lover on the veranda waved at him. He raised his hand back behind the windscreen. He told the driver to wait in the bar on the corner and stepped out into the salty neighbourhood of laughing mammies and loud Tupac playing and kids trailing wire contraptions on wheels. The pair watched him. The jeep took off and the woman led the men inside, placed the Fanta bottles in the kitchen sink, locked the back door behind her.

They were holding each other on the bed when the woman's voice rang out. They kissed. They crawled apart and began to dress. This time he did not watch the other man pull on his worn clothes, but sat there, elbowing into his T-shirt, inhaling traces of their entwined skins. They embraced. He was given a fresh Fanta from the fridge while his lover finished one of the warm bottles that had been left there.

He walked alone down the street and came to the bar on the corner. It was empty. For a moment his innards seized and he nearly stumbled on the ridge of the gutter. He felt obscenely visible, his crimes written in colossal scrolls on his person. He ordered a beer and threw it back, grateful for the chemical swilling; he looked for options in the degraded sky. Then the jeep pulled over and the driver was most apologetic, saying he'd been to a timber yard.

He climbed in, said he preferred the windows open, realised he didn't have a single bead to show for the afternoon.

Now the soldiers turned to stare as their vehicle crawled past in the tired file back from the beaches. One soldier pointed to his white face as they inched by, and urged them off the road. The soldiers were always looking for easy money. The driver swung over untroubled, jerking on the handbrake, glancing at his boss for what would happen next. But he was already grinding his jaw, thinking of colleagues he could call if they were hassled too hard. Papers were fished out; they were all in order. His documents were pored over with a theatrical intensity that set him on edge.

A soldier in a badly-fitting uniform commanded the driver to step down. The driver looked across, swept with worry. His panic increased. But he could only think of his lover being harangued by these young bastards, the ripples he had tongued along this man's beautiful throat, the unguarded facial expressions he had received as gifts. He tried to step down and follow the driver, but was stopped by a second soldier standing by the window shaking his head.

'What's going on here?' His voice nearly failed him. 'What's the problem?'

They marched the driver down the incline into a pit in the land, beyond the stream of traffic. As he watched his head began to spin and the faintness spread in tingles to his hands and legs. Again, he pushed on the door; again the stern soldier shook his head. The man turned laughing to the group fixed in a circle of olive-green shirts and blue tassels on muscular shoulders, berets on gleaming foreheads, guns dangling.

The driver was pushed to his knees.

'Stop this!' he cried from the vehicle.

The driver raised his hands, long fingers with bony joints. On the kneeling man's face he could read no expression, hear no sound through this horrible act.

One soldier playfully raised a gun.

He sat there watching the scene, compelled. He thought of a gun raised to his lover's temple and this shocking vision wet him through: he would rather feel the cold steel in his own mouth. He pulled out a fan of cash from the glove compartment and waved it at the soldier's flanks. Begged him.

The soldiers fell away laughing, ribbing each other, guns thwacked against lean spines. The driver stood and dusted himself.

They drove back to the steaming city, which was soon awash with stormy gusts and red-swilling streets. The driver accepted his apology for this random singling out. As the car crawled on he looked at the young man's angular face and wondered what thoughts he had summoned in those unlawful moments. But the driver held the steering wheel and was unreadable. He turned away, staring out of the window at the splattered shacks. He now saw the lovemaking earlier as fragrant with doom, prologue to the staged execution. The two contexts overlapped and he saw the beach road with its bloody memories as a poisoned conduit through the afternoon. As the rain pelted down, and the city passed in filthy prisms with half-dressed children caught in doorways, he saw their fervent bodies on the soaked bed and knew he would never risk seeing the man he craved again.

In those weeks he worked long hours and went home directly. He wrote jaunty emails to friends, contacted a woman who had wanted to marry him, who sent him photographs of her twins. He looked up house prices in his old city and considered doing an online language course in Chinese. His sister wrote to him: *I'm so glad you liked the book. It was great, wasn't it? Thanks for the photos. The house looks rather swish, at least you're not sweating all day. What about a shot of this famous man you've met? A wife (and kid?) this time? Something tells me you are barking up a very thorny tree. I'm so glad to have left everything and more behind. Here the deserts are crazy with flowers...*

But in the night he dreamed of being raped in a cell and woke up floundering, uncertain of his senses. Another time he saw himself surrounded by soldiers, prone on the sand, anticipating ecstasy. It repulsed him.

When two months had passed he knew there would be no more envelopes or hotel names written in slanted letters. He remained calm. After work the driver took him to the tennis courts, where he met a young waiter who slipped him his telephone number as he paid for a round of drinks. He watched this man's alluring spine and the clipped back of his skull disappearing into the kitchens. That night he called him up and gave him his address.

The Healing of Santo Yeboah

About halfway down Via Mazzini, just before the train tracks, a van pulled out of a side street, knocking Santo's bike and collecting his back wheel for a scudding stretch. Santo hit the ground with an elbow, one foot drawn under the tyre's frilled circumference and his head bouncing off the rain-drenched tar. They said these things happened in slow motion: it took an age to screen that limpid personal Judgement Day while you were adrift. But there wasn't an instant between the time he was peddling home and when he was the stunned target for the next slithering vehicle.

A car screeched. Veered around, took off.

Santo tried to work out which of his parts was still working. There was a wet mash on one side of his face, now burning. His legs were cobbled to him and one arm he could lever slightly, so he dragged his body between the bumpers of two parked cars. He saw his bicycle squeezed together, pinned over itself, the leather seat spun out into the middle of the road. Seeing reds and blacks he began to pray for the flight of his soul.

He heard people on the footpath. *Sergio, secondo me la Laura è incapace...* Then, hours later, or perhaps it was the same woman talking, *Ma non era qui il posto...* He started to call them. But he knew they would think he was just another begging black drunkard. Santo's hand like an uncouth device was always left in the air when he collected change. His calls collapsed in his throat as though he'd never spoken their tongue.

Cars kept passing. Giant leaves spilled onto the ill-lit street. Soon enough, another black would pass by to see if the bike's detritus could be revived, if there were parts to be taken. He would swipe up the leather seat in the middle of the road and hurry from the body. No police. *Trovato nero, trovato colpevole.* Santo felt the beginnings of a cold dread coming up from his legs. In the hospital, would they dress him in good clothing instead of this putrid work gear? His wife would feel so assailed if he were wheeled in with these rags upon him. They would never understand the concocted verbs that would fly from her.

He tried to reach something, to haul himself up and become visible. He hooked his hand onto the plastic bumper but it careered off. He concentrated harder, coaxing his fingers into a dirty gap where there were tubes and frets. He tugged himself up, but lolled back down, head snapping as though it were filled with barbs.

Ama would be so vexed. She would be convinced he was with Raymond in his crammed apartment on the divans, laughing and grooving to videos on his enormous TV, those two Nigerian hairdressers from downstairs sipping their rum Cokes. Ama would be moaning in prayer now, the stew and *banku* cooled. Their place was a block away over the train tracks.

Last night Santo had heard the high horrible frenzy of the tongues as she pummelled her fists on the floor. He had covered his head again. At the clinic they had explained that the baby was growing, but a tiny arm was trapped within a membrane that had formed across her womb. The doctor had shown them the screen but Ama's face turned away. Even Santo could see only the child's heavy head and clustered, curled limbs. Then when Ama had tried to throw herself on the floor the nurses rushed at her.

They had left that place to catch the bus.

Heal me, OH LORD, and I will be healed; save me and I will be saved, for You are the one I praise.

Santo discovered he could no longer move, and that each breath had become a slow summons, a voyage or issuing. He heard bells. Now even the sound reaching his single lifted ear was a thing he had to unravel into tones.

What he could not think of was Ama who would be left here.

A light switched on in one of the shops, just beyond the undercarriage of the first car. He felt a shower of splinters and at first thought the light had moved above him and was pooling there. But it was an agitation behind his eyelids which fluttered green, fluttered violet. It was a florist's shop. There were plants and flowers backlit against the window and a person moving about, towards whom Santo again tried to lift a hand. He saw his fingers in the air, gravel sewn into the palm. He watched the digits striving in the rain, unaware of his body's capitulation. Throngs of pain amassed in his abdomen.

He had lived here these ten years, had proven to those at home that he was not wretched.

Santo saw his telephone flashing on the road. He had not even thought to use it, but now saw it would serve him no purpose. He whispered towards the voices gathered inside. Told them to hush. For if it was Ama reminding him that his firstborn's arm might fall uselessly along his body, he would let go of this harrowing suspension and slide away. Or if it was Raymond, telling of the dripping pussy of the hairdresser girl, he knew he would feel a tremendous toll or blazing wires through him.

Confess your faults one to another, and pray one for another, that ye may be healed.

He smelled his long-dead mother above his forehead. She used to reserve fat mangoes for him, brought him back a puppy they were going to slaughter on the road.

He saw hands snatch up the leather bicycle seat from the road. And remove the flashing phone. *Fratello mio.*

Of this last flight ahead, he knew nothing.

Santo could see his son's face moving within his wife's womb. He saw the child's arm caught in a cloudy weft. He could sense the furious circuits of the blood, see the scant coverage of skin; the eyes embedded in the miniscule skull, the features in a soft oil.

There were hills where he had been a small boy. Long ago, there had been a forest, since chopped down by the timber cutters. The old folk spoke of the spirits of the slaves dissolved into the land, from the time before they were *pikin.* They remembered how these people had been beaten down from the north, how they had cried in their chains and these chains had made sores on their skin, and some women had gone over to anoint them.

He had thought he would never return to that blustery place.

Pia Tortora

When he travels with his father, Cam is reminded of the wheelchair-bound American Jew who was shot and thrown off the *Achille Lauro* in the '80s, deep in the Mediterranean Sea. Earlier, the steward helped his father out of his chair and coaxed him up the steps of the aircraft. Vicious-eyed, his father had been thankless. Cam has looked up the cruise ship hijacking, read that the irate American hostage had triggered something in his young inept executioners: singled out, he had been taken on deck and shot twice. A Portuguese waiter had been forced to haul his body overboard, and the man's wheelchair had followed him into the sea.

Mid-flight, Cam looks over the icy mountains of Western Europe. He thinks of warriors seizing villages, pointing filthy digits at those they would rape or enslave, a history of selection. That bright afternoon on the ship's deck, he thinks his father, too, would have railed at the young terrorists, reminding them of the wrath of their own fathers. Cam imagines the shock of the killers as life left the American paraplegic; he sees his father's body dropping through the air. Next to him, the old man stares at the strip of emergency measures affixed to the seat in front.

In London another steward wheels them through the airport where they meet Dominic, Cam's son, banked against the railing where passengers flood into the main hall. Dominic is an effigy in a black T-shirt, grown immense. He embraces Cam, bends to kiss his grandfather's cheeks, allows the old man's hands to mould themselves around his. They are in London for Dominic's graduation tomorrow, which Cam feels as a marker in his own life. When the young man turns, Cam sees the flesh amassed across his upper back, and the haunches of an overweight woman. Cam suspects drugs, too much dope, or the same inertia that nestles within his wife's psyche. Dominic is half a head taller than Cam; he smells unwashed.

Dominic delivers them to the hotel desk then says he has to meet a friend and backs off, heading out to the street. Cam watches his bulk cross the window, as alien to him as any of the people pushing past.

Three months ago, Cam's wife booked their hotel rooms for the trip. But even then Cam would have wagered on her absence. His wife has chosen well. They are in a Hyde Park hotel overlooking a bus-jammed avenue, the building surges over treetops. Cam hands over his credit card to be swiped and says that the third member of the party is not with them, and could their rooms be on the same floor? However this cannot be altered as the hotel is full. Cam considers sleeping in his father's room on an extra bed but cannot abide the idea of shitting or pissing with his father beyond the wall. Besides, his father says he wants to be able to wheel to the window. What else is there for him to do here? Cam knows that he is mobile enough to look after himself.

Upstairs his view is a wider stage, hazy with light. He throws his bag on the rack. The room smells of fixtures and laundered fabric. He pauses at the window, watching a woman charge across the grass in the Park below. He texts his son to arrange a meeting at the flat in an hour. He could call his wife, though there is little chance she would answer. Cam turns away to the bathroom but the woman below still tugs his eye. Is she being chased? He watches her sprinting further and further along the green plain, until she dips under a fringe of trees and he will never know.

Down on the street he walks by the rim of the Park to the Underground station. There is something wafting across from the greenery, adrift above the street. It showers over him and he feels warm air on his neck. He'd never thought of London as a sensual city, coming from baroque, whimsical Rome, but he feels a shiver of horny youth. New breath coming from an unknown mouth. The scent of underarms, fingertips. Rome, for all her girlish sculptures and fervent overtures, makes him feel ancient, living in the mouth of death. At night, when his wife sleeps, he looks at porn. He likes agile, breastless women with dyed black hair. Lately, when Cam has travelled across Europe for work, an otherness propels through him, carrying gusts of the lives he might have lived, while a clawing starts through the territories of his body. He feels the plateau of his age and the pressing of his soul for release. He thinks, if his soul has inhabited other men, he knows that one of them has been lawless. The porn makes him relaxed. There are certain women he would recognise if they passed him in the street. He would wish to speak with them, that is all.

He has been to Dominic's flat once at the outset, when there was only a cheap desk and a pile of books, but he hasn't been over there in a good eight or nine months. Three years ago he assembled the Ikea bed and improved the lighting, led his son down to the student kitchen where he showed him how to prepare a *soffritto* for pasta sauce. Dominic was less weighty then, worried about his choice of course; he stuttered a little. Cam was shocked when Dominic said he was afraid of getting beaten up by thugs. Cam said, 'It won't happen to you!' But it had, not a month afterwards. The boy had been knocked to the ground, kicked, his phone and wallet taken. Dominic lives in a shared house now, and Cam supposes he has mastered cooking, hopes he has savoured sex. Cam hasn't asked if there is a girlfriend. But he thinks back to the clammy man in the black T-shirt he embraced this morning, with his odour of fried food and folded skin. There is no girlfriend. His son is a child of the flat, groaning underworld of the internet.

Dominic opens the door. He stands there a moment too long, filling the doorway, a little unsteady, or perhaps Cam imagines this. Who could have known the boy would grow so huge? Dominic's eyes are bloodshot and half-closed. He is stoned.

'Come in,' he says.

In the kitchen, Dominic lights a cigarette and lets the lighter drop to the counter. Cam watches him smoke, hands in pockets. They drink cans of foamy beer. Cam's thoughts flounder. How is this done? He tries to untangle his parental will from his sense of insult and realises this is too large, the scale of this. He wants to abdicate, he wants to pace back along the street to the train station and pretend he never came here, never stood in this foul kitchen drinking Slovakian beer, staring at his fat son staring back at him.

In Dominic's plunging eyes, he sees this challenge.

Dominic's mobile phone rings and he steps outside through the half-rotten door to take the call. As he walks up and down the path Cam watches, insulating his emotion, slowing it such that it ticks inside of him, an atomic energy. When his son enters again he is calm.

'Let's have a look at your room then,' Cam says.

They march upstairs where the situation is full-blown. A screen sits on the desk, a game console and headphones; all else has been elbowed away or tumbled onto the floor. Towels, bedding, food wrappers and containers; clothing in mounds along with unopened letters and curling books. Cam thought as much. He thinks of the combat between fathers and sons, displayed here as surely as shouts and punches.

They stare at each other. Then Cam shunts up the window and the stale smell escapes. He swings around in a fury. His hand falls upon a shoe on the desk, which he picks up and launches through the window. He begins throwing his son's belongings wide into the garden. Books, clothing, shoes are flying. Cam sees the controlled fist and mangled grin on Dominic's face. His son had wanted this trial, even though he swears at him.

Dominic watches his junk sail out into the weeds.

When he is just abreast of the hotel, he notices a woman staring. For an instant the air muddles him; it is evening-scented now, and the mass gathered over the Park sheds upon him.

'Camillo—' the woman says. It's his given name, used by a handful of people in his neighbourhood.

'Pia?'

He crosses the street, jolted. This is London. This is Pia. Pia Tortora. Arms wide, light kisses. So far from the Rome days when their social circles had interwoven.

'What are you doing here?'

'My son is graduating from university tomorrow. We're staying in the hotel.'

Pia stills before him, a magnet for his eyes. Her skin, buttery once, has collections of stains, she is swept with them; too much sun, years of tobacco. Their paths crossed one summer on the islands. Cam grows bashful as that time flares in his memory and ignites. They both glance aside.

'You look well,' Pia says.

Cam has never gone back to those days. It was when he and his girlfriend were estranged, and then that winter he had married her.

He sees Pia's fine hair plugged into her scalp. Did they ever have children?

'My husband – Gerard – is no longer alive. You may not have heard this.'

Cam, who was picturing Gerard's face, now feels a wilting in the gut.

'I'm truly sorry,' he replies.

'It happened not far from here,' she says, her head motioning down the road. 'A heart attack. There were problems that should have been taken more seriously. But Gerard thought the doctors were being overzealous.'

Still shocked, Cam can't engage Pia's eyes. She is glad to be telling her story afresh. On either side of her, people are waiting for buses. Cam imagines a man with a shaven, burnished head propped against the spear-headed fence; hears the sirens crashing through.

'This must be rather recent,' Cam says.

'It's been a year now, or just over that. I usually come here on Mondays. That was the day it happened. I catch the Tube up here, then walk through the Park back home.'

Early on, their socialising lapsed when Gerard had outmanoeuvred Cam at work, leapfrogging ahead abroad. At work Gerard had been bloody-minded. Cam's wife had felt she was disliked. Cam follows Pia's eyes into the Park, noticing a pair of sneakers strung over electricity wires.

'I'm truly sorry, Pia,' he says again. 'Are you alone now?'

'My daughter is studying in Montreal. We don't get along very well. It's really so pleasant to see you, Camillo. How is your wife?'

Cam knows he has time for a drink with her in the hotel lobby across the road, but does he want to? The theatre with Dominic has all but emptied him. He wants to remove his shoes, throw his body onto the bed, shave again and shower. Before him, he has an evening with his father.

'You are still married?' Pia says.

Cam nods. He wonders if she has had some sort of surgery. He pushes it back but the past returns in grainy, mute frames. On the island, he and Gerard scaled the volcano with a group of hikers. They spent the night in sleeping bags on the summit as the lava roared and rats scampered over their feet. The whole time Cam had thought of Pia's tits swaying as she unrolled the cane mat she took to the beach, or their displacement over her ribs as she read. For those first days the three of them had cooked and ate and slumbered with the warmth of siblings.

Cam touches Pia's forearm. 'Listen, why don't we catch up later on?' He tells her he has to get back to his father upstairs, taking her telephone number which he knows he will delete the moment he passes through the doors. Cam has a habit of ruling people out. And Pia, there is nothing he wishes to renew with her. As they stand there and Pia's eyes begin to dance into his, he feels aversion, and the sense that she has stolen from him. Tomorrow Cam's buoyancy will not return and he will hear the defibrillator pads smacking Gerard's chest.

'Camillo, may I hug you?' Pia says.

Her arms rise to him and their torsos connect, necks linking. He encloses this woman, alarmed that his senses recall her smell and skin with quaking fondness. Cam's lips open on her hair. The three of them had become brazen playthings of the island, he had always left it at that. Pia feels stronger than he would have assumed, stronger than a woman who visits an unmarked shrine every week.

'Who was that woman you were talking to?'

It comes as a relief to see his father slumped in his wheelchair, his red-rimmed eyes landing upon him. The old man's stomach rumbles.

'Pia Tortora. I knew her years ago in Rome. Her husband has died of a heart attack. It happened very close to this spot, it seems.'

His father ignores this. Most of his friends have passed away. Cam remembers those who congregated until the end at the local bar, the marbled skin clinging to their skulls. Sometimes, his father will speak of the early ones who died long before their bodies became wrecks. There was a chap called Guido, pinioned between two train carriages, whom his father spoke to while he was dying. His father says that in the last moments Guido's voice came from somewhere above, that from his crushed frame he had taken flight. His father has towed his own body for years now.

'I'd like a good meal,' his father says. 'None of that English rubbish.'

They leave the hotel and the evening air is warm. Cam ties a sweater around his father's shoulders which the man pulls off. It is a fawn colour, it lies in his lap. Dominic says he can't join them for dinner, that he'll lunch with them after the ceremony at the university. Cam will collect him in a taxi tomorrow morning. He never asked if Dominic had his garments ready. After his dramatic jettisoning of Dominic's belongings out of the window, Cam had just told him not to turn up stoned.

There is an Italian place among a group of restaurants. It is empty; there is a struggle to introduce the wheelchair into the room. The waiter is disinclined to help and the cook is leaning on a counter lodged in the back wall. Behind him, the bright lighting of the kitchen is framed.

'Could you help me move some of these chairs?' Cam says to the waiter who unfolds his arms.

The young man is slight and bandy-legged, the skin polished over his face. His hair is gelled in spikes around the exposed scalp atop his head and his eyebrows are plucked into arches. It's a common look in Italy, but over here the man seems androgynous and feline. Cam looks around at the hanging Chianti bottles and sepia photographs of Vesuvius.

'Are you sure you want to eat here?' he asks his father.

Cam would just as soon eat at the hotel but his father is already combing the menu.

They return to the hotel and his father banishes Cam from his suite. He says he needs to use the bathroom. Cam smells urine. He tells his father it is okay and he wants to help. He doesn't mention the word 'urine' because he knows his father abhors any language of the body. His father admonishes him for choosing such an unpleasant restaurant. Upstairs in his room, Cam sits on the bed and finishes a beer.

He turns on his computer. He resists. In the bathroom he splashes his face. Cam thinks of Pia Tortora in her flat across the Park. He has deleted her number. He takes the lift down to the hotel bar, where he orders a whisky. He calls Dominic and the boy answers. He's in a pub, a chaotic backdrop until he steps outside. Then Cam is not sure what to say to him after his wild gestures this afternoon. Dominic laughs, but the laugh is meant for a friend, not Cam who stands there waiting until his son's wheezing giggles have ended.

'Well, tomorrow then,' Dominic says and rings off.

Cam is straddling a stool, watching a rugby match played out under driving rain, when he becomes aware of a shape and scent behind him. It is Pia Tortora. She stands there in a black blouson dress drawn at the neck and waist, a dark plum motif scattered over the fabric. He notices the cloth first, how the pattern represents some kinder variation of the swastika. He has seen this geometric form before. Pia looks more relaxed than this afternoon. In this light he can see the direction that her skin has been tugged and stitched back.

'I was quite certain you weren't going to call me so I decided to take my chances and turn up. Am I right?' Pia asks.

'Yes,' he replies. 'You are right.'

She orders a whisky and sits next to him. 'Gerard would have been very happy to see you again. You haven't thought very much about us, have you, over the years?'

'Quite honestly, no.'

'There's no need to worry, Camillo. I haven't come to transport you back to our devilish past,' she says. 'You're just a link to Gerard, whom I do miss. Tell me, did we not corrupt you that time on the island? Not even a little?'

'I don't believe so.' Cam shies away to the drenched rugby.

Pia rattles her drink. Beyond the street, the Park is blackness. He thinks he should have called the laundry downstairs, or at least taken his father's clothing down there in a plastic bag. The old man's piss, it is rancid.

'How did you get here?' he asks.

'Taxi,' she replies. 'Where's your son? He must be around the same age as Chiara.'

Cam's arm swings over the unoccupied bar stool next to him.

Pia laughs. 'And why is your wife not with you?'

'My wife? My wife no longer travels.' Cam looks at Pia's face and realises she will be the first person to whom he tells the truth. 'My wife hasn't left our apartment in three months,' he says. Cam tells Pia about his wife quitting her job at the journal and her self-imposed exile from the outside world. About her fears of bomb blasts in the train stations, and black-masked terrorists breaking into offices. A colleague of hers was gunned down in Paris.

His eyes return to the rugby; Pia's stray into her drink.

'It's easy to become afraid these days,' she says after a while.

Cam watches the players fly on top of one another, grateful her reply goes no further. The pattern on her dress vibrates on the outskirts of his vision.

'You know, Camillo, I still enjoy thinking of Gerard,' she continues. 'Gerard was enchanted by you.'

'Please. I'd prefer not to revisit any of that,' Cam says, his gaze pulling away from the screen and falling down her front.

'Are you looking at my breasts?' she asks.

'Yes, I am looking at your breasts.'

'My breasts are good. I've had work done.'

'Have you come here for me to invite you upstairs?' Cam says. 'You want that, don't you?'

'Yes.'

'I think not,' he replies. 'I am married, Pia. It's still a marriage of sorts.'

Pia finishes her drink. The barman glides before them and Cam nods, but Pia's hand draws across the air. She watches the young man reach for the whisky and the liquid slinking in the bottle.

'Camillo,' she says. 'I think I misinterpreted what happened on the pavement this afternoon. Is that so?'

She looks at him, her face groomed and tawny; her eyes are dark cul-de-sacs. She says, 'I'm going to walk to the door now, and not turn back. Are you okay with that? Camillo?'

'I am,' he replies, while thinking he would have her on her knees with her bosoms rocking. 'I think it's for the best.'

The barman glances at their frank faces. Pia pulls up the strap of her bag. She leans in. 'Let me tell you this,' she says. 'There's no good reason to, but I will. For many years Gerard used to bring home young men. They all resembled you. The length of their thighs and torsos, more than the size of their members. You know he had a professional interest in proportion.'

Pia steps down from the stool, kisses him on both cheeks. Again, her scent produces an undoing and he feels his armpits sting and dampen. Pia moves back and looks towards the doors as if to confirm her course.

'The boys became younger and younger,' she says. 'While we became older and older. Until one day Gerard said there would be no more men and we would no longer sleep together, and we did not. We called that day *The End of Camillo.*'

At first light Cam stands at the window in his pyjamas. He finds relief in the reappearance of the cityscape. He wants to project himself out there, needs to get walking. He has been waiting for the natural light to dismantle his thoughts. All through the night hours the mass of memory, cut free, extruded through his being, has blown up as visions in this room. Cam remembers Gerard's phone call when he was shattered in Rome after the breakup. The ferry trip from Naples. He sees the house that belonged to someone in Gerard's family. The building's solitary prominence on the hillside as you walked up from the bay. The volcano looming behind, an immortal trembling.

It takes Cam a long time to furnish this setting with their beings. He remembers the pair of them barely dressed, emerging on the balcony and calling down, a display of genitalia even in those initial moments. Pia's bare arms washing peaches in the wide flat sink. The arabesque floor tiles and ceramic plates hooked to the walls. Finally, he admits Gerard, his rich, bronzed torso coated with sun-bleached hair.

Outside the light rises into blooms in the sky. Cam fixes himself a horrid instant coffee that burns his mouth. He watches traffic circling the Park. He decides he will walk in the direction of Dominic's house, then catch a cab the rest of the way when his thoughts have cleared. Bring him back here for a decent breakfast with his grandfather. The three of them, together at least, to get the day started. Cam regrets going downstairs to the bar last night, but no more than he regrets refuting her. He had known all along that Pia would show.

He remembers Gerard's first challenge, 'Kiss my wife'. The rest emits a squall inside of him. But he makes himself travel to the end, to the last night when the three of them had slept tossed together, to the final morning when their bodies had lain interlocked on the tiles. When his memories complete their course Cam reaches the same vantage point, he feels the same soft expulsion as the day they waved him down the trail. He sees himself board the ferry back to Naples. He sees the wedding dress and the young precarious bride, the inanimate cosmos he had chosen.

The Cliffs of Bandiagara

A woman, her son, her boyfriend and a trader drive north to Mali to interview a musician for an English record company. The woman is a freelance journalist, the man a photographer. She does not know that the musician is sick and leaving for a concert in Denmark in a matter of days. The interview has been arranged, or half-arranged, by a man in London whose French is not good, who thinks he has spoken to the right person in Bamako. This is pre-internet, pre-kidnappings, pre-terror videos. The Twin Towers have fallen weeks ago. The land is flat and soundless with her history manifest in adobe mosques crumbling along the bloodied slave routes, and painted *Boulangerie* signs in villages where commendable baguettes are sold. The road is a silver spear. The days are dense contracts between these four people.

Between the messy, unscripted towns there are baobabs. Once, the boy makes them stop the car on the side of the road. The engine tickers. The boy has a new front tooth that has come down crooked, which his mother intends to have fixed. The boy leaps onto the dust and declares he is running to the tree, the bow-oh-bab tree, that one there, and he begins to elbow the dry air and his sneakers produce orange puffs. The woman had known there would be moments with the boy.

'Let him go,' the man says, stretching his legs and focussing his camera on the tree's distant barrel and arms. The man comes from a coastal West African city; he has been her lover for five months.

The boy grows smaller and smaller, a white wafting on the scrub, almost bodiless. The woman watches. The boy once popped his tongue into her mouth, but she knows it was copied from some guy she was seeing. Because it pleased her, this mix of animal and man, she told no one. She wonders, when her son turns back to the group by the jeep, what compulsion he might feel towards her: slim, defiant, wearing a short, disrespectful T-shirt. Will he recall this scene when he is a man, staring back at the woman he loves?

The trader, who is named Cissé, remains in the car. He is dressed in a clean shift and cradles his head. At least once a day Cissé claims he has malaria.

Cissé has them stop outside a city he says he knows well. It is Sikasso; they have just driven for miles and miles over rucks of sand. He says they should first buy their baguettes *ici*, pointing to a stall where a girl lies on her arm asleep. The photographer does not like to follow Cissé's recommendations. He is not convinced the trader will be of any use to them on this journey, and dislikes the sing–song of Cissé's French. Instead the woman, who once lived in Paris, sees the irony of perfect baguettes under her arm and greasy notes with a northern figurehead flattened on the counter. She lifts herself back into the jeep and gives a heel of bread to the boy.

Cissé leads them to a place where he says there is excellent sheep meat. They are installed in a hot back room on benches and given four bottles of Coke that sit in pools. The green walls are smeared with hand prints to shoulder height. The prints are vigorous, a record of past feasts.

A platter of mutton bones piled high is served by a man in a grubby shirt.

In the neighbourhood the blonde boy is chased by other children and his flat hair is touched. He begs Cissé to tell him how to say, *Don't touch me. Please.* Cissé, who is a vulgar man, more vulgar than his companions know, tells him to repeat this in local language: *My mother, she is horny.*

In the morning a dog attacks Cissé on his way back from the mosque. The reddish animal lunges out from behind a shed, sinking canines into his tendons and tearing the surface flesh. It is only just dawn and the sellers are out on the road. A busty girl comes up and he does not understand her dialect, so they speak in French. Cissé is petrified, his temples are wet. The girl shoos away the growling dog and brings Cissé to her room where she raises his torn ankle and pours warm salted water over it, then stinging alcohol. She is young and her kindness makes Cissé wish for his wife. He hobbles back to the hotel where the others are asleep. He walks through the compound. He asks a woman bent over sweeping for some tea, but the woman scowls.

Inside the room the boy lies in a netted cot that is just longer than his outstretched body. He sleeps on his back, motionless. The couple made love in the dark of morning and now lie in repose. The photographer awakens. He covers their bodies and stares up into the netting. He wants to put his fingers inside of the woman next to him but he does not want her consciousness alive or her body animated. He lies still. His cock is soft and he cups it in his hand. There was a woman from his city a few years ago who had fallen pregnant with his child. It happened just when his love for her had begun to blaze. Each day he had photographed every region of her body. Her manly shoulders and short, humpy breasts; the knuckles of her spine as she crouched to wash her sex, fingering herself as she squatted. But the young woman came home one afternoon and said she'd had an abortion. Said they were living in a bubble. She left him for an American journalist who was later shot. What he was told was this: the man had arranged an interview with an opposition leader in a nearby country and drove up to the politician's house. A police officer put his pistol through the window and discharged.

If he concentrates he can still cry for her. He used to believe that the photographs of her body were his most intimate images, but his work has improved and now he sees that his obsession made her hidden to him, and these photos were bereft of craft. In one she has a white cloth knotted around her neck. She has a boxy forehead and she turns away, her body twists; she does not belong to him. She stands before a half-built house on the salt flats out of town. It was not the story he had seen or wished to tell, but it had emerged. He has learned that much of his work is subterranean, that he must lie in wait. Recently, he was told that she has given birth to a daughter.

The singer that his new girlfriend is to interview was groomed by one of the icons of Malian music, a man who lived for decades within the embrace of the West. At 60, he grew tired of concerts in Bercy and the clucking of people and the breasts of white women. He dreamed of irrigating the barren fields around his village with channelled well water; he heard the sound of gushing water in every moment. The old man severed his record contract and returned home to his wives, and his absence left a vacuum that was filled by the young disciple. This man, in the music world, quickly became known for his immense talent and rudeness. Many journalists, given fraudulent directions, have failed to negotiate the dusty warren of Bamako's back streets.

After breakfast she leads him to the shower recess where a trickle falls over their necks. He rises to her, they grapple and laugh, he pierces her and knows the shower taps are grazing her back, but she likes the pain; he has seen this. He dislikes her biting, he prefers fluid love-making. The child watches them return to the room half-dressed. She tells him to brush his teeth. He is disgusted that the child enters the bathroom where they have just fucked, then his disgust separates from him. It's her child. His children will never be subjected to this. In fact, their affair is instructing him how to correct his life in advance. Looking ahead he suspects they will last a few more months before the sex is spent and the boy becomes paramount to her. When the boy goes out into the sunlight, he savages her lips.

Outside they see the boy is speaking with a man on a bicycle who is wearing a wooden mask. The mask is elongated, chalky white with sea-blue dots; inverted triangular incisions for eyes and two hare ears curling forward. Standing astride the bicycle, the man holds the mask to his face, tilting down to the boy's captivation. He talks in muffled phrases. The woman paces over to the man who can only be a seller. She does not know that the cyclist is the brother of the busty girl who bathed Cissé's ankle that morning. Cissé, by way of thanks, had told the girl he was travelling with a white woman when he saw a pile of artefacts on the floor. He had given her the name of the hotel.

'You want buy? *Tu veux acheter?*' the hare man is saying to the boy.

His mother holds his shoulders, pulls him back. The large-headed man frightens her with his turbulent voice. Cissé watches from a stool in an alcove. The photographer thinks that perhaps there is a shot if the woman and child would move away. The hare man on a bicycle as a mythical outlaw. He sees that his woman is braless, accessible; she has told him she can be no other way. Now he sees Cissé staring at her evident breasts. The hotel manager flies out and chases the cyclist back onto the street.

The woman drives. They reach the outskirts of the town and head forth along a sealed road into the scrub. There are fewer baobabs and ruins in this area, and they have brought bottles of bright orange Fanta and grilled peanuts in newspaper cones. After an hour she stops the car on the side of the road. There is waist-high grass and she goes off to pee, unzipping her jeans as she walks away from the jeep. She is gone a while and her lover grows edgy, thinking of snakes. He looks out but she has crouched down and he can't see her. It is not concern that he feels, but exasperation with her flights. She emerges from the grass calling his name, tells him to bring his camera. Leads him along the trampled column she has made through the growth. At a distance from the car she pulls off her T-shirt and throws herself down in the grass, topless in her jeans.

'Photograph me,' she says. 'Photograph me.'

He captures her arms on the scratchy pressed halo, her plum nipples and the contortions of her face. Her skin is a shimmering, colourless garment. He brings her torso into focus, thinking of her organs overlapping in shades of violet and red. She wants him to straddle her but he will not. She pulls him to her and their faces are ill-aligned, bitter.

In the car, the boy empties a Fanta bottle and hands it to Cissé, who throws it wide into the grass. The boy asks Cissé why he wears a dress like a woman.

Bamako rises like a defeated cloud before them. The heat repels them, traffic pushes them to and fro. Cissé, who claimed he lived here as an adolescent, tells him to swing right. 'No, swing left! *À gauche! Ici!*' The photographer drives now; his lover is solemn at the window and the boy asleep. Scant directions were sent by the London office but Cissé says they are all wrong, says that the musician she is to interview lives at the opposite end of town from where they are headed. The photographer mentions the quartier of his colleague Sami, married to a French air hostess, where they have been invited to stay. Cissé's hands fly out again – '*À gauche! À gauche!*' – and it is clear that he is clueless. The woman rolls her eyes. Cissé finally sits back, smiling out of the window at the clutter of bars and dwindled pan-African monuments along the boulevards. The boy wakes, climbs over the front seat, curls into his mother's arms.

Sami's house is a cool bungalow with concrete support struts throughout the main room. The front veranda has been screened off and writhes with contented plants. They are seated out here. Sami's house-girl serves them duty-free *pastis* from France before bringing out a round of local beer. Cissé's hands jostle between his legs. He drinks a bottle of Sprite. The photographer knows Sami from a major exhibition, held in Bamako, where both of their images were praised. Sami runs a gallery that he would like to support. The woman feels her lover is distant from her now, even inconsiderate; she sees he is relieved to be in different company. He laughs hard at Sami's jokes. He asks of Sami's wife, the French air hostess Kitty, who is doing the Dubai–Paris–Rio route this week.

She takes her son to the bathroom so she can look through the house.

She sees the couple are childless. She sees that Kitty has a deep love of antique beads, which are arranged on coffee tables; that she collects the indigo-stained cloth they weave here; that she admires the blocky Dogon horsemen who ride across their porous constellations. Kitty, too, has perhaps read of the reaches of the Dogon universe, their preternatural knowledge of the galaxies above. There is a framed photo of a European woman with a fringe that brushes the top of her sunglasses. There are prints of Sami's work on the walls. They are tight, sharp portraits of Malians. She wonders if Kitty is fleshy and broad, a vivid juxtaposition to Sami's work. She wonders how it would be to spend most of the day in the air, groundless.

Her son is hungry. In the kitchen she asks the young girl for *une banane*, absurdly happy she has produced a riff of French without thought. Her son peels the banana and eats it. The girl's hand moves over his blond straight hair. The boy says the words Cissé told him and her hand jerks back.

In the evening a woman named Maryam comes to Sami's house. She is a local singer and she knows the musician the journalist has come to interview. She knows him well. She knows his compound, it is on the other side of Bamako and it is very difficult to find. But she will show them. Do they know he has a concert in Denmark this week?

Maryam's hair is shaped into two splendid coils that entwine at the back of her head. The boy wants to touch these elaborate, necking snakes. He kneels on the couch beside her, his clear hands reaching through the air. Maryam arches her neck in his direction.

The photographer has spent the afternoon speaking of his current project with Sami. It is a political work with an Algerian colleague, which will document the offspring of the generals executed during the coup in his country. Now he is fascinated by the tilting of Maryam's body. The asymmetry of her face and shoulders and one breast below the other, its form compressed. He wants to study the itinerary of Maryam's movements. He feels a transaction is already in place. He feels this sense of exchange with the best of his subjects.

Maryam sang last night until the early hours in a low-ceilinged bar in central Bamako where she has followers. Maryam is tired of speech, though she enjoys the white starfish of the boy's hands straying over her neck and upper arms, they are cool.

When Kitty is abroad Maryam stays with Sami. Her hair lotion and face cream and brassieres and lacy thongs are in a locked cabinet in the maid's room. A few dresses are at the back of the house-girl's wardrobe. Maryam wants to make love with Sami before her body falls to the bed and her throat is gripped by the heavy hand that troubles her dreams. Sami's tongue will render her blind and lifeless. Maryam lifts herself. She walks barefoot to Sami's bedroom and closes the door.

Sami's gardener has taken their bags from the jeep and placed them at the foot of a double bed in a converted garage at the side of the property. The room is narrow and a ceiling fan makes low swoops. Sami announces that Kitty's brother is an anthropologist, Philippe, working in the north, and they should disregard *ses affaires*. When Sami bids them goodnight the woman tugs off her clothes and walks naked to the attached outhouse, where her lover hears the smattering of water on tiles. She does not call him. He and the boy look at each other. The boy stares into his eyes in the absorbent way of children. The man lies down on the bed.

The boy throws his pillow to the floor. He cradles himself on top of the sheets and turns to the wall.

When the woman comes out still dripping the man is already dreaming: he has seen her vanish into blades of grass; he has left the metallic vehicle behind and the calls of the others.

She opens his trousers and makes him erect, bounds on and off him, brings him into her gut, spears herself with him.

He is ashamed. Her fury does not break, even when he has burst inside of her. He thinks of her body stained with tears and dust. For the first time he sees an image of her that he wants to make. Then, when their bellies are still joined, he feels the indentation of her touch reaching through his skin, making a passage within him. She has felt it too. She looks into him, and he feels he has been spared; they may endure. He wants to fly beyond himself and watch their grace from the other end of the room. He wants to roll her thin body in dirt and hear the words fall from his mouth, 'I will cherish you'.

After prayers Cissé follows a busy road leading to a boulevard that crosses the city. The wound from the dog bite sends arrows up his leg as he walks. He raises his shift and looks at the jagged skin. A woman passes, a tier of folded cloth on her head. She clucks her tongue as she rolls by. Cissé releases the shift onto the ground. He does not yet feel fever. Cissé's life began upcountry by the rivers. Though he told them he knew the city well he has never lived here. Delivered by an older brother to his uncle's compound in Bamako, it was thought that Cissé would gather fare money from passers–by, for one of the uncle's many buses that roped through the town. But on Cissé's first night the uncle made use of the boy in a violent way, then whipped his buttocks with his belt. Cissé was 12 years old when he ran away to the south.

Cissé cannot remember the face of his mother.

He reaches the main boulevard where minibuses fly past and cars stream at speed across all the lanes. People in the buses sit hunched forward and he sees a goat in a woman's arms. When he had run away to the south the vehicle had lurched before a piglet squealing over the road, then careered into a ditch where it lay upended. A large wailing woman had pinned Cissé beneath her. This woman pushed his bones together until he was an airless shape. At night he still wakes with the pressure of this woman upon him.

A ticket boy hanging out of a minibus waves bills in his face and urges him to get on. Calls him a stupid shepherd when he just stands there.

He sits down. The bars and shops all along here are French. He drinks another Sprite and it is warmer than the one they gave him at the house. He eats a croissant which tastes of oily salt. He throws it down and asks the girl to get him a sweet cake.

At first Cissé thought that the white woman was interested in him as a man. He had worn a checked shirt under his shift, purchased from the Indian stalls. He had sprayed on perfume when he brought his wares to her house. The boy played outside but she disregarded his wild running.

When she asked him if he could be their guide on this trip he said, 'Of course, Bamako, *je la connais*.'

Cissé had told them he had family to stay with in Bamako. But he will never go back to his uncle's house here. When a beggar comes up he asks him where he can buy something that will ease the pain in his foot. Something fast, something cheap. The fever has started in his spine. He follows this crumpled man into the back streets.

She awakes thinking they should never have come here together. She looks at Sami's slow fan turning. Their skins do not touch. She knows he wants to photograph Maryam's rolling, superb body. She has been there when it has flared in him, the desire to approach subjects for his work. Once, two women in a slum bar drunkenly began to kiss. He bought them beers and asked the women if he could snap them. It was arousing, a courting. They were young with bright white teeth. She had watched his dance around them as tongues flickered, as cheeks and breasts were touched. She had asked him if he'd had a hard-on. He'd said his work never made him hard. He said it wasn't that at all.

She didn't believe this. Watching these two women with their bold dresses and market sandals had made her slippery wet.

He had produced an astounding sepia image of two dissolving profiles. The magnificence of closed eyelids; granular planes beneath the promontories of cheeks. The connection of a kiss. She could never have foreseen this vision.

She regrets flailing on the grass yesterday, begging him to photograph her. She is so desperate to enter the canon of his work. Flattened on the burning grass, the sunlight a vicious bath on her torso, she had thought she was granting him an image. But as she lay there she realised she had no understanding of what he sought, of how it became disinterred. He had clicked a few times, even bent to her, but his eyes had refuted her and grown annoyed. He had not even wanted her sex. Today she will ruin those negatives.

She rubs her spit onto his fingers and pushes them inside of her, feels them enliven.

As they fuck she thinks of Maryam's nude body. She thinks of Kitty's photograph turned to the wall. She thinks of Maryam's purple vulva. She climaxes in a gradual, head-kicking way, feels herself spurt onto him; he licks her face and she feels choked.

She thinks that Cissé hasn't turned up, even though he said he would come after morning prayers.

The boy wakes when her lover goes off to shower and she wonders if, in the future, she can make amends for the way she has half-forgotten his father and has had a series of men. She still thinks there is a window where she can. The boy does not pull across the netting and come to her. He lies staring upward, little legs bent and hair she cannot bear to cut straying on the pillow.

The boy tells her that Cissé was bitten by a dog.

Sami provides them with a young man who will lead them through the city to where the musician lives. The interview is today. The photographer looks for Maryam down the hall where Sami's bedroom is located. But the bedroom door is closed. Sami wears an indigo blue shirt with ironing creases and embroidered filigree on the pockets. The photographer imagines this is a shirt that Maryam has given him recently. Sami does not speak of Maryam and their conversation resumes where it had left off before Maryam arrived at the house. Sami says he is working with a subject today, a woman who was kidnapped as a girl by the Tuaregs in the north, and held for nine years on the rim of the Sahara. He says he met this woman selling dried fish, that there was a captive isolation in her eyes. The photographer is listening, he has often seen these sentiments within his subjects' eyes; his passion lies in the extrication of this.

The woman interrupts the two men talking and says that if Cissé doesn't turn up they will go without him, and good luck to him. She will manage with her stilted French. Her equipment bag is at the door with her Dictaphone and battery charger.

The boy is grumpy and will not eat his food.

The woman's parts are swollen and burning and her lover extends his hand with long fingers and bitten-down nails across the table. He rests it on her forearm. The textures of their two skins meet.

Maryam appears in the hallway. Her hair is unmoved, the same weighted sculpture as it was last night, and she has little yellow balls of sleep in the corners of her eyes. Her body sways under her kaftan and her breath is thick and stale. Maryam comes to the table and folds herself next to the boy, asks him if she can share his breakfast. She and the boy eat up mango slices, then divide a roll of fleecy white bread with groundnut paste. Maryam asks the boy if she can touch his hair and he says, 'Yes.'

At the gate, Cissé is leaning against a mango tree in the shade.

The photographer drives out onto a main road. The woman and her son are beside him. Sami's guide sits in the back seat with Cissé. It feels strange to be driving again after being static in the house. Sami has said that they can return there to sleep, but he does not like to turn back, ever. He feels uncomfortable about the violence of their rapport this morning in Sami's converted garage. It feels like his come is still seeping out of him, as though there is a leak he cannot stop into his jeans, onto the seat. He touches his balls and his pants are dry. He wants to tell her, 'We don't have to be like this'.

He remembers in the beginning she asked him to enter her when she was bleeding and this disgusted him, though he had done it, then watched his red member subsiding on her stained belly. He wants to tell her, 'This can stop. We can have something other than this'.

The photographer looks into the mirror and asks Cissé how his family was. Cissé replies that they were well and happy to see him.

From a polythene shopping bag he draws a hand towel and passes it to the woman in the front seat.

'From my mother,' Cissé says to her.

The woman thanks him. Then she turns around and says, 'Were you bitten by a dog? My son woke up saying you were bitten by a dog. Is that true?'

Cissé sinks back, laughs. He knows they would take him to some clinic and leave him there. Then the injections would start. The nurses, they would worry him.

'No, madam, that is not true.'

She tells him she doesn't need his help for the interview.

The contours of the city rise into the sky. There are monuments that look like bones scraped together, and many beaten-up cars. The minibuses scissor between them. There is a river of heads along the footpath.

When they have been driving for an hour Sami's helper indicates a mud-bricked wall where the road narrows, each side banked with orange sand. For the last 30 minutes they have passed along many streets like this. The man steps down from the jeep and walks away. The wall has an opening onto a courtyard where they see three women sitting on plastic chairs, a girl bent over sweeping, a stunted tree.

They follow the musician's youngest wife into the broad house, along hallways and past rooms where they hear murmuring or glimpse sleeping children spread-eagled on the floor. There is a pounding somewhere, a long wooden pestle driving cassava and yam into a pulp, massaged around a mortar by swift hands. The journalist knows this much. She smells sauce boiling away, thinks it is made with dried fish or smoky crushed prawns. With the bitterness of leaves, baobab leaves perhaps. She checks the boy is following them. The photographer's equipment bag whistles against his thigh. The walls are bare and powdery, an impermanent substance. Her nipples contract with the slight chill, she feels it cross her shoulders. On the sleeve of the CD they gave her, the whites of the musician's eyes have been unrealistically enhanced.

The musician is hooked up to a drip in one of the dim back rooms. He lies on a mattress on the floor and does not respond when his wife calls him. She raises her voice. The man snuffles and lifts himself onto an elbow.

The room smells of illness, even shit. Apart from the mattress and drip stand, there is a chest of drawers piled with papers and rubbish, a mound of clothes on the cement floor and a bucket. The musician wears a turban and his black shirt ripples into his skin. He looks at them. The photographer wants to pull out his camera.

The musician's wife tells them that her husband has typhus and they should not go too close. She says he is catching the plane to Denmark this evening and clucks her tongue. He has a big concert in two days. She says she has to cook now and the boy should come with her outside. The journalist tells the boy to go with her.

The couple take respectful steps further into the room and settle their bags on the floor. The journalist introduces herself. The photographer kneels to his bag, changes a lens. The metal rims slide together.

She cannot decide whether she should crouch or stand to take her notes. She sits cross-legged on the floor, opening her notepad, running over the points she has made and the brief the record company gave her, months back. She has been warned not to mention the old guy, the mentor. They are at loggerheads now. She prepares her Dictaphone.

The photographer wants to capture the stench of sickness. He sees maps of inky colour. The man's mouth opens and it is a tender rose cage.

The woman is distracted by the way the photographer has begun to move. She studies the musician, looking for the image that she will see printed, framed on a wall, far from here. She has worked with photographers before, but it usually comes after the interview, when the subject is fatigued and barriers have fallen. She wants to tell the photographer to pull back, to give her some space, but he has seen something and she no longer exists, none of them do, it is just the light flare on a chemical-laced scroll, the unalterable narrative of exposure.

She says her lover's name. Asks him to leave the room and let him do her work.

The musician watches their discomfort.

She changes position, sitting back on her haunches. There are chinks of midday light scattered close to the wall beneath the half-closed shutters. The musician rolls a joint, lights up and inhales a couple of times, tugging on the tube so that the drip stand shivers. He holds out the smoking thing towards her. She rises on her knees and takes it.

She sits back, pulls up her spine.

The photographer hears the boy's voice out in the courtyard between buildings. He is thinking of Maryam and her body smeared by the night of lovemaking. Maryam's stale smell runs along his nerves. Like his lover in the past, he wants to photograph her crouched, rinsing her body, an intimate ellipse.

Cissé sits in the shade on one of the plastic chairs, given to him by a woman with lavish gold earrings. He has a chewing stick in his mouth. The musician's youngest wife settles the boy by her side as she squats on a stool over her pots. The boy asks where her children are, so that he could play. He asks her over and over again. Cissé guesses that she is childless or has recently lost a child. He knows the musician makes her work hard for him, harder than his senior wives. He thinks the musician has given her an illness that the doctor said has damaged her womb.

The young wife slaps the face of the white child.

The photographer hears the boy crying out in the daylight. He throws his bag over his shoulder and hurries on. He sees the boy nursing his cheek and the young woman storms into the kitchen rooms.

The boy hugs him hard and a knot rises in the photographer's throat. He was abandoned in a boarding school in England when he was four. In the summer his mother, who was a diplomat, never arrived. He was farmed out to older couples with silent houses, who devised games.

'Come with me,' the photographer says to the stricken face.

In a corner of the blue-painted veranda the photographer deposits his bag and notices an overturned calabash and a four-legged cooking stool. He places them before the intersecting blue planes; they are glazed by reflected light. He sets up his Hasselblad, inching around the composition until the tension peaks between objects. He shows the boy the viewfinder, makes him listen to the collapse of the shutter.

He asks the boy to go to the stool. The grooved calabash sits overturned by his dirty knees and his cascade of blonde hair falls sweaty around his face. There are shadowy rings under the child's eyes he has never noticed. The boy sits with hands locked.

He tells the boy more about the camera, given to him by a German photographer before he returned to Berlin. The man had been called Henning. He remembers this man had one night invited him to a beach bar, and they had taken their beer bottles onto the sand. There the German had pulled him to his body and kissed him as he fought. A strong, straight-backed man, he had released his shoulders and walked off into the darkness.

The boy jumps up and pins a gecko to the wall.

He looks down at the box of the camera, rubs his thumb over one of the sides. He does not feel the photographs he took of the musician are worthy. There was no quickening, no communion. He thinks that to photograph his lover he will have to wound her. Then revive her, resuscitate her. He feels love in his groin, a passion.

The boy shows him the gecko in his palm. He pulls up his shirt and entices the gecko onto his tummy. It adheres there, pulsing. 'Snap me! Snap me!' he says. The boy calls over to Cissé to see. Cissé's chair is tilted against a wall but he is watching. He throws up a hand that fans the air.

The journalist comes out of the doorway into the courtyard. Cissé sees the other women look across at her as an unkempt idol from Europe, they know the musician will go there and fuck women like this.

She locates her son and her lover on the veranda. She pauses, observes the man kneeling, the boy holding up his shirt. All along she tried to get the musician to talk, while the man released meagre answers. The musician has suggested they follow him to the airport and finish up at the VIP room inside. She isn't sure, but perhaps she heard the boy cry out before.

'What are you doing to him?' she says to the photographer.

The boy sees her and begins to whimper. She rushes to him and his embrace feels awful, an endless pledge. He will not tell her what the matter is.

'I think you can put that away now,' she says, indicating the camera between her lover's legs.

The young wife slips outside and tends to her pots. She gives the journalist an extraordinary smile and says they are welcome to eat. She says her baobab leaf stew is the best in the quartier. She invites them to sit down and commence washing their hands. Cissé wanders over.

As they eat in a wordless group the musician passes through the compound and the journalist sees the majestic man at his full height. He is dressed in smart jeans and a printed shirt, wears black wrap-around sunglasses and carries nothing. The wives on the plastic chairs watch him move. He speaks to no one. They hear a jeep revving outside the walls.

At the airport they have no access to the private lot where they can see the musician's jeep is parked. The journalist shows her press card, which is looked over and handed back. None of the guards will tell them where the famous man has gone. The interview is suspended and they buy iced yoghurt sachets from a seller on the street.

The escarpment of Bandiagara rises above the Sahel plains, pocked with the pillbox granaries of the Dogon people. Here, the god Amma gave life to the brown clay of the earth and produced twins called Nommo, hermaphrodite fish-like beings. To establish gender, the twins were circumcised. The foreskin of the male became a black and white lizard; from the excised clitoris and labia minora of the female, the first scorpion was born.

That night they drive across this highland. They have visited Mopti, a Venice on the banks of the Niger. They stood before the adobe mosque with her crest of vertical fingers. For the first time the journalist is stared at in a different way. Her boldness wavers and she wants to cover herself.

They have little money left and the photographer's half-brother in the UK sends them a transfer. She has almost finished her travel funds from the record company. They are going to drive all night, hopefully make it to the border.

The photographer is at the wheel. He feels relaxed, the woman is placid at this altitude, far away from Bamako. The landscape is a lunar surface. The road is singular, it drops and climbs over glades tessellated with glowing rocks. He would be content to stand out there in the wind, and speak of the arc of these days with her.

The woman's hand rests on her belly. She recognises changes in her breasts and skin and knows he has left his seed within her. He has told her there are twins in his family. Conceived here, in this land where twins embody the cardinal forces of the heavens. She thinks: this has to stop when we get back to the coast. She will expel these beads inside of her. And yet, perhaps she will not. Perhaps she will speak to him and they will allow these beings to uncurl.

As they drive Cissé sees two men walking, they are wearing tall wooden masks that reach into the black sky. Their robes are flattened against their bodies. It is clear that they are spirits roving the earth. Cissé's ankle sends a charge the length of his leg, into his spine.

The photographer stops the car on a broad stretch, he wants to walk with her. The couple wander ahead along the lightless road. The wind enwraps them – it is stronger than he thought – it whirs and vibrates. She turns around to look at the car tilted on the verge.

'Why? Why?' she says. 'We must go back.' She is not thinking of the sleeping boy, she is thinking that this place is too immense for them, too primordial. She wants the enclosure of the vehicle, the boy within her limbs. She would rather endure smaller things.

She remembers that the Dogon people discovered a hidden star, a blind star, using knowledge sifted down from the Egyptians, knowledge that the Westerners pored over and found a way to dismantle. And yet she knows it remains there, part of a universe beyond. They stand awhile beneath an infinite net of constellations, galaxies printed upon galaxies, a celestial harvesting.

Acknowledgements

I would like to thank Imogen Pelham for believing in this collection, and John Mitchinson and the team at Unbound; endless thanks to the many generous, patient and often faraway supporters of *The Cartography of Others*, for you have made this book possible. Enormous thanks to Hilary Mantel and David Rogers; thank you Cathy Galvin, Annemarie Neary, Tom Vowler and Eric Akoto; to Cathy, Paul, Zoe, Sophie and the wonderful Word Factory community; to the hard-working magazine editors and competition judges who gave these stories a first breath of life. Thank you Stef, Agnes, Stuart, Maurizio, FC. Huge thanks to Susi and Kay for always being there, to my family, and to my readers Omar, Stuart, Rachel, Lisa, Arrigo, Jim.

'Adieu, Mon Doux Rivage' was a finalist for the Short Fiction Prize and a version was published in Issue 8 of *Short Fiction*. 'The Wild Beasts of the Earth Will Adore Him' was a finalist in the Kingston Writing School Hilary Mantel International Short Story Competition and published in the anthology *What Lies Beneath* (Kingston University Press). 'The Ukrainian Girl' appeared in Issue 4 of *The Lonely Crowd*. 'Three Days in Hong Kong' was published in the anthology *Fugue II* (The Siren Press, London). 'The Book of Bruises' appeared in Issue 14 of *Structo*. 'Magaly Park' received a Pushcart nomination and appeared in *Gem Street: Collector's Edition* (Labello Press, Dublin). 'Enfolded' was a finalist in the Love on the Road Short Story Competition and appeared in *Love on the Road 2015* (Liberties Press, Dublin). 'Love and Death and Cell Division' was published in Issue 222 of *Ambit*. 'The Kingdom of Fassa' was Story of the Month with Seren Books. 'Yann at Night' appeared in Issue 1 of *Flight Journal*. 'Return from Salt Pond' was published in *Two Thirds North 2015*. 'They Came from the East' won first prize in The Short Story Competition and appeared in *The Short Story*. 'Astragàl' appeared in Issue 7 of *Trafika Europe*. 'The Architecture of Humans' appeared online in

Litro. 'The Bamboo Furnace' was published in Volume 75 Number 3 of *Southerly*. 'Hotel de Californie' appeared in Issue 1 of *The Nottingham Review*. 'Pia Tortora' was a finalist in the Royal Academy and Pin Drop Short Story Award. 'The Cliffs of Bandiagara' was a finalist in the International Willesden Herald Short Story Prize and published in *Willesden Herald: New Short Stories 9*. The author wishes to thank the editors of these journals.

Acknowledgment is made to the following copyright proprietors: David Higham Associates for the lines from *Under Milk Wood: The Definitive Edition* by Dylan Thomas (Phoenix). Edwin Marion Cox for the translation of Sappho's verse on page 189 from *The Poems of Sappho: with Historical and Critical Notes, Translations and a Bibliography* (Williams and Norgate, London; Charles Scribner's Sons, 1924). Giacomo Meyerbeer for the aria 'Adieu, Mon Doux Rivage' from the opera *L'Africaine*, Act I. Epigraph quotation is from John Donne's *Letters to Several Personages: Sappho to Philaenis.*

Patrons

David Andrew
Lane Ashfeldt
Morten Auklend
Lerah Mae Barcenilla
Susmita Bhattacharya
Emily Booth
Louise Buchler
Lesley Burt
Mary Byrne
Jonathan Cardew
Freeborn Caron
Mariateresa Cascino
Elaine Chiew
Rebekah Clarkson
Georgia Annie Conzato
Isabel Costello
Dan Coxon
Gary Duncan
Lidia Dussena
Ken Elkes
Gilla Evans
Jennifer Faddy
Joanna Atherfold Finn
Nod Ghosh
Zoe Gilbert
Shauna Gilligan
Melissa Goode
David Goodman
David Griffin
Francoise Harvey
Sophie Haydock
Charlie Hill

Alva Holland
Mary Jane Holmes
Peter Jordan
Elena Kaufman
Cate Kennedy
Sophie van Llewyn
Barbara Lovric
Adnan Mahmutovic
Alan McMonagle
Steve Moran
Francesca Muir
David Nicholls
Susan Harbage Page
Nastasya Parker
Cat Payne
Hannah Persaud
Sylvia Petter
Alex Preston
Santino Prinzi
Leanne Radojkovich
Cameron Raynes
Liesje Ridley
Helen Rye
Anthony Sattin
Elisabetta Scala
Jo Simmonds
Valerie Sirr
Rachael Smart
Ruby Speechley
Rebecca Swirsky
Rosy Thornton
Louise Tondeur
Chloe Turner
Mariarosaria Valente
Melanie whipman

Charmaine Wilkerson
Lisa Williams